Happy Reading

Craig

X

DRIVING NOWHERE

Craig McCabe

ISBN 978-0-9557417-0-8

Acknowledgements

Thanks to family and friends. Fergie for the tip on the humming, Brian 'Bomber' Harris the only real life character and who's story is a whole other book. All my critical acquaintances who laughed when I told them I was writing a book ' git it right up ye'. And a special thanks to 'The View' for their inspirational tunes and energy.

Cover design by Ryan McPhail
www.ryanmcphail.co.uk

www.craigmccabe.co.uk

CONTENTS

1) Not the greatest job in the world

I've been on all day and this miserable looking bastard, who happens to be my next customer, is actually struggling to get his fat arse in the car. It's not that I have anything against fat people but if I was finding it hard to get in or out of a car I'm quite sure I would do something about it. I can smell his foul body odour before he even shuts the door, a swift movement of the trigger finger on the window button should help…should, but more than likely…wont. I have a strong air freshener, my window is open and yet stinky man here is still over powering the smell. This is definitely my last fare today, I've had a text from Gaz saying that everyone's in the East View bar and that's more than enough encouragement for me to finish. As soon as I drop off stinky man I'll be heading there for a well deserved drink.

Once he's in and his breathing eventually settles down he says "sorry eh hae chist problems, gees is trouble breathin an that."

Yeah you're too fat, loose some fucking weight. He now comes out with the classic line that I get asked from nearly every second customer.

"So have ye been busy then?"

I don't want to answer him as I am afraid if I open my mouth I'll inhale his bad odour.

"It's not been too bad." I say as I veer my head towards the window.

I have a slight grin every time I answer this as I know this is everyone's ice breaker to let me know they want to talk but don't know what to talk to me about.

"So do ye like drivin the taxis then?"

"It's like any job really, it gets to you after a while."
The bad part is having to picking up people like you, you smelly fucker.

"I don't like it because you have got to work all the unsociable hours, you know, the ones when everybody's out on the piss."
Total lies. I work whenever I feel like it.

"You see that's the busy time when you make your money. Then there's the arsehole drunks that you have to put up with. Also the junkies and the general moaning bastards"
...And the nosey cunts like you fatso.

"Also if you don't work you don't get paid, as there's no holiday pay in this job, apart from all that it's okay, I mean it's better than signing on as, a jobs a job as long as it pays your bills right."

This must be too much information for him as he's not answering to that, or maybe he's searching his tiny mind for something else to ask me. When I first started I would have said that this was the greatest fucking job in the world because all you do is sit on your arse and drive around all day. You work if and when you feel like it with no bosses on your back all day telling you what to do. My job before this was in a factory which was that bad the bastards timed me when I went to the toilet. The place had no windows and during the winter it was dark when i went in and dark when i came out. I only saw daylight at the weekends and even then I was up out all night to ever appreciate it.

"You're a bit young ti be on the taxis are ye no?"

And there it is...over two years on the taxis and at least once a week without fail somebody will ask me that, he must have thought long and hard to come up with that one. I don't actually mind when it's a good looking girl asking but when it's a wanker like this, I feel there trying to be a bit patronizing towards me. I remember when I had just started on the taxis, some guy wouldn't get in the car because he thought I was a joy rider…must have been the hooded top.

I suppose it is a bit unusual to see a young guy with his own taxi as most of them are usually fat, old baldy men and I hate every one of them. They are all arrogant, moaning, greedy, two faced bastards and deep down I know they all fucking hate me. Sometimes if I'm sitting behind another taxi on the rank, the customers see me and will walk past the car in front to get in mine and the other drivers hate this as there is nothing they can do about it. Don't get me wrong they do get out of their car and shout to the customer that they are first in line for a pick up, but the customer usually just tells them to 'fuck off'. The other drivers act as if it's my fault and they all hate me for this. The amount of arguments I've had and sometimes near punch ups because of them blocking my car and stealing my jobs is unbelievable, nothing ever comes of it though as most of them are all mouth.

"Eh'll bet you dae a lot o shaggin in this joab?. Ah they young lassies wah pretend that they dinna hae enough money fir the fare."

He now starts to tell me some story that another driver told him about a customer who offered him a blow job instead of paying the fare. What the fuck is this guy all about? It's usually young people who ask me that and you have a laugh about it because they know the score but this cunt is about fifty years old and is just being a nosey, dirty old bastard. He must be waiting on me telling him some filthy story so that he can go home and have a good wank about it. The thought makes me sick…oh no, maybe that's just his very bad body odour that's now starting to turn my stomach.

"You know what, the people that tell those stories are full of shit, probably those fat, old, baldy drivers. If they are true, you can imagine what those fucking women look like if they are willing to lower themselves to do something like that."

He appears to be a bit disappointed at my answer, of course

I do a lot of shagging, but I'll be fucked If I'm going to let this old pervert know the perks of my job.

I arrive at fat mans destination and I cant get away quick enough and get to the pub, so that I can forget about all these sad depressing customers lives that I've had to endure today. As I speed off along the road I forget to log off my computer and it beeps to give me another job. Out of habit I press the button and accept the job. It's the train station. I tell myself that this is definitely the last one and drive off towards the centre of town. I have all the windows down to release the foul stench that's left behind but it appears to be lingering around. I get a little paranoid when I have another fare after someone like that has been in my car, as I feel that the next customer thinks that the smell is coming from me. As I pull up at the train station there are several people waiting in the taxi queue but I notice a girl standing back from them with a holdall . She is small with dark hair and even from a distance I can tell she is really pretty. I get out the car to shout the name while looking at the queue for confirmation from my customer but the dark haired girl acknowledges me that she is my fare. I smile back but feel that this is not my usual put on smile that I reserve for all my other customers. She takes her holdall in the back with her and tells me her destination. I drive off but can't help looking in the mirror at her. I am not usually one to be stuck for words but this girl is stunning, in a real natural way.

"By the way if there's a horrible smell in the car it's not me, my last customer was this big fat smelly man."

She looks at me and I know as soon as somebody says anything like that people will start to sniff to try and smell it.

"Do you say that to everybody who gets into your car?" She says in a very polite Dundee accent and gives me a cheeky smile.

"Nah, I can only smell your air freshener."

"Lucky you, I can still smell him."

"That's because the particles will still be up your nose. Instead of trying to smell other things to get it away you'll have to blow your nose first."

"You are just full of useful information aren't you."

"I love that song, is that a C.D. or the radio?"

"C.D."

"Are you into Indie music?"

"I like a bit of everything really, but yeah, I listen to Indie quite a lot."

"Do you ever go to live gigs?"

"I go to T in the park."

"No I mean to see local bands."

"Not really, no."

"Here." She says handing me a flyer with a list of bands on it.

"What is this?"

"My friend organises bands to play at this pub. They are really good, you should come along."

"Thanks, maybe I will."

I look at the flyer. 'The Doghouse' and think how am I ever going to persuade the guys to go there. Just as the conversation gets going I arrive at her destination. She hands me the fare with a few quid extra and tells me to keep it.

"Thanks."

"It's alright, hopefully I'll see you at the gig. Oh, if you do go and you are there early enough to catch the first band. Be prepared."

"Prepared for what?"

"'The View.' Their fans could be a bit wild."

As she walks away I smile but think to myself that I don't know what the hell she is talking about. I turn to drive off and see a car full of evil looking wide-o's drive past and stare at me. I look back around to see the girl but she's gone. I switch off the computer and drive away in the direction of the pub. On the way I can't get the picture of the girl out of my head and feel quite stupid as I didn't even ask her name. I look in my mirror and she soon disappears from my mind as I see that the car of wide-o's has doubled back and is now following me. I arrive at the East View and park the car a few streets away. It should be safe enough until the morning. As I walk towards the front of the pub the same car passes and slows down. I keep looking ahead and walk through the door without turning around.

2) No introduction

I don't know why this pub is called The East View as it
doesn't actually have a view except to look onto an old
derelict building and it isn't even in the East of the city, it's
more in the middle.

As soon as I walk into the pub, I spy Gaz in the corner
slavering in some girls ear. Gaz is my best mate whom I've
known for most of my life, to look at him you would never
guess that he is one of the major drug dealers in the city. No-
one knows this except me and his supplier, some big shot
from Glasgow. Jamie, Kyle, Joey and Mickey are just sitting
over from him. Jamie is my younger half brother, he's only
nineteen but has been hanging around with us for a couple of
years. He walks about thinking he's some sort of gangster
and is constantly being put in his place by me or Gaz. Kyle is
a mate whom I've known for several years. I got to know
him through some girl I was seeing as he was going out with
her friend. Kyle is the type of person who never gives anybody any shit and gets involved in fighting whatsoever. I
trust Kyle more than I would trust Mickey or Joey, which is
quite strange as I grew up with them, actually I trust Kyle
more than I trust my own brother. Mickey is a funny guy
who can handle himself but knows his limits. He is not afraid
to let you know what's on his mind. Joey has always been really tall but was never a fighter and he always hung around
with us so that nobody else would bully him. He is a student
who works in the gym and gets us in for free. Since he's
worked there we have noticed him putting on the beef. We all
take the piss that he is on the steroids, which he constantly

denies. As I sit down Gaz slides over to me accompanied with the girl that he's probably been promising the world to, to get in her knickers. I get the nods from everyone and Jamie passes me a bottle.

"Ahright mate, how's it goin? This is Donna, Donna this is Shane."

"Eh ken wah Shane is. He doesna need introduced ti me." She says in her squeaky voice that sounds as if she is about thirteen. Gaz looks at me as if I know her or that maybe I've given her one, but I've never seen her before in my life. Not that Gaz would bother if I had as it wouldn't be the first time we've shagged the same girl. Gaz is a couple of years older and used to live across the road from me when we were growing up. He was brought up by his gran and granda, Kate and Big Danny. Gaz is very switched on and for someone who was thrown out of school many, many times and left with no qualifications whatsoever he is one of the most intelligent people I know...well except from Big Danny. Gaz is the type of person who watches Countdown and does better than the contestants. It is really funny when he watches it with Big Danny as they continue to rattle out these unusually long words that nobody in their right mind would think of. I remember once Gaz saying that you can get by with a little knowledge as long as you have a lot of common sense as common sense can be disguised as knowledge and someone with common sense can always gain knowledge. But having a lot of knowledge is nothing without common sense. Once this was broken down and explained to me. I understood...the cunt was right. Gaz is the type of person who will do anything for you and wouldn't expect anything in return. He's also a chancer with girls and will tell them anything to get in their knickers... I guess we are very alike in one sense.

As I take a swig out of my bottle my face drops as I look up to see the wide-o's who were following me walk into the pub. There is one who has his stare fixed on me and he seems very familiar. He has the stereo typical hard man features with the shaved head, the stocky build where it looks like he has no neck and the deep slanted eyes with not much going on behind them.

"Gaz I think something's away to kick off."

"Why?"

"Those guys who just walked in, they've been following me since I dropped off my last fare."

"That's Murdo. He'll no dae anything if he kens yer we me."

"Murdo, Dek Murdo."

"Eh, he jist got oot a few weeks back."

"What do you mean if he knows I'm with you?"

"Watch. Awright Dek." Gaz shouts across the pub.

Murdo nods and turns away back to the rest of his schemie looking friends.

"How do you know him?"

"I've had a few dealings with him in the past. He knows people that I know, so it's cool"

"I couldn't give a shit Gaz, If he starts he'll get it the same as any other wide-o would."

"Calm doon and keep yer voice doon tae. Do ye ken what he's jist done time fir?"

I am about to tell him that I couldn't care less but Kyle interrupts

"He stabbed some poor guy for shagging his missus."

Suddenly my aggressive manner seems to fade a little.

"He's lost a bit of weight, looks like a ponsy body builder now." I say trying not to look over at him.

Dek Murdo was one of those guys that when you were growing up had the reputation of being hard as fuck. He was about ten years older than all of us and we had listened for years about stories of him being 'Off his head' and a 'Fuckin nut job'. As we grew up we all learned that he was just a bullying bastard who picked on the younger ones. Anyway as things go, some people that he bullied over the years grew up to be a lot harder than him and stopped taking any of his shit, that's when the knives started to get pulled. This all goes hand in hand with his reputation and also his nickname 'Mad Dog', which he evidently gave himself.

As more drinks are passed over from the bar Gaz moves away from Donna and gives me the full story of what happened. The evil bastard was working as a bouncer on a club and his missus was talking to some guy so Dek starts on him. The poor guy was actually giving Dek a good go until he 'surprise surprise' pulled out a blade and stuck it in him. He's got previous for stabbing and loads of other shit but all he's served is four years."

"I fucking hate people that use blades, they usually tend to be the ones who act all tough but can't fight sleep."

"Do ye want ti find oot?" Gaz says with a big grin on his face.

"Nah, maybe later."

The both of us have a little snigger then I down my drink and get up to order another round. While at the bar I get a text from Lisa,...I FINISH IN AN HOUR IF U WANT 2 POP UP L8R 4 A DRINK XXX... She's a girl I've been seeing the past little while. I've been trying to end it but when I am out with the guys I end up taking to many drugs and find myself knocking on her door. She works the phones and computers in the same taxi office that I work from.
Lisa is quite small and slim with the long blonde hair and a sun bed tan...typical Barbie doll. Since I started shagging her I seem to be getting loads more work sent my way. If she's working during the night and a big out of town job comes off. She phones me and gets me out of bed to go and do it. We were only friends at first and I would see her out at the weekends but I never tried it on, although she did flirt with me a bit. I think I was really pissed one night when I ended

up back at her flat. I thought she knew the crack, that it was all just a bit of fun but after a few weeks she changed. The downside being that she became very clingy…well actually she was more like a possessive control freak. Whenever I was out she would turn up and get jealous if I was talking to other girls. If I was having people back to mine she would go crazy because I invited other girls up. I had to make excuses so that she wouldn't come up to mine because once she was in, she wouldn't leave. All my mates hate her and all she does is bitch about her own mates. When I don't want to see her I can't use the excuse that I'm working because she knows whether I am or not. If my computer is on in the car this registers with the main computer in the office. There is also a tracking device connected to this which means she knows exactly where I am. This was designed to determine which car is the closest to whatever jobs come in. I think the other drivers are starting to get suspicious though, as it's always my car that gets the call to the office at the end of her shift to pick her up …but she is a great shag.

After several rounds of drinks and a few more desperate texts from Lisa I tell Gaz that I'm leaving after this drink and he starts moaning that I just got here.

"We're ah headin in the toon the night, eh though ye were up for it. Whare are ye sneakin aff ti anywey?…Oh shit it's no her fae the office again is it? That fuckin Lisa Yer wee spunk bucket."

I look at him with the schoolboy grin like I'm trying to hide something and then the both of us just snigger.

"It's gettin a bit regular again mate? you canna stand her an we canna stand her so how do ye no jist tell her to fuck off?"

"What do you mean 'WE' can't stand her. If she walked in here right now and asked you to shag her, you would have you dick out before she even finished her sentence."

"Nah nah Jamie would hae his oot well before me."

"That's true." I say while nodding.

Gaz hates me seeing Lisa, well he actually hates me seeing any girl regularly because after a club I always end up going back to hers and he has nowhere to go when he's pulled. He lives with his gran and she doesn't like him taking girls back there...she doesn't mind him walking about her house with a joint hanging out his mouth but bringing a girl back is not on. I will have to ditch Lisa though, as I miss shagging the girls that Gaz pulls. When he pulls a bird he always makes sure she has a friend for you and they are usually the type of girls that when they walk in your flat their knickers just fall off. If he can't find one for you he'll pull one that will be up for it from both of us. The downside to this, is that sometimes these girls are big, fat and ugly... but most of all, they usually stink. The worse part is that I get left with them in the morning as Gaz always sneaks off home after shooting his load to take his fucking dog out. He has one of those Staffy dogs which he calls Biscuit and takes it everywhere. He treats it like a fucking baby and even lets it sleep in his bed. If we are going to a party after a club no matter who's it is. He'll go home and bring it back with him. Don't get me wrong it's a cracker of a dog, all black and very cute. It looks the way a Staffy should look, the type that you would see in a picture book, not like the ugly cross breeds that you see going around...Although most around this end of town have probably come from Biscuit due to the amount humping it does. When Gaz doesn't have him on his lead, which is quite often and it sees another dog. It bounds over and tries to ride it...male or female. Gaz gets the piss ripped out of him for this as we all blame it on the dog sleeping in his bed.

How Gaz got into dealing wasn't by thinking 'Oh I'm going to start selling drugs and make loads of money'. He had dabbled in recreational drugs like most of us since we were young teenagers and after he eventually left school he had started work on the government's Youth Training Scheme...slave labour jobs. This was a scheme where employers took on sixteen or seventeen year olds and their wages were paid by the government. This was supposedly an incentive for the employer to take them on after a two year period. This system was abused by employers who took on these people and used them for slave labour with a promise that they would be offered a full apprenticeship after their two years training. They had no intention of offering them full employment and they would be terminated before the two years were up. The employers would make a phone call and would receive another young naïve school leaver. Gaz had went through several of these jobs as he had the employers figured out within a week and would either be sacked or had walked out for refusing to do their meaningless errands of making them tea or cleaning the toilets. During this time Gaz used to supply the hash between our close circle of friends we had at that time. He never made any money out of it as he only sold enough to get his own for free. Our circle of friends gradually got bigger and they all ended up coming to Gaz. Once the speed and e's came on the scene Gaz saw an opportunity. Several years down the line he was the main man in the area and had three to four people selling it for him. There was never any trouble and the people who sold for him only sold to trusted buyers. He never touched smack and coke wasn't around in those days like it is now.

This went on for years until Gaz's supplier got busted. He was sent down for several years, which gave Gaz an opportunity. His suppliers supplier was a big shot from Glasgow and he asked Gaz if he wanted to take over. Gaz agreed but being the paranoid guy that he is he told him that it was under his conditions. The big shot loved it as Gaz found out he was just as paranoid as him. So the set up was started where there was no contact between either of them. They picked their gofers, people they trusted to do the drop offs and pick ups. The introduction of mobile phones was the key to this whole system working between Gaz and his new found employer.

Gaz contacted a dealer in Dundee and told him that a supplier from Glasgow was looking for a dealer. He did not mention names but told the dealer that he would get a phone call to where and when the drop off would be. Someone from Glasgow would travel through to Dundee either by train or bus. They would receive instructions by text to go to a pub in the centre. It was different pubs each time. Gaz would be close by, driving a taxi. He would wait until he was next in line to get a job and then phone a taxi to the pub that the guy was in. Gaz would then pull up outside the pub, he would shout in the door a pre arranged name and the guy would get in the taxi. The package would be left in the back and Gaz would drop the guy off at another pub in the town. The guy would have a quick drink in this pub and then head back to Glasgow. Gaz would then have to contact his dealer in Dundee and arrange for his guy to phone a taxi and coincidently, it would be Gaz's taxi that would get the job. If the dealer in Dundee ever happened to get busted they would not know who Gaz was or who the main supplier was.

Before this arrangement with the big shot, Gaz did plan on calling it a day at one point. This was when he met Debbie, she was a nice girl who didn't appreciate her partner being a drug dealer. Although she never complained when he was spending loads of his cash on expensive gifts for her. Within a few months of meeting Debbie they had moved into a flat and were talking about settling down and having kids. They took on Biscuit who was only six weeks old and nearly fitted into the palm of your hand. Gaz was still handling the drugs himself and he had people knocking on his door at all hours of the day and night looking for gear. It got too much for Debbie and she gave him an ultimatum, stop dealing or she was leaving. Obviously Gaz didn't stop dealing as the money was too easy and it paid for the lifestyle he wanted. The furnished flat, all the expensive clothes and nights out on the town four or five times a week. The typical drug dealers lifestyle. Although it has to be said, the more money he spent on clothes the more he would still look like a schemie as Gaz is the type of person who if you put in a made to measure designer suit he would still look scruffy.

Debbie couldn't live with the threat of the flat being busted by the police so she left. Personally I think she was seeing someone else but I've never said that to Gaz. She packed her bags and took off leaving him with Biscuit, who was six months old by this time. It was actually her idea to get a dog and walked away without a second thought. Gaz couldn't give him up as he had become attached to it. After his supplier got busted it turned Gaz into a paranoid wreck. He had to ditch the flat and move back with Kate and Big Danny. If the drug squad were onto his supplier at the time, then they were onto him. If they had looked at his lifestyle, he was fucked. Now he just keeps enough to keep him going and the rest he gives to me to put away. He has no bank account, no credit cards or anything that can be attached to his name. Most drug busts come from tip offs or grassers wanting a reduced sentence. He knows the only way he can ever get caught is if word of his arrangement ever got out, but as far as I know the only people that know about it are me and the big shot. If nobody else knows about it, then nobody can grass. The only way he can get busted is if the police did a random check on the taxi when he was doing a drop...which is highly unlikely.

I go to sneak out the door before anyone notices as Gaz is keeping everyone amused by ripping the piss out of Jamie, who just so happens to spy me sneaking away and tries to divert the attention onto me.

"Whare are you goin?"

"Lisa's."

"Hmm, you lucky bastard eh'd love ti shag her."

"I'll be sure to mention that when I see her then."

We both laugh as I go out the door but at the back of my

mind I'm thinking, brother or no brother I'll bet if that cunt got half a chance he would shag her while I was seeing her. I walk off leaving them listen to Gaz telling them about how when Jamie was younger he used to hide his skiddy undies under the bed.

3) Rock n roll star

It's only a short walk to Lisa's block from the East View, which in one way is a good thing as I don't have too far to walk but in another way it's too convenient at closing time when I am fuelled up looking for my hole. When she first started at the taxi office I didn't take much notice of her until one night when I was out on the town a bit worse for wear I seemingly made a pass at her. She came up the road with me and I have regretted it ever since. She told me her friends knew me and to stay away as I was a bit of player. I didn't argue, I just told her straight that I was only wanting my hole. She joked that once I had been with her, I wouldn't want anybody else. I didn't know that in her mind she actually meant it. She started turning up everywhere I went and flirting with me. I thought she knew the score but It's like she thinks that the more we have sex the more I'll want to be with her. She hates all of my mates as they apparently stop us from having a proper relationship but she couldn't be more wrong. Being with them actually drives me to go and see her. Although If I wasn't getting sex handed on a plate I wouldn't even bother. I feel really confused when I think about all this as when I am with my mates all I want to do is be with a girl and when I'm with a girl and just shot my load I can't wait to get back to my mates. There is the odd occasion where I've met a girl at the weekend and agreed to go to the pictures or go for a quiet drink during the week with them and the whole time all I am thinking is that I can't wait to get her back to my flat and give her one. As soon as this happens I can't get her out of my flat quick enough. I hear people tell me that they would love my lifestyle and they are resentful that I have no kids, no ties, I go out when I want, do what I want and I have no woman nagging at me to do this or that. Although at the same time I feel envious of their relationship.

These thoughts are getting way too deep, I knew I shouldn't have taken that coke Gaz laid out for me in the toilet. He put out two monster lines on the cistern for me and Joey and I thought I was being the smart arse by taking them both to piss off Joey. Now look where the fuck I am.

I press the intercom and she lets me in. The landings have the usual stench of alcohol and piss, which I don't understand as the security door is supposed to stop the fucking schemie's getting in, unless it's one of her minky neighbours, or even worse…Lisa herself. I get to the top floor and press the buzzer

"Hi come in, would you like a vodka?"

"I wouldn't mind."

As Lisa goes through to the kitchen I go into the living room and sit on the couch. For how much of a state this block is in Lisa's flat is very nice. She's got her Robbie DVD on …GREAT! Looks like I'm going to be shagging while listening to this shite again.

It's like she has everything set up for me coming up here, she's obviously after her hole as well. This is so fucked up, both of us have sex on our minds but for two totally different reasons. Mines is because I am coked up and need to release my urges and hers is to please me so that I'll stay with her.

"Were you in the East view?" Lisa shouts from the kitchen.

"Yeah I only had a couple, I've not long finished work."

"I know, I saw that you had logged off and I couldn't wait to finish so I could see you."

Fuck, this has got to stop she's getting way to into this…well maybe after tonight.
She hands me the vodka, which I quickly devour, then she squeezes in behind me on the couch and starts rubbing my

neck and shoulders.

"Would you like to lie on the floor and I'll give you a massage." She says.

"Okay" I say, but I ask her to get me another vodka, and a large one this time.

As she goes to the kitchen, I take off my top and lie on her large fluffy rug. She brings me the drink and I sit up and take a large gulp. She sits on my lower back and pours a little oil on my shoulders then starts to rub. The shivers tingle down my spine as she continues rubbing down my back to the top of my arse.

"Turn over." She says, raising up so that I can move.

As I turn over I reach for my drink and take another large gulp. I put down the glass and she pours oil over my chest and starts rubbing it all over. When she reaches the top of my jeans she strokes across my stomach and then up my sides, this goes on for a while as I think she is enjoying teasing me …the little bitch. Eventually she starts kissing my chest and working her way down with her tongue. She opens my buttons and pulls down my jeans and boxers. She keeps stroking my balls while kissing my dick, teasing me more and more. I lean over for my drink and she takes it from me, she takes a little sip and hands it back to me. As I'm swallowing another large gulp she puts my dick in her mouth but she hasn't swallowed the vodka.

"Ahhhhh."

This is fucking heaven, the vodka is really cold but her tongue is hot. She works me up until I nearly come and then lets it go. I pull her up to me and we start kissing. I start to undress her slowly, stroking her lovely toned body. She picks up the remote from the television, turns up the volume and then grabs my hand leading me through to the bedroom. I walk back and pick up my jeans, take out my wallet and slide out a condom from behind my credit card.

"It's okay just leave it."

"Yeah right." I mumble as I walk back into the bedroom. The last thing I need is for her to get pregnant.

We move onto the bed and try out a few positions. The sweat is dripping down my head so I stop and go to the bathroom to wipe it, on the way back I go to the kitchen for another vodka. As I'm pouring a drink I notice that I'm humming along to a fucking Robbie song…I quickly stop. I take my drink through to the bedroom and lie on the bed. Lisa starts playing with my semi to get it hard again but as I look at her I get a reality check of where I am and I suddenly realise that this was a big mistake. I guess the coke is wearing off.

"What's wrong?"

"Nothing. Why?"

"This is not like you."

"What?"

"Well it doesn't normally take you that long to get hard."

I don't answer but reach up and take a large gulp from the glass. I look at Lisa but I am thinking about someone else, if she knew she would probably kill me. I have to put her out of my mind just now and finish what I started here. I pull her close to me and put in a little effort of foreplay until I eventully get hard again. I sit on the edge of the bed with her legs rapped around me. I slide forward while holding her up with my hands on her arse. She puts her arms around my neck as I thrust faster and get into a rhythm. Her groaning gets very loud then she shouts in a very shaky voice.

"I'M AWAY TO COME."

"Ahhhhh."

The both of us let out similar noises as we lie back on the bed. Lisa feeling fucked and me feeling fucked up. I role over, drink the rest of the vodka and curl up with Lisa's arms around me and go to sleep.

I waken up in the morning feeling rough as fuck and still have that Robbie song going round in my head. I go to the toilet and as I pee it comes out in every fucking direction, all over the seat, floor and wall.

"Oh fuck." Why does that always happen after I've shot my load?

I quickly grab a load of toilet roll and give it a wipe.

"Would you like a cup of coffee?"

"Nah I'd better go I have to go to work soon."

I can't get out of here quick enough. I would usually tell myself that this was worth while and that I had a great shag but not this time. This time I just feel guilt, guilt for coming up here in the first place and stupid for taking that fucking coke. I put the rest of my clothes on and head to the door. She follows me and tries to kiss me, I give her a quick peck and tell her I'll phone her.

"I don't want you to go, please stay."

"I can't Lisa, I have to go to work."

"No you don't. You work when you want. Take the day off and stay with me."

"Don't do this again Lisa."

"What? I just want to see you. Can we meet up again tonight then?"

"I don't know. I'll see"

I walk to the door and try to get out before she turns nasty

"Fuck" She's locked the door. Here we go.

"Open the door Lisa."

"Just stay a while longer Shane, please." She says opening her bathrobe revealing her naked body.

"I can't Lisa please, open the door."

"Oh so now you've got what you want, that's it."

I knew this would happen, why did I take that fucking coke.

"Lisa give me the key."

"No you're staying here."

"Lisa I have to go to work." I say a bit louder as I start to get angry.

"No you don't. You just want away from me."

She leans forward and puts her arms around me but I don't return the hug. She starts crying as she knows the waterworks get to me as i fell for her act before. I put my arms around her and she hugs me tighter. I reach into her robe pocket and gently take out the front door key. I release my arms and walk quickly putting the key into the lock. I hear a scream and feel my hair being pulled from behind. I grab her wrist tightly to stop her and she lets go. I release my grip and then she attacks me with her fists and feet, punching, kicking and screaming all at the same time. Nothing lands on me as I block most of it with my elbows and knees. She screams again louder and runs off into the bathroom locking the door. I stand for a minute and listen to her crying. The last time she done this I ended up staying for hours to make sure she was okay. I put my head to the door and contemplate whether to knock and ask if she is alright but I know this is what she wants. This is like a fucking déjà vu. I'm not falling for it this time. I walk to the door and unlock it, I look back one last time and then head off down the stairs. I hold my breath so that I don't breathe in the smell as it's a bit much when you are hung over. I walk back towards the East view and get my car, I know I shouldn't be driving as I still feel half pissed but fuck it. As I'm driving I feel my phone vibrating all the way home. I know it's Lisa so I don't even bother to look at it.

I walk into my flat, which is in an overpriced building just off the Perth Road and a few snotty nosed neighbours look me up and down. I know they hate that someone like me can afford a flat like this, especially when they see people like Gaz walking in and out of their building. They probably think I just rent it but little do they know I own the flat outright with no mortgage. If it wasn't for that pathetic piece of shit that calls himself my stepfather throwing me out at eighteen I wouldn't be in this position and I know it bugs him too the amount of money I have made buying and selling flats. This current one is the business though, it has a large living room with a balcony that gives views of Dundee which is amazing at night. The master bedroom has views across the Tay and over to fife which at times is just as good. As soon as I get in I go straight to the stereo put Oasis on and blast it out to get that fucking Robbie tune out of my head. I strip off and go in the shower …"I'm a rock 'n' roll star."

4) Customer No.221
Junkies

I know this address, there fucking junkies...great. This is Broughty Ferry, the so called posh outskirts of Dundee. Some of the residents I pick up talk to you like you are a piece of shit and they think because of where they live they are better than you. In reality they live in a scheme that is full of junkies just like everyone else. They probably don't know that their original neighbour is renting out their house to someone who has been evicted from a council house and is now renting privately. What they don't know is that the rent money is actually paid through housing benefit and their high council tax payments are going towards keeping these junkie's as their new unsociable neighbours. The guy swaggers out of his house and gets in the front seat. Before he tells me where he's going he slides and tilts the seat back. This is not because he needs more leg room as the cunt is smaller than me. He sits in a way that he has his elbow up on the side panel and has his row of sovereigns on show. They blend in well with his new tracksuit with the newly added hash burns along with his hundred pound trainers...this is the stereotypical Chav.

"Eh'm goin ti Maryfield Medical Centre. Eh'll no be a menit an then onti the hulltoon ti the chemist, then hame."

"Why do you not use the chemist in Maryfield?"

"Nah cause eh'm banned fae the three o them. Eh'm banned fae the ain at the hulltoon tae, bit they let is in though."

I drive to the medical centre where he's out the car and

back in a couple of minutes after picking up his prescription. Next is the chemist, where I wait a little bit longer. On the journey back he tries to make conversation with me but my answers are very blunt as I can't stand this guy and what he is all about. His whole way of life revolves around the world owing him something. This parasite sits on his arse all day and claims every benefit possible. He has a house with a large front and back garden which is rent free, no council tax, free drugs and to top it all he has told me in the past that he receives extra money to live on because he is a registered drug addict. Because he has kids this opens a whole new list of benefits for him compared to the average junkie.

I have several junkies in my taxi a week as they go for their daily dose of free methadone and all they ever talk about is how to claim for this or that so that they'll get extra money. They know everyone's business and what they are all claiming for. I agree there are some unfortunate people who end up with a drug habit and with the correct help and change of attitude, they beat it. The average person who pays their taxes would agree that the money put aside to help these people is not grudged if it was going to be used correctly but it is being abused by the same people that it was designed to help.

These junkies are not mugs, they are quite intelligent people and have learned over the years how to screw the system. If they put as much effort into cleaning themselves up and getting a job instead of scamming everyone and everything they would probably be quite successful. Judging by the amount of junkies I have encountered over the years I would say that nine out of ten don't actually want to come off drugs. I arrive back at this guys house and stop outside his long drive-way. He pulls a huge wad of notes from his pocket and hands me a tenner.

"Jist keep the cheenge." He says as he winks at me before swaggering back to his plush house.

I can't tell if it's all in the mind with some of these junkies as when they get in your car when they are strung out. They are very nasty, rude and sometimes aggressive, dangerous people. They go from house to house trying to get drugs and they get more abusive if they are unsuccessful. The minute they score and get back in the taxi their attitude totally changes. They give you all the 'Hey man' and call you 'Mate' when only minutes before they were ready to start on you because they couldn't get a hold of some drugs. I would hate to think what would happen if they didn't get them as who knows what these people are capable of when they are strung out.

Customer No.269
Priorities

The social workers in Douglas and my customer is a woman waiting outside with her three young boys. She gets in the front and her three young boys climb over each other to dive in the back

"Eh'm goin ti Dunmore street in Kirtin."
Before I even drive off, one of the boys dives up onto the parcel shelf at the back window. I turn around to tell him to get down and see the other two with chocolate on their fingers and wiping them all over the windows and down the back seat

"RIGHT THE THREE OF YOU SIT DOWN AND GET YOUR SEAT BELTS ON OR YOUR GOING NOWHERE."
I shout quite angrily but feel even more contempt for their mother who sits in the front and doesn't even turn to see why I am getting onto her kids.

During the journey I hear the seat belts clicking open and the boys start laying into each other on the back seat. One of them has squeezed into the space between the front and back seat while one of the other boys is on top punching his lights out. The swearing and filthy language from these boys would put Gaz to shame. Their mother sitting in the front has her mobile phone out and is happily chatting away to someone. She has the latest flip model phone definitely worth a few hundred at least and her kids look and smell like they haven't seen a bar of soap in weeks…easy to see where her priorities lie. I'm nearly in Kirkton or kirtin as my customer would say and I try to switch off to the noise from them as I speed up to get to their destination as fast as I can. My mother would have booted my arse if I behaved like that when I was younger…well actually Jamie's dad would have kicked the shit out of me more like.

I feel sorry for these kids as they have a mother who obviously doesn't give a fuck about them and can't teach them how to behave or even a simple right from wrong. She would have known all about it if I had thrown the little fuckers out. What kind of start in life have these boys got? They are going to grow up hassled by social workers and they have a mother who thinks that going around stinking of pish and shite is okay. I can only wonder why there isn't a father around.

Customer No.340
Tayside's finest

"Where are you off to then?"

"Hulltoon please."

"Oh I'm getting a please this time."

I've picked up these two schemie's before. Mother and daughter. I would definitely do them both. The mother is at an age where she's still considered young, and the daughter is working so she must be old enough for me to give her a good shag. Gaz would probably say they were mingers as he likes to pretend he has standards, but I have witnessed some of the girls he pulls due to him turning up at my door with them.

The are both talking about going out tonight so I will have to make sure I give them my number so that I can pick them up later.

"Oh fuck, what the hell are they wanting?" I say as I clock a blue light flashing in my mirror.

"Ohh what have you been up ti?" the girl in the back says trying to be funny.

I watch the cunt get out of his car so I do the same.

"Do you know you have a break light out?" The man with the face of stone says.

"No. No I didn't."

"Where's your badge?"

"What, my taxi badge?"

"YES" The clown in the ill fitting uniform says very abruptly.

"It's in the car."

"You're supposed to wear your badge at all times when you are plying for hire. NOW GET IT ON."

I want to shout, yes sir and do the Hitler salute but I don't think that would go down to well. The cunt is on his own so I could probably just tell him to fuck off but then he would just make a call and have about five cars here in minutes the fascist cunt. He starts ranting and raving about how I should check the car before every shift. Do you think I have a bionic fucking eye that can see the back off the car while I'm sitting in it with my foot on the brake you stupid cunt. What is his problem anyway? He's pulled me over because I have a break light out, which is fair enough but he's going a bit over the top. I see those boy racers ripping about the streets every night with all the illegal crap on their cars and they do fuck all.

"Have you polis no got anythin better ti dae?" The young girl in the back shouts out of the window.

"How many hooses have been screwed in the time you've been standin there?" The mother adds.

"When you've dropped off your passenger, go and get the light fixed and if I see you driving later on and it's not fixed I'm going to put you off the road."

"No problem." I say through gritted teeth.

I look at him before getting back in the car thinking I would love to meet you in a dark alley on your own so that I could smash your face in you arrogant prick.

The woman and daughter are still shouting abuse at him out the window.

"What the fuck did he git oot o that? Fuckin nothing better ti dae that's what their problem is. They want ti go an catch some real fuckin criminals."

The woman in the back is right, I really wonder what was on that cunts mind when he decided to stop me. Somehow I don't think he stops every car in front of him that has a brake light not working. What's bothering me more is not what he stopped me for but the way he was talking to me. Young taxi driver in a flashy car maybe? I would say that most of the time I am an easy going guy but when someone with a bit of authority becomes a bullying bastard it really gets me worked up and makes me hate them even more. Because of that happening it put a bit of a downer on the banter I was having with my customers so I never got the chance to give them my number…the fascist cunt.

Customer No.388
The bully

I sit for a while waiting on my next job, which is a good thing as I'm feeling quite rough from last night. The sore head kicked in several jobs back and that's after taking a few pain killers. I never thought I had that much to drink last night. It's a good job I didn't get breathalysed earlier because there could have been a chance I was slightly over the limit.

Eventually my computer beeps, it's Asda for Milne. As I approach the entrance I can see there is already a taxi with the boot open and the driver is loading the bags of shopping. I hope that's not my fucking fare. I drive into a space on the rank as the other taxi is about to drive off.

"Taxi for Milne."

The old lady in the back hears me as her window is open and says "Oh that's me."

I recognise the drive's face but it's not until I read the name on the side of the car that I recognise him, Macintosh.

This happens to be the same loud mouth who I had to endure abuse from in my first week on the taxis. I pulled up on the rank one day and this cunt started shouting his mouth off at me to fuck off and find some other place to sit. If there wasn't two other taxis on the rank and a load of other witnesses that day I would have got out and smashed the cunt. I told him to piss off and that I'll sit wherever I fucking want. I've seen him a few times over the years while I've waited on jobs but he hasn't said a word. He's a big guy with one of those hard looking faces and a big 'Desperate Dan' chin. I've watched him mouth off at other drivers and they've all put their heads down and walked away from him. I could have said something then but they are all wanker's anyway and they all deserve each other.

"SHE WIS WAITIN FIR AGES, YE SHOULD HAVE

GOT HERE QUICKER."

Macintosh shouts out his window and looks at me with a large smug grin, which makes his chin appear even bigger.

"Is that right?" I say while getting out my car as fast as I can and storming over to him. He drives off before I get near him and he keeps the same smug look on his ugly face before giving me the finger out of the window.

I don't know what I would have done if he hadn't drove off as I couldn't exactly do anything with about fifty shoppers walking past me. As I watch him drive off I feel a slight anger rush through my body. This is mixed with adrenaline as I can feel my heart beating faster and my finger tips stating to tingle. I get violent thoughts through my mind of what I'll do to him the next time I see him. I knew he would eventually get wide with me again. I know his type, they can't help themselves. It's like they have something to prove by bullying a weaker or smaller person. Well it's about time he got his comeuppance.

When I've seen him mouth off to other people it's never directly affected me so I've never got involved, but not this time. The only thing I know about him is that he's from Lochee and drinks in the Ivanhoe, which to me means a double chip on his shoulder. Every time I have a customer going to or from the Hoe I seem to get shit off them. It doesn't matter whether it's young guys or old men with walking sticks or women, they all have the same arrogant attitude. I've seen me not drive fifty yards from the pub and having to drag some drunken prick out of my car for being wide. On the odd occasion when I've had to go into the pub to shout on a customer, I've seen Macintosh sitting there with his mates, being loud and aggressive. He's looked up and just given me his stupid smug grin, well to me it felt more like a sneer.

I have to wait for quite a while until my next job but this is a good thing as it gives me some time to calm down. All the other taxi drivers see is this young guy with the flashy car moving in on their job and they don't like it. If I was driving for one of them and making them money there wouldn't be a problem. But as I have my own car, in which customers prefer to get in rather than their buckets of shite, they don't like it so they think they can bully and take the piss...Well one of them has done it to the wrong fucking person and he's soon going to know about it. They say what goes around comes around, well I've waited a long time on this coming around.

My customer gets in and they start blabbing on and on all the way through their journey and I don't know what the fuck they are talking about. I am agreeing with everything they say by nodding now and again but the whole time all I am thinking about is Macintosh.

5) The workout

Text from Joey.

"ARE YOU STILL UP FOR IT MATE, TIME YOU
PICKIN ME UP?"

Oh shit I must have mentioned to him last night in the pub
that I would go to the gym with him today. I really can't be
bothered but after all that shit with Lisa this morning and
then that cunt Macintosh being wide I think maybe a break
from the taxi would be a good idea. I'll head home for my
gear and pick him up.

Joey is a mate from school who was always big for his age.
He was a bit of a wimp and this resulted in him being bullied
constantly. He always hung around me and Gaz but we both
know this was so that nobody went near him. He started col-
lege a few years ago after many dead end jobs and he ended
up working in a gym. Since then we've seen him put on a lot
of weight and now has the bulging biceps and six pack.
Which he tries to say is down to his training program and a
good diet. I wouldn't trust Joey as far as I could throw him,
but when we go out it's good to have him hanging around as
his size intimidates people and they think twice before starting any shit. We all know he can't fight sleep but other people don't. When he started at the gym and building himself
up we noticed his swagger got bigger and he had a bit of an
attitude. Around this time I once heard him getting a bit
wide with Kyle, but he was soon put in his place. Kyle is the
type of person who doesn't bother anybody and along with
Gaz they are the only people I really trust. Joey works at the
gym part-time and gets us in free. He's always complaining

about money…typical student. He explained to me once about the student loan he gets, which is to pay for his rent and is also meant to feed and clothe him during term time…how students manage this without any extra income is fucking beyond me. The worse part about it is that once he finishes studying and gets a job, he has to pay it all back.

I always wondered why Joey kept asking me to the gym and not Gaz or Mickey. At first I thought it was because I had transport to pick him up and then I thought the cunt was bent…well I still do. But I later found out it was because when he takes Gaz or Mickey they just muck about or sit in the saunas and shout rude comments to all the females. From our point of view this is not really a bad thing but Joey's boss gave him loads of shit as he was the one who signed them in. The only thing I don't like about going to these gyms are those bodybuilders with their stripy pants. They stand and look at themselves in the mirror while doing a set and then chat for about ten minutes before their next one. The life of a stereo typical bodybuilder. Jab some steroids in their arse, lift a few weights, take a job as doorman and then walk about thinking they can fight the world. I have no time for them whatsoever.

I go to sound the horn but see him standing waiting at his gate.

"Ahright mate. Are ye ready fir a hard work oot?"

"Not really, I'm a bit hung over."

"Whare did you sneak aff ti last night?"

"Where do you think?"

"Ahh nah, you werna shaggin ti Robbie again were ye?"

I give him a funny look as I can't remember telling him about Lisa's Robbie obsession.

"Eh jist dinna git you Shane. Ah ye dae is moan aboot her. Yet ye still go up ti her flat fir a shag. You winna let her in your flat cause once she's in, she winna leave, which eh really dinna understand as anybody else widna want somebody as stunnin as that ti leave. Personally eh'd want her ted up in meh fuckin bed so she couldna fuckin leave. Eh would love ti ken how ye manage ti pull ah these good looking women. Ye blatanly tell them you are only eftir yer hole an yet they still come back for mare…Well maist o them. Eh think you've found oot we Lisa that no ah burds want the same thing though eh. Do ye ken what? See when eh'm oot in a club it feels like there are burds hingin aboot you just waitin ti be asked up the road. Eh sometimes wonder aboot the burds that eh pull, if they are jist we me ti git near you."

"Joey, you don't half talk some shite mate" I say as we arrive at the gym.

We get changed and as soon as we walk in I see them. The all gruntin, all swaggerin, poofy bodybuilders, with their muscle vests and stripy baggy pants. They stare over with their heads back makin their necks swell out but I don't even look over as they would just get me worked up. I start stretching off and when I look around Joey has fucked off to talk to them. I just carry on doing my own thing but I glance over catching Joey comparing his biceps with one of them…What a fucking nonce. I could just imagine their conversation as there's not a brain cell between the lot of them.

"Oh you're back, I thought I was training on my own."

"Eh only went over ti say hi."

"More like bend over." I mumble

"What."

"Nothing."

"You're set."

As Joey gets himself into position to lift I watch one of his friends walk over to use the punch bag. He puts on his gloves and starts hitting the bag. I immediately feel embarrassed for him. He throws several pathetic punches and stops for a breath. I watch as he swings one arm from behind his body towards the bag and it hardly moves. I smile to myself and look away.

"These are the guys who are supposed to protect the public from drunken louts who are out to start trouble. If I was one of them what the fuck would he do if he came up against someone like me."

"Go and show him how it's done then Shane." Joey says nodding over to the bag.

"Nah not just now, I wouldn't want to put all you're real friends to shame."

As we finish our sets I think to myself that we must have lifted more weights in ten minutes than those bodybuilders did in the whole hour that we have been here.

I walk over to the punch bag and Joey tells me he is off to work on his six pack. I know the bodybuilders are all watching so I take it easy by throwing a few jabs and hooks. I work around the bag and start to pick up the pace. I throw a few big hooks but keep on the move. I get flashes of Macintosh in my mind and then I really start to hit it. I forget about who's watching and before I now it Joey is tapping me on the shoulder.

"Ye had enough yet Rocky."

I look around and see that all the bodybuilders are standing watching me, I'm surprised they can stop looking at themselves in the mirror long enough to bother. I take off my mitts and follow Joey to the changing rooms.

While driving home we are having a laugh about the bodybuilders in the gym when my face drops. I turn the car around.

"Whare are ye goin? Are ye no drappin me aff first?"

"Yeah, I'm just checking something out, that's all."

I thought it was him. Macintosh is sitting at the front of a rank on his own. I stop on the opposite side of the road and roll down my window.

"OH MACINTOSH. Who the fuck do you think you are stealing my job this morning?"

Joey is unaware as to what is going on and sits next to me

smiling as if I know the guy.

"PISS OFF. Ye we prick. What the fuck are you gonna dae aboot it anywey?"

I turn to see Joey's face drop as he realises it's not a joke.

As I step out of the car I hear Joey shouting 'leave it' but I am off in a rage marching across the road. Macintosh gets out of his car and squares up to me.

"What the fuck are you gonna dae ye wee p…"

I jump up and smack him in the side of the head with everything I have. He falls across the front of his car but comes back with a big hook scuffing the top of my head. I lean in with a punch to his stomach which makes him bent slightly. His face is more in my reach now and I throw a few more punches before he crumbles to the ground.

I feel my arms being pulled from behind. It's Joey who is using his weight to drag me back across the road.

"I'll fucking kill you, you wee prick." Macintosh shouts as he picks himself up.

I struggle free from Joey and run back over the road. We trade a few punches until I land one on his chin putting him on his arse again.

"Think you're a hard man? You're not that fucking hard are you? You fucking mouthy cunt."

I go to walk away but he still mouths off. I lose it and lay into him with fists and feet and don't stop until I am pulled off once again by Joey. I look down to see Macintosh's face covered in blood and his body lays still as Joey pushes me towards my car.

Joey opens my car door and shouts at me to get in then runs back towards Macintosh. At first I think he's about to hit him but he crouches down and puts him into the recovery position.

"What the fuck did you do that for?" I say as we speed off.

"Because if he chokes on his own blood you'll be up for murder."

I don't say anything until we arrive at Joey's flat and the whole time I can feel my hands and legs shaking with adrenaline. I tell Joey to put the kettle on as I go to skin up.

"Give it here. You make the tea." He says as he sees me struggling to put the skins together with my shaky hands.

I come through with the tea and Joey passes me the joint. I know the rule about taking two puffs and passing it back but fuck him. Joey has a few puffs and passes it back to me. I can tell Joey's not happy with me and even after a smoke I can feel the tension from him. I finish my cup of tea and get up to leave.

"Let is ken if you hear anythin?" He says. But what he really means is, let me know if i have to watch my back from now on because of you. But it's a different story when someone is giving him shit and he turns to me to help him out.

"No probs mate." I say as I head off out the door.

I've always thought that if someone like Macintosh goes about like he does he must have something to back it up. It's on my mind that I could have hurt him bad as Joey said he was out cold but fuck him he was a bullying bastard and given half the chance he would have done the same to me. I check my phone before going back to work and have about five messages from Lisa, I don't even read them I just press delete all.

Customer No. 643
Money was money

The Mains of Claverhouse is a pub that is situated on the borderline between Kirkton and Mill of Mains. Two schemes in Dundee. The pub is across a busy road from Caird Park golf course. This used to be a respectable pub, where in the summer the golfers would go for a well deserved pint. Half a mile along the road in the Kirkton direction was another pub, 'The Claverhouse'. This pub, in it's day was one of the roughest pubs in Dundee where every would-be hard cunt in the area would gather to talk about who they had smashed or who they were about to smash. Women included. The good thing about this pub is that it kept all these nut jobs in one place. It eventually shut down, which resulted in these people having to drink elsewhere. For most of them that meant going along the road to the Mains of Claverhouse. Within weeks the whole clientele had changed and this was now known unofficially as the new Claverhouse.

I enter the front door and shout the customers name.

"TAXI FOR DAVIE."

This scrawny little rough looking man pipes up from a stool at the bar.

"EH THAT'S ME."

Before I walk back out I notice a bit of a scuffle near the pool table and I recognise their faces form years back but I can't put a name to them.

I get back in the car and the scrawny little man is not far behind me.

"Right drevir, eh'm goin inti the toon."

"Where about in the town?"

"Anywhare, stop at the bank on the wey though wull ye?"

"What about the bank in the town around from commercial street?"

"Eh that'll dae. Eh hae enough fir the taxi but eh still need mare money. Eh mind when money was money."

"What do you mean? When money was money, what is it now?"

"IT'S WORTH FUCK ALL" He shouts.

"Eh got mare fir a pound in the seventies than eh would the day."

"Obviously, that's called inflation mate."

"What's that?" He asks.

"What?."

"Inflation" He says.

I can't tell if this guy is really pissed and talking shit or if he's some sort of retard and talking shit.

"Well you obviously earn more mow than you did in the seventies, so the more your wages go up the more everything else goes up."

"Di ye ken what? Yer fuckin right" He says. He hears a familiar song on the radio and starts singing out loud. This carries on for a while as he makes up his own words and starts to get louder.

"Those guys in the pub arguing over the pool, what's their names again? I think I know them." I say trying to get him to stop singing.

"WHA HIM HE'S A FUCKIN BAM." He shouts.

"Yeah but what's their names?"

"HE'S A FUCKIN BAM, HE'S NO EVEN IN THE HUNS."

Jees, what the fuck is this guy on? I really hope this guy is just pissed, I'd hate to think he was like this all the time.

"EH'LL BANG YER PUSS" he shouts looking straight at me.

"You'll what?" I say smiling. I think this guy has either got a lot of bottle due to too much drink or he has a few screws loose.

"EH'LL BOOT YER BAHS, YE PRICK."

"Are you speaking to me?"

"Me, eh, eh'm fine, yersel?"

"I'm alright, but I seriously think there's something not right with you though mate."

I can't tell if this guy is taking the piss or what.

"Dinna worry aboot me. Eh'm in the Kirtin huns."

I reach the bank in the town without having to stop and give this guy a slap.

"RIGHT YOU, OOTSIDE, SQUARE GO."

I start laughing at him.

"DO YE SEE ME LAUGHIN, NO, NOW GIT OOT THE CAR AN WE'LL HAE A SQUARE GO."

"Look mate I suggest you pay this fare then you can go and have a square go with anybody you want. It's five fifty."

He pulls out his wallet and opens it to find that it's empty. He then puts his hand down his sock and pulls out a roll of money. He hands me a twenty.

"The things ye huv to dae when ye drink in yer local. JIST KEEP IT YE BAM" he shouts as he gets out of the taxi.

I go to drive off and he stands at my car window.

"COME ON THEN, COME AHEAD YE BAM." He shouts.

I put the twenty in my pocket and laugh as I watch him swagger down the street shouting abuse at random people to 'Come ahead.'

6) The stripper/exotic dancer

My next customer appears from her tenement door with two large bags. She is a stunning blonde and looks totally out of place living in a junkie infested block on Park Avenue in Stobswell.

I get out of the car to open the boot but she informs me that she'll take them into the back with her. I clock the cowboy hat on top of one of the bags as she gets in.

"So where are you off to them?"

"The fantasy bar please."

It now registers that she is a stripper, I was a bit slow there, I should have realised when I saw the hat.

"Is that you away to start?"

"Well, I was supposed to start at nine but I'm a bit late. What about you? Is that you on all night?"

"Me, no, I'm actually away to finish. Have you worked at that place long?"

"No it's only my second night, I usually work in Edinburgh but I thought I would give this one a go."

"So what is it like?"

"I hate it, some of the other girls are really bitchy towards me. The customers are much sleazier and the money isn't that great either"

Just by looking at this girl I can see why the other strippers are bitchy towards her. Although she has jeans on I can tell she has a great body. I've picked up strippers in the past an none of them have ever looked like her.

"Do you ever go to the fantasy bar?"

"I've been in them but they are not really my thing"

"What do you mean?"

"Well when you have nightclubs in Dundee where the girls get their tits out after a few vodka and cokes. There's not really much chance of getting me to pay for someone to get them out…at least I would have more chance of shagging the burds from the nightclub."

"Yeah, you're probably right." She says as she looks at me in the mirror and smiles.

"So what nightclub do you go to them?"

"Slims."

"Oh I don't like Slims now, I go there when I'm not working but it's only because there's nowhere else to go."

"What about the Mardi?"

"Yeah right, that's like an underage disco."

We arrive at the Fantasy bar and she says "Will you be back working again later on tonight? It's just that you could pick me up when I finish…if you happen to be in the area."

"Oh I don't know, me work late. That could cost you a bit extra."

"I'm sure we could negotiate."

No fucking about, I dive straight in.

"What, like a free dance?"

This makes her smile again and I feel a tingle in my balls without her even touching me. We exchange numbers and I tell her if she's stuck for a lift just to give me a call

"My names Shona, by the way."

"Oh right, my names Shane."

As soon as I drive off I realise I have all those spacers coming up to my flat tonight for a smoke. Not to worry, most of them head off about two. She won't finish until half two so that should work out fine.

***

I'm glad I didn't have too much to smoke tonight as there's no way I would have been capable of driving. Everybody left except Gaz. He crashed out on the couch so I just through a cover over him and sneaked out. Shona text me three times tonight asking if I was definitely going to pick her up. I was going to let the others know what was going on but fuck them. If this turns out to be a no show I would never hear the end of it.

I park up outside and watch as other taxi's pull up and some real mingers come out. They've probably got great bodys and are good at what they do but from where I am sitting they are real ugly. Shona appears with her bags and puts them in the back but this time she gets in the front.

"What do you think you're doing?" I say very serious.

"What do you mean?" She says sounding quite worried.

"Why aren't you dressed to give me a free dance?" I say smiling.

"Maybe later."

"So where are we going?"

"You know where I live, unless you have somewhere better to go?"

"We could go to mine."

"Okay."

I drive off felling quite excited but trying hard not to show it. As I pull up outside my block she says "Is this where you live?"

I nod and smile and help her with her bags as she follows me upstairs. We get in the flat but Gaz doesn't waken up.

"Don't mind him, that's my mate. Come through to the kitchen I'll make you drink, vodka okay?"

"Yeah. Is this your flat?" She says as she looks through the curtains that lead onto the balcony.

I don't answer, but I nod and smile.

"How much are you a month for this place?"

"Eh'm, nothing."

"Yeah right, this must cost you a bomb."

"No, I swear, I pay nothing, I own it."

"What did you win the lottery or something?"

"I wish it was that easy. I used to buy and sell flats, I bought them really cheap and sold them at a profit. Don't worry I'm not a drug dealer or anything like that. I can't speak for the piece of shit crashed on my sofa but that's a whole other story."

"Speaking about drugs, I have some coke if you want a line?" She says as she pulls a wrap out from her purse.

"Yeah, cool."

"It fell out of someone's pocket when they were getting their wallet out to pay me, so I sneakily crouched down and put it in my boot."

When she says this I suddenly get a mental picture in my head of this lovely girl dancing for a bunch of sleazy men all paying good money for her to get her kit off. Some of them even offering to meet her later by using the latest cheesy chat up lines. Every one of them dying to touch her and here she is in my kitchen.

She opens the wrap and I can tell someone is going to be rally pissed off tonight at losing this as it's a lot of coke. She cuts up several lines on my bunker and takes a crisp new tenner from her purse. This has probably come from someone's wallet that they have departed with to see her flash her fanny at them. She rolls it tightly and hands it to me.

"You first." She says.

I lean forward and snort a line up each nostril. Shona leans forward and does the same. There are still a few lines left on the table which I am sure will not last long.

We stand chatting for a while in the kitchen until the coke fully kicks in. she leans forward and kisses me and before I know it she has her hands down opening my jeans.

"Wait a minute. What happened to the dance I was getting?"

"Oh yeah, I forgot about that. Go and put some music on and wait through there. Oh, but what about your friend?"

"I'm sure he won't mind."

I walk through with my vodka and put the stereo on. Gaz's rap music starts to blast out of the speakers and he wakens up. I put my finger to my lips and nod towards the kitchen. He puts his head back down as if he is still sleeping. A few minutes later Shona appears wearing her sexy cowboy outfit. She climbs onto the coffee table and touching herself as she does a sexy dance. I have a fly look at Gaz who is making faces at me wondering what the fuck is going on. Shona climbs down off the table and sits on my knee while slowly taking off her clothes. She starts to rub me through my jeans and it is only a matter of seconds before she has me hard. Shona gets naked and throws a cushion down at my feet for her to kneel on. She opens my buttons and starts licking all around my balls. I lean forward and take off my shirt as Shona pulls my jeans and boxers down to my ankles. She leans over to the skirt she had on and pulls out a condom, opening it and carefully sliding it on me. She sits on top of my thighs and wraps her legs around me. I look over to Gaz and at first I think I'm tripping or something but he has his jeans open and is having a wank. He looks up at me and I burst out laughing.

"What? What are you laughing at?"

I nod in the direction of Gaz.

"Was it getting too much for you, was it?"

Gaz gets up and hobbles over with his jeans falling to his knees, while still wanking. He stands in front of Shona and I think he was hoping she would suck it, but she puts her hands on top of his and helps him along.

"You had better not come on me." She says.

He turns away disappointed and hobbles back to the sofa to carry on his thrashing. I stand up lifting Shona in the process and kick my jeans and boxers off my ankles. I put Shona down and lead her by the hand to the bedroom and leave Gaz to finish himself off.

I wake up in the morning with her still lying next to me. I offer to get her some coffee but after some fondling and a little foreplay we end up having sex again before we both get up and I give her a lift home.

***

The weekend can't come quick enough for Gaz who has been doing my head in about going to the Fantasy bar after me bringing Shona back to the flat. I kept in touch with her but it was a one off and I don't really want to make it a regular thing with her. Although she would be good for the odd occasion. I told him most of them are ugly and nothing like Shona but he still insists that we all go and check it out. Kyle and Mickey are up for it too and after a few drinks up the west end I now find myself in a taxi on the way to the Fantasy bar. Gaz told me he has a few grams of coke on him and when I told him I didn't want any he snapped at me.

"It's not for you, it's for the strippers."

We go in and Shona comes straight over and introduces us to another couple of girls. They are not too pretty but they have very sexy toned body's. I hand Shona a tenner and as I pass Gaz he hands me the wrap with the coke. Shona leads me to a small room and closes the curtain. I pull out the coke and she takes a hefty line up each nostril. We have a quick hug and kiss before heading back to the bar. I hand the wrap back to Gaz and in a spit second he is off to another small room with one of the ugly girls he was introduced to. Kyle and Mickey are like kids in a sweet shop as they pay for dance after dance with all these ugly strippers.

Gaz pays for a few more dances but chooses the same girls every time.

"They lassies are comin back ti yours fir a perty" Gaz says.

"What lassies?"

"The ains that huv been chargin me a tenner ti go in the wee rooms an snort meh coke."

"What, you've been paying for a dance but actually just going in there to take coke?"

"Eh" he says with a big smile on his face.

"What are you up to?"

"Nothin. Eh've spent over a hundred pound an that's no in-cludin the coke. But hey, eh'll get ah that back."

The night goes in quick as the bouncers shout that it is about to close. We have a taxi waiting on us outside but we physically have to drag Gaz away from the place. We head up to mine where we tuck into the crate of lager that we left earlier. Shona and the other two girls come up about half an hour after us and are welcomed into the kitchen by Gaz who has been waiting impatiently on them. He has several lines of coke all laid out for them. Gaz offers them a drink and they all say vodka which is a relief for me and Gaz for two totally different reasons.

Shortly after the girls comment on how good the coke was and ask for another line.

"That was fae meh mate, eh always get good stuff fae him. It's no been cut too much. There's no much left but eh could phone him an git him ti drap some aff. The onay problem is that eh'm runnin oot o cash as eh used it ti pey fir you strip-pers" Gaz says giving me a funny look.

One of the girls turns to Gaz and quite seriously says "We are not strippers. We are exotic dancers."

The girls all chip in to buy some more coke and Gaz nips out to meet his 'friend'. While he's out the music is turned up and the girls all have a laugh by taking turns to dance on my coffee table.

"This is what eh call a perty." Gaz says as he bounces back in the flat with another wrap of coke. He cuts them up a few more lines and rushes about topping up their drinks.

"Gaz what are you up to? I had a line of that coke and it's nothing special." I say as I pull him aside.

"Yeah but that's only because you never had a vodka with it, it's magic coke. You only get an effect when you follow up the line with a vodka. Here, drink this." He says as he hands me a small glass with, what looks like vodka and orange juice.

"Hey your right enough, that does make a difference." I say.

"But maybe that's down to the fucking G.H.B. that you've been putting in it".

"Shhhh." He says as he winks at me.

Several lines and drinks later with my head feeling a little fuzzy, I eventually end up in my bedroom with Shona. I lie back as Shona goes down on me but I start to get bored and my mind starts to wander. The next thing I know she is on top of me and I am inside her without a condom. I can't believe I'm doing this, those cunts are all next door swapping around without condoms and they are the one's that'll go through life not giving a fuck and never catch a thing. Where I'll be the one that'll not use one just the once on some spunk bucket and end up with the fucking virus.

I don't last long as I feel I am about to shoot my load and whisper it in her ear that I will have to stop as I am about to come.

"No, keep going." She shouts.

"I don't have a condom on."

"It's okay, keep going."

I shoot my load up her and roll onto my back. Shona moves down and starts sucking me off again.

"Does that not taste horrible."

"Not really, just a bit salty"

She comes back up to give me a kiss but I pull back as I feel her tongue.

"I don't want to taste it."

"Why?" She says as she puts her hand down and scoops up some of my sperm from her onto her fingers and starts licking them. For all those nice thoughts I had about this girl, they virtually vanished in the split second that I witnessed her doing this. I get up and walk through to the living room naked and am surprised to see that everyone else is naked or near enough. If anyone walked into my flat they would think there was a full scale orgy going on.

After all the coke has been consumed and the alcohol level is at a minimum the girls decided to leave. They get a taxi together and I have to lend them money after they spent it on the so called 'best ever coke'. I really thought these girls had been around and seen it all but I was obviously mistaken as they were so naive not to notice they were being spiked with G.H.B.

"You're a cunt Gaz, we could have been onto a good thing with them. And you're due me the money I had to give them for the taxi" I say as we both laugh.

Mickey and Kyle are looking confused as to what's going on.

"You guys didn't think that was just coke making them feel like that did you?"

"Gaz, you never, did you crush up e's and mix it with the coke?" Kyle says.

"No, it was G.H.B. in the vodka" I say.

We all laugh as Gaz pulls a wad of notes out of his pocket.

"The strippers charged me a tenner a dance and I basically charged them a tenner a line of the finest COKE a cola around." He says as he pulls out the empty bottle of G.H.B.

"You're forgetting one thing." I say.

"What's that?"

"They're not strippers…They're exotic dancers."
"Wooooh"

7) A typical night out

CUMIN DOWN?
I text back…HALF AN HOUR

I'll do another job, go home to drop off the car and walk to Laings. I hope I don't see Lisa tonight, she has been texting and phoning all day. She was actually in the office and called me through the car radio while I was working just to talk to me. I said I would call her later as I was busy but fuck that, I can't be bothered with her. I get calls from withheld numbers as if I don't know it's her. She actually phoned from a phone box and I thought it was a number I knew so I answered it. It was her and all she did was cry, she was trying to talk but I couldn't make out what she was saying so I hung up.

Customer No. 378
Tins of beer

Another smelly fucker. I can tell this even before he even gets into the car

"Aright mate? Is it aright if eh smoke?"

On every window of the taxi there is a no smoking sticker and everybody knows that you're not allowed to smoke in taxi's anymore anyway…Actually, you're not allowed to smoke anywhere.

"Nah, sorry mate."

"Fuck, eh've jist lit up tae."

Just lit it up. It's a fucking nipper. The smelly fucker looks at me as if it's my fault as he pinches the top of it to nip it again. It's actually not worth fucking nipping as there's less than an inch left to smoke. Why do people light up if they've just phone for a taxi? The journey is less than five minutes but they can't wait that long to have their nicotine rush. He gets in the car and sure as fuck he's a stinker. His clothes smell like they've not been washed in weeks.

"Eh'm onay goin ti Asda. But will ye wait fir is? Eh'll onay be fev meenits an then eh'm comin back."

"Yeah sure, no problem."

On the way to Asda he informs me that he is only going for cans of beer.

"There's a shop across the road from your house. Why did you not get them out of there?"

"Cause eh grudge gein the Paki shop the extra twenty pence he pits on each can."

I pull up outside Asda and wait impatiently as the smelly man saunters in for his cheap beer. I watch the front door and expect him to come out with several crates which would justify the fare but no, he slowly walks out with a twelve pack. If you compare the prices he has saved himself two pound forty by purchasing the cans from the supermarket…but when I return back to where I picked him up, his taxi fare comes to four pound sixty. Due to his refusal to line the pockets of his local ethnic minority shop his crate of beer has now cost him an extra two pound twenty. He reaches into his filthy jacket pocket and hands me a fiver from his yellow nicotine stained fingers and his long dirty fingernails. I go to hand him the change.

"Nah jist keep it mate."

"Cheers."

Before he walks off. The fag he nipped before the journey is quickly pulled back out of his pocket and lit up. He swaggers off towards his house with his cans of beer and leaves behind his disgusting smell still lingering in the car.

I eventually get to the pub after a short walk along the Perth road, I forgot how close the pub actually was. As I go through the large glass doors I see Jamie is at the bar, I go to shout over the music but decide to walk around and give him a friendly little slap in the head and tell him to get me a pint.

Jamie is my younger half brother, well I used to say little but he is actually bigger than me now. Jamie is only nineteen but looks and acts much older, this could be due to him hanging around with Gaz as they still live a few doors from one another. When Jamie is with Gaz the two of them can sit wasted for days on end…a real couple of stoners. We have the same mother but although I've never met my dad. Jamie's dad has been with my mother since I was a toddler but I still don't think of him as my dad. I've had a lot of problems with him when I was growing up and I still can't stand the cunt. I was about sixteen when I first knocked him out for his constant bullying. There was a few more knockouts after that until he learned to back off. He was always on my case. He was worse when Gaz was around, like he was trying to show off that he was in charge or something. He used to do the same with Jamie when he was growing up but that started to fade not long after I hit him, I guess he must have realised that if I was capable of growing up and doing that to him then here's to what Jamie would fucking do to him.

Jamie is served the drinks and I help him carry the round over to the table where Gaz, Kyle, Joey and Mickey are sitting.

As I go over to the table Gaz shouts "Guys, watch what you say it's the psycho comin over."

They all laugh except Joey who looks at me all serious, I smile back but he knows I'm pissed off because his version of what happened will obviously be exaggerated and make me out to be some sort of thug who beat up a guy for mouthing off, when he knows it wasn't like that.

We only have one drink in Laing's and Gaz has us moving onto the next pub down, Rafael's. During this time I am continually getting texts from Lisa asking where I am. I show them to Gaz who gives me a smug look as if to say I told you not to keep seeing her.

On the way to Rafael's Gaz pulls me up about Macintosh.

"So what's the story aboot the guy ye smashed?"

"He a prick, he's been on my case a few times and he pushed it too far this time"

"Wah is he?"

"He's just another taxi driver, Macintosh. He drinks in the Hoe."

"The Hoe, in Lochee. Are you aff yer fuckin haed?"

"Why?"

"They cunts fea the Hoe are ah fuckin mental."

I just shrug my shoulders at him.

"Eh'm no jokin mate. You better watch oot, they'll be looking fir ye."

I don't take much notice as Gaz is totally flying out of his head. He's had a few e's and is blabbing on and on about a load of shit and no one is really listening to him.

We get into Rafael's and he starts pawing at me to get my attention and puts his hand to my ear like he's away to tell me a big secret but he knows no matter what it is I'm going to tell everybody anyway.

"Shane do you see that girl at the bar?"

There is a tall girl with a short skirt, long hair and a very pretty face but you can tell she is the type who knows it, a real 'look at me.'

"Yeah, what about her?"

"Eh hud meh tongue in her knickers last week."

"Fuck off."

"Honestly."

"There's no way she would let you shag her."

"Eh nivir said eh shagged her. Eh said eh hud meh tongue in her knickers."

There is a long silence then I say to him.

"Come on then spill the fuckin beans, tell is how you managed to get your tongue in her knickers."

With both of us staring at this girl Gaz explains to me that one day last week while working on the taxis he gets a job into the town. It was the girl at the bar, she had been shopping and had a lot of bags. Gaz starts putting them into the boot when he notices in one of the bags some new lingerie that she's been treating herself to. Gaz says to her

"Dinna worry hen, eh'll pit them awa." And she stupidly leaves Gaz alone with her shopping. As the girl is getting in the car Gaz reaches into the bag and pulls out a kinky pair of red lace knickers. He leans forward with his head nearly in the boot, gathers a load of saliva in his mouth and proceeds to lick the crotch of these knickers. He places them back into the bag shuts the boot then drives the girl home...so technically he has had his tongue in her knickers.

"You're fucking sick, do you know that?."

"That's good coming fae you...Psycho-boy."

I laugh this off as I know if I try to explain myself when Gaz is in this state it will just go in one ear and out the other. We have another drink in Rafael's then head down the road to Nero's bar.

As we walk in Dek 'Mad Dog' Murdo is standing at the bar with a few of his mates. He looks up and gives Gaz a nod of the head but when he sees me he puts on the usual hard man 'Eh want ti fight the world' stare. I don't know what they're up this end of the town for and really I don't want to know. We walk past and find an empty table in the corner. I watch as Murdo says something to his mates and they all turn and stare over at me. I mention it to Gaz but he tells me to ignore it.

"Dinna lowerin yersel ti that shite mate. Eh've telt ye before. He's a blade man and theres only one wey that a fight we him would turn oot. Tak ain o these an forget aboot it." Gaz says handing me a couple of e's.

"Honestly mate, eh huvna hud a hit like this in a lang time. Eh'm totally wasted. They're the business. They're like the ains we used ti tak years ago."

That's enough encouragement for me. I take the two of them and pop one in my mouth and put one in my pocket. After a few drinks I start to mellow out a little even though I keep catching Murdo looking over at me. If he wanted to do anything I'm sure he would have started by now. I pop the other e and get up to go to the toilet as i have a sudden desire to pee. On the way I notice Murdo in deep conversation with the bouncer, he's probably taking about who has the biggest blade on them. I stand at the urinal and unzip waiting on this rush of pee to come out but although my bladder detects that somethin wants to come out, it just doesn't happen. I stand for about ten minutes and still nothing.

"Fuck." This is getting annoying.

I go back upstairs and who has decided to show up…none other than Lisa, my wee stalker.

"Shane, I want to talk to you."

"I've nothing to say."

"Please Shane." She says grabbing my shirt to stop me from walking away.

"Lisa, LEAVE ME ALONE."

She starts to get louder now and her eyes fill up with tears. People have started looking over wonderin what's going on. I looks over to the guys and nod in the direction of the door. Gaz nods back and then shakes his head at me. They all stand up to walk out and I go to follow them with Lisa still holding my shirt. As I walk past the bar she pulls on my arm quite hard and in frustration i turn a little to tell her her to let go but as I turn who does my arm catch on the way round? None other than Dek 'Mad Dog' Murdo.

"Ho watch what your fuckin dein, you wee prick." He says.

I don't even look up but apologise anyway. I go to keep walking towards the door but feel myself being thrown forward.

"EH'M FUCKIN TALKING TI YOU, YE WEE PRICK."

I have never had an e drain from my body so quickly in all my life. I turn to see Murdo standing with his face like thunder.

"COME ON THEN." He shouts.

I feel the anger ready to burst out of me and just as I take a step forward Gaz pulls me back and steps in front.

"Laiv it Dek. He's we me." Gaz says as the bouncer steps in front of Murdo.

"Eh couldna gee a fuck. You tell that wee prick ti stey oot meh fuckin road." He shouts as I am ushered out of the door.

"Why did you do that Gaz?, I'm not scared of that cunt."

"Dinna be so fuckin stupid, if you start we him yell never hear the end o it."

"What do you mean?"

"Look one on one, yeah mibbe you could smash him. But you ken he's the type wah would come back again an again. He's just come oot o jail fir stabbin some cunt, does that no tell ye somethin…Like he's capable o dein it again an remember he winna just go fir you, whahever you are we will git it tae."

We walk a bit further down the road and Gaz lights up a joint, which i feel is badly needed. He passes it to me to calm me down. He's known me all my life and he knows that it's on my mind to go back there.

"What wis ah that aboot?" Jamie says shouting at me.

"But mare important wah was the wee stunner that ye were chatting up?"

"Eh hope you're no referring ti Shane's spunk bucket."

"That wisna that Lisa that yev been tryin ti get rid o was

it?"

I give Jamie a nod.

"You're a fuckin prick. What would ye want ti dump her fir? She's fuckin lovely."

"Jamie you say that every time you see her. Why don't you go and get her?" I say in a sarcastic tone.

"Eh would, but she was standin we that wanker Murdo when we left."

"Good, they fucking deserve each other."

We get to the Parliamentary Bar and I feel quite calm after what happened with Murdo but this is obviously due to the joint that Gaz passed around on the way. Gaz hands around more e's but I don't take any. I don't want to be too wasted in case I run into Murdo again or worse end up shagging Lisa again. We have another couple of drinks and then head off to Slims.

8) Slims

Slimjims is now just another commercialised night club, but a few years ago to us regulars it was just Slims...our little heaven. This was definitely the place to be on a Saturday night, although we were actually here sometimes Friday, Saturday and Sunday. It used to be the type of place were if your face didn't fit you didn't get in. It was always full of lovely friendly people. Girls that wanted to talk to you and get to know you and guys who weren't out to start a fight or cause bother. I was always invited back to party's afterwards not that I always went as I usually had my own party to go to. It didn't matter how fucked you were someone always made sure you were alright.

Slims door policy must have been very good as there was never much trouble in the club. I've lost count of the number of times people were in front of me in the queue and the doorman would say 'Sorry, regulars only.' There would be a bit of mouthing and occasionally a bit of trouble but to me it was as if the doormen could tell who the trouble makers were by there appearance. This was a good thing as it meant they didn't have the aggravation of having to throw them out later.

This has all changed now as new owners have extended the club by renovating the space under and above the original building. This extra space is a considerable size, which means the owners have to let in anybody to fill it. All the schemie's that wouldn't normally get past the front door are now swaggering about like they own the place. They can now wander through from the extension to the original Slims where they bang into people purposefully to start trouble.

Slavering over girls who wouldn't look twice at them. The girls down stairs would maybe fall for that because they are also schemies 'Sweengin thir chewy.'

In the past I've heard people comment that Slims is 'full of posers' and the girls are all stuck up bitches who don't even talk to you. I look at them and think no fucking wonder they don't talk to you. The girls that they were referring to are not stuck up, they shag just as much as the schemie girls. To the schemies it's maybe because these girls talk more polite but to me, it's because they have a bit of class. The type of girls who want to better themselves by not going up the road with some wanker who cant handle their drink and swaggers about wanting to fight the world. I think to myself, what's stuck up about that?…fucking schemies.

When we get to Slims and the queue is very long, Gaz is totally flying and has a word with the doorman that he knows from years back.

"Any chance o lettin a few old regulars ti the front."

"No probs Gaz, is it just the six of you." Gaz nods and the doorman points to the other side of the entrance. Before going in Jamie goes to walk away and says "I'll see you guys later." And walks off in the direction of the Mardi.
Kyle shouts on him "Oh where are you going?" He doesn't answer but turns, gives the sly grin and keeps walking. We all know he's away to the Mardi to get a few under agers. We'll meet him later.

Gaz has a word with the doorman about Murdo, just in case he comes in and starts his shit. The doorman tells Gaz not to worry about it as he's banned from Slims for years anyway. We go straight upstairs and head for the bar to get the drinks in. Kyle follows me and Gaz heads to the toilet but Mickey and Joey are on the dance floor with their hands in the air, bouncing from the e's that they took earlier. Kyle has had a couple of e's too but he doesn't dance, he's one of those peo-ple that stands at the bar and gibbers a load of shit to everyone.

The place starts to fill up and after several bottles poured down my neck I'm starting to feel more relaxed and put all that shit earlier with Murdo out of my head.

As I walk around the club nodding to the usual faces added with the occasional handshake but I know what I am looking for. The little honey from my taxi. I walk through the three levels of the club with no one coming even close to looking like her. I notice Emma standing at the bar, well it's actually her lovely sexy legs that I notice first, she has on a very short skirt and is leaning over the bar trying to get served. I go over and rub my hand up her leg, I see the expression from the side of her face ready to give a me a mouthful but she soon changes that to a smile when she realises who it is.

"Oh it's you Shane, I thought it was some sleazy bastard, they were away to get a good slap."

Straight away I can see that Emma is wasted as her eyes are popping out of her head and she is chewing her gum at about 100mph. While talking to her I'm really quite jealous of the state that she's in, I've had a few e's from Gaz but I'm not getting anywhere near the hit she's having. I decide to wait with Emma until she gets served but the DJ plays an old tune, which makes Emma grab my hand and pulls me to the dance floor near her friends. The tune has everyone on their feet with their hands in the air. The club is jumping and I can't believe how good I feel after such a shit start to my night. As I'm dancing, Emma's friend Stacey is there and comes closer to talk to me. She has to lean into my ear so that I can hear her and out the corner of my eye I can see Emma staring.

"Hi Shane, what happened to my phone call, I'm still waiting." She says in her sexy polite voice, I look at her next to Emma and think how did they end up as friends because Emma is a 'look at me' blonde bimbo type girl and Stacey is more of a quiet reserved student type.

"Sorry I've had a few things to sort out…" I don't get a chance to say anymore as Emma puts her arm around my neck and pulls me gently saying to Stacey in a friendly tone

"You're not getting him. He's with me."

Stacey smiles at me and says "Good luck."

I have thoughts going through my mind of how much of a good night this is turning out to be, until I hear a voice behind me shout in a very aggressive tone.

"Get your fucking hands off him. He's with me."

I turn to see Lisa standing with a look of pure anger. She then shouts at Emma

"You wee slapper, get your hands off him."

"Lisa what are you doing? These are friends of mine. Why don't you fuck and off leave me alone?"

As soon as the last part comes out of my mouth I regret it as I know it's enough to get her started. I see the rage in her as she goes for Emma and grabs her by the hair pulling her to the ground. The bouncer sees it all and steps forward grabbing Lisa and throwing her out. I turn to the girls and apologise for what happened but Stacey takes my hand and says "Don't be daft Shane it's not you're fault."

"If you follow me to the bar I'll get you all a drink."

I head off the dance floor and go straight to the bar, with Stacey and Emma and the rest of her friends walking swiftly behind. I get to the bar and shout up a round of drinks for them and I can hear Emma behind me asking all the questions

"Who the fuck was that Shane? What was that all about ?"

I turn and start handing out the drinks and say "Look, it was someone I was seeing. I'm really sorry about that, I hope these drinks make up for it."

"No they won't, but if you invite us back to yours after here I'm sure that would make up for it" Emma says as she strokes my arm.

"Yeah sure, I'll meet you all outside at the end." As I say

this I go to walk away but Emma pulls me close so that she can talk in my ear

"Just thought I'd let you know. I don't have any knickers on."

I move in close to her ear and tell her "You're a durty girl."

"DUURTY, I like that."

I'll bet you do.

I smile and walk away as I have to find the others to tell them to go back to mine. As I'm walking around the club looking for them, at the back of my mind I am still hoping to bump into the girl from my taxi. Although at the same time I can't stop thinking about Emma with her short skirt and no knickers. I know I feel as though I made a connection with her in the short time she was in my car I don't even know her. She could be married with kids for all I know. I eventually find Kyle at the top bar, still wasted and talking shit to some girl who looks under age and who is also wasted. How she managed to get past the doorman I don't know, but I guess if she has I.D. then there's nothing they can do. I pull him aside to tell him to come up to mine but if he is he'd better not fucking bring her with him.

"What's wrong with her?"

"How wasted are you Kyle? She looks about fifteen. Anyway Emma and her friends are coming up so if you see any of the others tell them"

"Yeah, no problem."

I wander around the club but I don't see any of the others and once I am satisfied that the girl I'm looking for is not here my attention is soon directed to Emma whom I see coming out the toilet. She comes over and asks me to go to the bar with her to find Stacey. I let her lead the way so that I can look at her arse as she walks. We get to the bar and it's very crowded but we find Stacey who is waiting to get served. As I am waiting with her I have my hand on Emma's arse and as her skirt is so short my fingers slip under easily. I work my way through until they slide inside her. She turns around and wraps her legs around me and I can feel her getting turned on. While this is happening Stacey is chatting away to which I am nodding in agreement but do not have the faintest ideal as to what she is talking about. Emma is now rubbing my semi through my jeans and I feel like shagging her at the bar in front of everyone…knowing Emma she would probably let me. Before it gets out of hand Stacey passes the drinks.

Before Slims finishes I ask Emma if she wants to leave early so that we could get a taxi easier. We both know it's to get to mine and have a shag before anyone else gets there. We sneak away without telling anyone. They all know where I live so they'll all get there eventually.

9) Back at mine

We get to the flat and I go straight into the bedroom and take off my top as it stinks of smoke and it's a bit sweaty from being on the crowded dance floor in Slims. Emma follows me and goes to the window.

"I love your view."

My bedroom window looks over the Tay and onto Fife. It looks good if you're trying to impress people but tonight... it's not needed. As Emma continues to look out the window I put my hands on her hips and slide up her skirt revealing her lovely tight arse.

"Hey calm down."

"What do you mean? You're the one that was teasing me by telling me you had no knickers on."

She turns around and starts kissing me. I pull her close to me and can feel myself getting turned on. She slides her hand down and rubs my semi through my jeans. She has me unbuttoned in seconds and is sliding down both my jeans and boxers. I slide on a condom and before I know it I am banging her from behind. As soon as I start to get into a rhythm my mind starts to wander. This seems to happen quite a lot when you take e's. I start to think that I have no connection with Emma except pure lust. I don't know anything about this girl. I don't even know her last name. She starts to groan a little louder and this puts my mind back on track again but just as I feel I am about to build up the buzzer goes on the intercom.

Emma groans "Don't stop."

I have to make a quick decision. If I don't let them in I'll keep shagging Emma for about another ten minutes maybe come, and then I'll be stuck with her for the rest of the night…fuck that!

I pull out and start taking off the condom, Emma sits down on the leather sofa opposite the bed with her legs spread wide and starts touching herself.

"Do you really want to answer that?"

"I'm very tempted not to."

I grab a t-shirt and go to answer the buzzer. When I come back Emma is fixing herself.

"I think you should be a porn star Emma."

She thrusts her arse towards me and puts her finger in her mouth

"Really."

"You're duuurty" I say drawing it out. We both smile as we hear people come in the front door.

"Thanks for waiting on us" Stacey says sarcastically.

I don't answer, I go straight to the stereo and put some music on. It doesn't matter what music it is, as I know when Gaz steps in the door the first thing he'll do is change it to his rap shite.

"If anyone wants a drink, just help yourself."

Kyle, Mickey and Joey turn up and say that Gaz has met up with Jamie and are away to pick up more alcohol. Joey shouts me through to the balcony for a smoke, If it's only hash I don't mind but it's grass and that stinks out the whole house. Stacey follows me out and Joey leaves once he passes the joint. I only have a few puffs when the phone rings.

"That'll be Gaz" I say as I walk back into the kitchen putting on a silly voice as if to imitate him and say "Ahright Shane eh'm awa ti pick up Biscuit."

But when I answer the smile is soon wiped from my face.

"Shane who is that you're with?"

"Who is this? Is that you Lisa? What the fuck do you want?"

"Shane is that why you don't want to see me, to be with her?"

"With who? What are you talking about?"

"The girl you are with on your balcony."

"WHAT?, ARE YOU WATCHING ME?" I shout.

"I wanted to see you." She says through her tears.

"LISA, GO AWAY."

"Please don't hang up."

"I've nothing to say to you."

"Please Shane don't hang up, I just want to see you." She is sounding really desperate now.

"Can I come up and see you."

"I don't think that would be a good idea do you?"

"Tell her to come up." Stacey says, trying to be funny. I give her a sarcastic smile but her comment does make me think for a second and stops me from getting angry. I try to calm Lisa down by telling her to go home and that I'll talk to her tomorrow but she is crying and breaking her heart down the phone.

"If you had any chance of ever seeing me again, you blew it by what you did earlier."

Through the noise of her crying I just make out the words 'Sorry.'

"Look, all this phoning and following me is not helping. It is pushing me further away. Why don't you go home and we'll talk about this tomorrow?"

"What do you mean? You'll come up and see me?"

"Look I have to go. I have people here. Go home and we'll talk tomorrow."

I have no intension of talking to her tomorrow but I just want her to go home before she does something stupid. Before I hang up Gaz walks in the door with Jamie. He puts a crate of lager on the kitchen table along with a bottle of vodka and due to the tension in the house as everyone has gone quiet he asks "Wah's on the phone?"

Before I get a chance to answer Stacey says "The stalker."
Gaz walks over to me and shouts down the phone.

"JIST FUCK OFF."

As he says this, he grabs the phone and hangs it up, he then walks out onto the balcony and takes what is left of the joint. I look at Stacey and we both laugh.

"What yous laughin at?" He says, as he exhales.

Before I get a chance to reply he takes a disc out of his pocket and walks into the living room. The music is turned off.

"Sorry, eh'm jist cheengin the disc, ken. Pittin some decent music on."

"Just make yourself at home Gaz. Will you?" I shout through from the balcony.

I go to walk back into the house but as I walk past Stacey she puts her hand on my hip and leans forward to kiss me...which I gladly return.

"Where's your bedroom?" She says with a cheeky grin.

"What about Emma?"

"What about her? She would do the same to me."

I go back inside and another of Stacey's friends comes up and starts blabbing away in her ear. This is my chance to sneak off and I find a seat next to Kyle who is being entertained by Gaz's story's. Stacey keeps looking over at me and nodding to the door. I lift up my hand to signal five minutes but in that time I am secretly checking her out. I look around the room at my friends and I know if I told any of them that I had been shagging Emma just over an hour ago and now her best friend is trying to get me into bed they would wonder what the fuck I was waiting on. I know an opportunity like this doesn't happen every day and I am beginning to wonder why I am still here thinking about it. Oh man, I have to stop taking these e's they make me think to much. I finish my drink and go to the toilet. When I come out Stacey is standing waiting on me. She leans into me and we start snogging.

"Which one is your bedroom?"

I nod behind her and she takes my hand to lead the way. We lie on the bed and she cuddles into me. We start fondling each other but somehow I hold back.

"What's wrong?"

"Nothing."

She can obviously tell something else is on my mind...or someone. What's wrong with me? I have this girl lying next to me wanting me to shag her and I'm hesitating because I don't feel a connection with her, because it doesn't feel right.

"Is it because of Emma?"

"Eh, eh'm. Well she is in the next room."

"Look, don't worry about it. As I said, she would do it to me."

Stacey puts her hand down to my groin and starts rubbing me. This sends tingles through my balls and all the negative thoughts suddenly disappear. My lustful thoughts are soon back and I am hard again. I start to take off Stacey's clothes but she stands up and takes them off herself. As she walks back to my bed I smile but am really checking out her body. I am lying on my bed with a raging hard on, a naked girl is climbing on top of me and I am thinking that her breasts are too saggy and her arse is too fat. I come to the conclusion that I just don't fancy her. I can tell she is trying to be dominant by telling me to do this or try that, like I've never done this before and it starts to annoy me a little. I feel that i just want to shoot my load and get it over with. I sit up with her legs wrapped around me and her arms around my neck. I move to the edge of the bed and tilt forward until she is about to fall back but I have my hands on her wobbly arse lifting her up and down. She starts groaning louder and this gets me into it, then she whispers through deep breaths that she is about to come...thank fuck. She pulls on my neck tightly and I keep going until she tells me to stop. She lies back on the bed and I get on top of her but after a few minutes she tells me to stop as she can't go on anymore. I still have a raging hard on and am now dying to come myself.

"You don't half know how to fuck me do you?" She says.

These words sound really strange coming from a girl who talks very polite. If she said them to me while we were fucking I maybe would have came. We lie back on the bed and she cuddles up to me again. I am about to dose off when there is a light knock on the bedroom door, I open it to see Joey standing with half a joint.

"Thought you might want this."

"Yeah, cheers mate."

I go to offer Stacey a smoke but she is out like a light. I stub out the joint and turn around to face Stacey. I start wanking as I touch her naked body and it gives me more of a thrill that she could wake up any minute and catch me. My thoughts keep drifting away so I give up and fall asleep. Several hours later I am vaguely woken by the bedroom door opening and I find myself curled up with Stacey's arm wrapped around me. This comfortable position is soon disturbed when Stacey jumps up with a scream as Biscuit jumps up on the bed, licking my face and nudging me to move so as he can get under the covers.

"Fuck off" I shout, more pissed off that I was woken up rather than the dog in my bed.

We both get up, put our clothes on and go through to find that everyone is still here except Emma, who apparently stormed off after she found out I was in bed with Stacey. I ask what happened to Jamie as I head to the kitchen for a drink and someone shouts through that he went for a sleep in the spare room. While in the kitchen I am passed a joint so I stay there chatting to Mickey as we pass it between us, then I think to myself Jamie, on an e, going for a sleep, somehow that just would not happen. I walk through to the spare bedroom and glance around the door. I walk back and signal with my hand for everyone to follow me but I also put my finger over my lips for them to be quiet. They all follow me to the spare room to find Jamie lying on the bed naked with his arm under Emma, who is fast asleep. He obviously couldn't move without waking her. We start laughing and this wakens Emma who looks up, smiles and pulls the cover over her head.

A few hours later after everyone has went home except Gaz and Jamie. I tell them what happened with Emma before they came up. Jamie thinks it's funny and starts all the little wisecracks while Gaz just shakes his head calling us 'sick bastards', I think he's just pissed off that he never got a shag last night. I'll have to get rid of these two shortly as I'm going to need a few more hours sleep before I start work.

Customer No. 1053
Tayside's finest #2

Sunday is hangover day. I always start late on a Sunday and work through until I have enough to pay the office fees. My next fare is at the Dundee Sports Centre where a very butch looking girl is waiting with her large sports bag. She gets in and starts chatting away about her football team who were very close to winning some sort of tournament. As she blabs on and on I comment with the usual 'Uh Huh' when she stops for a breath. This is only to keep the conversation going and to make me sound interested in her story. I don't actually hear a word she says as I am too busy clocking the traffic police following me. I start to get a little paranoid as every turn I make they are right up my arse. I make a detour down a few narrow back streets and sure enough, there they are. Tayside's finest right up my arse…again. What the fuck do they want?

I approach a mini roundabout, which is more like a speed

bump in the road. As the area around this is so small it is very difficult to manoeuvre. As I drive around it my rear wheels go over the edge of it. Within seconds the blue lights are flashing behind me. I pull over.

"What's wrong, why are they stopping you?" My customers says.

Because they have got fucking nothing better to do.

"I don't know" I say as I step out of the car to see what the fuck they want.

The officer who was in the passenger seat is out of the police car and marches over to me.

"Is this your car?" He asks quite aggressively.

"Yeah."

"Is it a taxi?"

How stupid is this tosser. He's just been following me for several miles, I have a sign on the back of my car which says 'Licensed Cab' and he asks me if it's a taxi. I don't want to be a smart arse here as I will just end up getting myself into more shit and the cunts will just lift me.

"Why didn't you go around the roundabout?"

"I did."

"No you never, you drove over the top of it." He says in his aggressive tone.

I feel a tremendous amount of anger towards him right now just for the way he is talking to me. I don't know if this is what his intension is but I'm not going to bite.

"If I did it was only my back wheels."

He becomes even more aggressive now and has his finger out pointing it in my face as he rants and raves. This has to be one of my pet hates and it reminds me of when teachers were telling me off at school and they soon got what was coming for doing it.

"Put your meter on hold and get in the back of the police car please."

I walk back to my car with my fists clenched and my teeth

gritted together.

"What's the matter? Why have they stopped you?" My customer says.

"Apparently for not going around the mini roundabout."

"What? You're fuckin jokin?."

I put my meter on hold and shrug my shoulders at her before walking back to the police car. As soon as I sit in the back, the big fat cunt in the drivers seat turns around and just like his partner has adopted the same aggressive attitude towards me and says "Do you see that sign back there?"

How can I see it if it's back there? You fat cunt.

"Uh Huh." I say.

"That's a mini roundabout. You approach it like you would any other roundabout. It's not a road bump that you drive over." He says staring at me with his wide eyes like he's high or something.

It's times like this I wish I had a secret camera to video these cunts attitude towards people. I would sell it to some dodgy cable channel just like they do with us. The only difference is, that their side wouldn't be edited to make them look good.

The anger in me is starting to build up with every word he says to me. If the cunt wasn't in the police and just some prick in the street he wouldn't last two minutes with an attitude like that. Somebody would be dancing on his fucking head by now. These cunts think…Well actually they know. That they can talk to you whatever way they want and if you talk back to them in the same manner, you get done for it. It's the same with bouncers, they act all tough when they stand on the door with their steroid built friends but when do you ever see them on a night out in a pub? Never, that's because they would be looking over their shoulder the whole night, waiting on someone they've been wide with to smash them.

Still staring at me, the fat driver says "It's a bad habit and it's one that just cost you thirty pounds."

He looks at his partner all smug with himself. It sounds as though he's been waiting to use that line all day and he's all chuffed with himself that he got a chance to use it. Now he can go home and get out his vast supply of kiddie porn like all those other sick coppers and wank himself to death. I am still in shock that they actually pulled me for something as petty as this. These cunts can sit here all day long and nine out of ten cars will go over the top of this fucking bump. The driver leans over and tells me to blow in the tube. He wait's a few seconds before showing the result to his partner. All clear you fucking pricks now give me my ticket and let me on my way. I smile at them as they let me out of the patrol car.

"Thank you very much." I say looking just as smug as them.

I cant let them have the satisfaction of knowing that they bother me. I get back in the taxi and drive off but they still follow me. My customer acts more angry than me when I explain about the fine.

"They want to go and catch some real bloody criminals. How many houses have been broken into in the time they've stopped you?"

I nod my head in agreement and smile at her but I am watching these cunt in my mirror as they are still driving up my arse. I signal to go into the cul de sac where my customer lives and they have the cheek to put the foot down as they pass me. With an attitude like that, no wonder people in this country have no respect for the them whatsoever.

Customer No. 1132
Dirty Stop-outs

This Sunday night is starting to drag out but I guess that's hangovers for you. Fintry Crescent for Munro. I wait for a while at the bottom of the flats and just as I am about to drive off thinking that it's a no-job I see the main door open. Two girls come out, they are in their late twenty's and look as rough as they come. Actually they look like I feel. They've obviously been up since last night. The one that gets in the front is very fat. She has on one of those tops that doesn't cover her waist and the spare tyre with the stretch marks is hanging out and nearly covering my handbrake. I can smell the B.O. wafting from her as the car sinks several inches due to her weight.

"Hi girls, where are you going?"

"Eh dinna ken. Hey Linda whare are we goin?"

Hopefully back in the sea you big fat fucking whale.

"Go ti yours if ye want."

"Eh, Stoby mate."

On the way the fat girl in the front is taking about the guy who's house they have just left. She is ripping into him but I think this is for the girl in the back's benefit as it sounds like she was the one who was supposedly getting it on with him.

"He was tryein ti neck we me when you were in the kitchen."

"Was he."

"Eh, he's hands were ah over is."

"What a prick, how did you no say something ti is?"

"Eh dinna ken. Eh think eh was jist shocked."

If some guy was coming on to this girl I can only imagine what he must look like if that is his taste in burds. She is absolutely horrible, her teeth are yellow and for someone to want to try and kiss her, they must have some serious mental health issues. I have known several overweight girls but they usually have plenty other quality's that has made me attracted to them. Sometimes it was a nice face or a good sense of humour or even just a great personality but this girl is one of the most ugly, nasty people I have ever encountered

"Here, are ye up fir goin oot the night?"

"Too right, eh'm aff work the morn. Eh'll hae ti cheenge meh claithes though, eh've hud these on last night."

A shower wouldn't go a miss. You smell like a cundie. Here's to what that guy would have encountered if she had let him put his hand down her knickers. She pulls down the sun visor to look in the mirror

"Oh meh gode. Check the state o meh hair."

I glance slightly over while driving and think to myself. This girl is so fat her layers are nearly hanging over my handbrake. Her B.O. is stinking out my car even though my windows are down. Her clothes are filthy, her teeth are yellow and most of all she is so ugly…and she is worried about her fucking hair.

10) Customer No. 434
Junkie city

Eh hae a delivery later so eh've got auld Wullie's car fir the night. He kens he always gits a good wee bundle at the end o meh shift, whether eh'm busy or no. He likes the grass so eh always leave him a enough fir a wee smoke as well.

Pitkerro road fir Stewart. Mare junkies. Eh've picked up this couple a few times before an they are a pain in the arse. They hae their bairn we them the day an as soon as they get in the car they start arguin aboot whare ti go first.

"Kirtin post office. We huv ti git there before it shuts." The fat ginger cow in the back says ti is.

It's nearly closin time but eh'm no awa ti speed fir them. It would be just meh luck ti that the traffic polis would clock is, an that's the last thing eh need. Eh git there on time an eh huvna even stopped the car but she's opened the door an treyin ti get oot.

"Hud on missis." Eh say, bit she just ignores is an storms awa inti the shop. She's back in the car within a few meenits, bit her man has been sittin fidgettin an lookin affay agitated. He tried ti talk ti is but eh cut him aff we blunt answers. Eh think he kens that eh dinna like him.

"Ah boot fuckin time." He say as she gits in the car.

"Shit yer puss you."

"Right alang this street an eh'll tell ye when ti stop." She hands him money, that has obviously just come fae the family allowance she gets. He tells me ti park ootside a hoose on the end o a row, but gets oot an runs around the corner ti another hoose.

These junkies always dae that, eh think it's cause whaever's hoose they are goin ti they dinna see them comin an naebody gets freaked oot when they see a strange car oot-side.

He's back in the car an starts whisperin ti her. Next she's on the phone…

"Go ti the hulltoon drevir." She shouts fae the back. Ah the wey ti the hulltoon eh kin feel the tension buildin up between them as they start gettin louder.

"What if he's no got any?"

"Then we'll trey…" Her voice lowers so that eh canna hear wahs name it is.

"Eh hate goin there."

"Eh'm no gein a fuck. If it comes ti it, yer fuckin goin." Ginger says.

We stop it a tenement block in Dundonald street an the guy bolts oot the car an up the stairs. He's back doon an inti the car within a couple o meenits lookin affay distressed. Eh canna tell if this is cause he hasna been fixed up or that he has ti face his fat ginger missus we nae drugs. The meter is tickin up an ah that's on meh mind is if eh'm gonna get peyed. Eh dinna gee a shit if they get their drugs an sit oot their haeds for days or it's a bad batch an they overdose an thir bairn finds them deid. Eh really coudna gee a fuck. That's the life they chose an that's the wey they want ti live it. But they had better pey fir this taxi or that fat ginger cow's man will be feelin meh fist in he's fuckin puss. At the back o meh mind eh'm actually hopin that they dinna hae enough money fir the taxi just so that eh hae an excuse ti hit the cunt. Then eh'll tak they're smack aff them an chuck it in the fuckin bin.

Eh'm directed ti a few mare dodgy hooses near the hull-toon area an during this time the ginger cow in the back is phonin around ti trey an find somebody ti fix them up. They are baith gettin affay agitated an it's turnin quite aggressive.

Eh feel fir the bairn wah is sittin in the back no openin he's mooth. She eventually finds somebody wah has what they want bit they winna be hame for anither twenty meenits.

"Right drevir, on ti Lochee."

Now there's a surprise, Lochee, fuckin junkie city.

"Eh telt ye, ye should huv phoned him first."

"Ah shit yer puss."

This arguin goes on ah the wey ti Lochee an at one point eh'm close ti throwin them oot. Eh look it the bairn in the back an eh feel really sorry on him so eh continue the journey.

"That'll be sixteen eighty please."

"Nah, were goin back again."

"No in this fuckin taxi yer no. This is as far as eh'm goin we ye."

She hands me seventeen pound an eh dig oot the twenty pence cheenge. As eh hand it ti her she grabs it oot o meh hand an storms oot the car slammin the door. It wouldna huv been the first time that eh've gave they junkies the benefit o the doubt an eftir they've peyed fir their drugs an drove them hame, they suddenly dinna hae enough ti pey fir the taxi.

Eh find it affay sad that there lives revolve aroond their next fix. Eh understand there are genuine hard luck stories o how people have ended up as junkies but they are in the minority. Eh feel sorry on their bairn growin up an seein ah this goin on. It maks me wonder if their bairn wakens up in the morning an has clean fresh claithes ti wear ti scale an something in the cupboards for he's breakfast or if he's parents even bather ti get up ti see them aff. It makes ye wonder what sort o up bringin they had to bring their ain bairn up in that kind o environment. The bairn is mibbe just a convenience ti help them receive extra benefits an less hassle for them ti find a joab. Eh'm onay workin the night cause eh hae a drap aff later an seein that makes me want ti walk awa fae it. But when eh think aboot it eh'm no dealin in smack an naebody telt them ti stick a needle in their airm.

Customer No. 497
Ruining my mood

Eh've been dragged aboot a mile an a half to pick up this
fat lazy cow and she's only goin to the fuckin bingo at the
end o the street. She's a grumpy bitch wha's moanin cause
she canna pit her seat belt on. Maybe if she got aff her arse
an walked now an again she would loose some weight an be
able to put her seat belt on. Eh drev to the main door o the
bingo an there is a large queue waitin ti git in.

"Looks busy the day, eh." Eh say treyin ti make conversation.

The ignorant cow doesna even answer, she looks up an
grunts.

"That'll be two pound twenty please."

She hands me the correct money.

"Thanks very much." Eh say as she looks at me again we a
face like a well skelped arse. She goes ti git oot o the car an
the hale queue is watchin as she struggles ti get her fat arse
up aff the front seat. It wouldn't be so bad if she lost some o
they spare tyres that are badly hidden beneath her lang over-
coat that she is wearing on ain o the hottest days we've had
ah summer. She eventually woddles oot o the car an eh shout
cheerio before she slams the door in meh face ignorin me. As
she canna walk that fast due to her size eh slowly reverse the
car as she heads for the back o the queue. She's obviously
haein a bad day so there's nae wey eh'm aboot ti drev aff an
let her leave her bad day we me. Eh shout again oot the
windee an several people turn ti look.

"Cheerio, I hope you have a nice day." Eh shout bit louder
in meh polite sarcastic tone. She doesna even turn her haed,
the ignorant bitch. Eh shout again an mare o the queue has
turned to see what's going on. She turns her haed slightly ti
see me we meh big smug grin on meh face an she says

through gritted teeth.

"Cheerio."

Eh laugh oot loud as eh drive aff kenin that the bitch didna put a downer on meh day. Eh canna believe eh drove ah that wey to pick up that grumpy bitch ti drev her aboot a hundred yairds doon her street. If she got aff her fat arse an walked ti the bingo mibbe she wouldna be so fuckin miserable. Eh huv always been brought up we the sayin that manners cost nothin, a simple hello, goodbye, please an thank you go a lang wey in meh book.

The drop off

Right that's the Glesgay cunt in Dundee now. Eh'v text him ti go ti The Scots Bar. It's the first ain he'll come ti when he gets aff the train. Eh'll text him again when ti get the staff ti phone him a taxi. They use meh firm so if eh time it right eh'll get the joab. He had better get the staff ti phone cause if he uses he's mobile an gets busted they'll ask him how he got that number. That's me just went number one so eh'll text him now.

Good that's the joab come through. Eh drev up ootside the pub an this wee weedgie cunt swaggers oot we a holdall ower he's shidder. He's the typical wee hard man, scars, skin-haed an ten bob swagger. Glasgow must be a rough place ti live cause nearly every weedgie that eh meet has dirty big fuckin scars doon thir face. He walks ower an gits inti the back o the taxi.

"Ahright mate, whare is it you're headin?"

"Aye awright pal, am going up the Perth road, any recom-mendations." He says in he's weedgie acccent.

"How aboot The Parliamentary."

"Aye, that'll dae, am just havin the one drink like, then am headin back." He says as he takes a package oot o he's holdall an leans forward puttin it on the front seat.

"I'll see you again some time pal." He says as he gets oot o the car.

"Eh, tak it easy mate." Eh say picking up the package an puttin it under meh seat.

Eh drev over towards Kirkton as that's whare it's gettin picked up fae. As eh'm drevin eh'm textin at the same time ti arrange the pick up. As eh drev over the Kingsway eh see the polis in meh mirror an the blue lights come on. Shit this is it, eh'm goin doon big time. Ten ti fifteen easy. Meh hert is goin like the clappers. Eh pick up the package fae under meh seat an wipe it doon we a cloth before throwin it in the back. Eh'll just plead ignorant. They canna prove fuck all. The wee weedgie cunt must have left it there, it's nothing ti dae we me. Eh wonder wha stuck is in. They must have been onti the weedgie that they've used for the drap.

Eh pull over an the polis boy gits oot an walks over ti meh windee.

"What's the problem?" Eh nearly choke ti say.

"Do you have a mobile phone on you?" He says.

"What? Eh how?"

"Can I see it please?"

Usually eh would start ti get wide an gee them loads o shite but right now meh hert feels like it's ready ti explode.

"Eh nae bother." Eh say handin him the phone.

"Can you come and take a seat in the back off the patrol car please."

Eh get oot o the taxi an walk ower ti the patrol car an meh legs are ready ti buckle as they feel like jelly. He opens the back door an eh get in, he gets in the front next ti he's partner.

"Under the traffic violation act…,we have reason to believe you were using your mobile phone while in control of a vehicle, registration number…, do you have anything to say?"

"Eh, no."

"We are issuing you with a fixed penalty of…"

Oh ye fucker, meh pumpin hert gradually starts ti settle back down. Eh thought eh had been busted. The polis hand me the fixed penalty an let me oot o their car. Eh get in the taxi an get ti fuck away fae them as quick as eh could. Any other time eh would huv got mesel lifted cause eh would huv argued we them an gave them loads o shite. But we that gear sittin on the back seat eh just shut meh puss an let them git on we it. And to think they daft polis were geein me a ticket for usin a mobile while drevin, an eh hud something on is that could huv put me awa fir years. It's a good joab eh wisna pickin meh nose cause eh'v actually seen mesel looking in the mirror ti get a wee cruster oot an endin up drevin on the other side o the road. As soon as the polis are oot o sight eh pull ower an text the cunt so that eh could get this gear awa.

Customer No. 679

Gaz's durty woman

Eh was gled ti git rid o that gear there e'll tell ye. Eh'll dae this one last joab an head aff ti the pub. Asda for McComskie. There's a young lassie waitin we a pile o shoppin bags an eh can tell there'll no be a bar o soap in any o them. The lassie would look no bad if she cleaned herself up a bit but Shane was right aboot kennin bey looking at somebody wah's gonna smell before they get in the car. Eftir eh load up the boot she gits in the back an eh notice the musty smell right away. The wee dirty mink.

"So whare are you goin hen?"

"Charleston."

"Nae bother."

"Listen when we git ti meh hoose, eh'll hae ti nip in fir the money like, ken."

"Eh, bit jist mind an come back oot again."

Eh drev up ti the hoose an as soon as eh see the gairden eh recognise it an eh've never even been here before. Eh mind o Shane tellin me aboot some lassie one night, she said ti him that she didna hae enough money fir the fare an that he could put his hand up her skirt an feel her cunt instaed if he wanted. Now Shane is no one ti be fussy aboot he's hole but she was apparently that bad he telt her he wouldna put he's hand up her skirt if he had a fuckin nuclear protective glove on. He also telt her ti pey the fuckin fare or he wis gonna phone the polis. It was dark but he remembers her gairden lookin like a scrap yaird we an auld B.M.W. in the drevway. Well surprise surprise in front o me now is a rusty auld B.M.W. Eh pick up her shoppin oot o the boot an follow her ti her front door. Fir a smelly mink she husna half got a bra pair o legs on her. She has got on ain o they wee denim skirts. As she opens her front door eh'm hit we a rancid smell that fills half meh lungs.

"Come in an e'll see if eh kin find some cheenge for ye." She says.

As eh go through the half papered, half scrapped lobby eh feel as though the soles o meh shoes are stickin ti the flair.

"Do ye want a cup o tea while yer here?" She says.

Eh look around the place an am shocked at the state o it. How anybody can live like this is incredible. Hygiene in a woman is no one o meh priorities like it is we Shane, but this place is mingin. Eh dinna think it taks much ti shower every-day. Eh'm talkin ten minutes topps an that includes emptyin your sacks. Eh try ti see past ah this an look at the lassie in front o is. She has a slim figure an a nice face…an nothing a good scrub wouldna put right.

"Sure e'll hae a cup o tea. Twa sugars an plenty o mulk please."

Well Shane, she might no be good enough fir you, but she's

certainly gittin it fae me. She puts the kettle on an before eh ken it, we are kissin in the middle o the kitchen. Eh hae meh hands on her arse an lift up her wee denim mini. She pulls awa fae is an gets doon on her knees ti suck is aff. Eh had a wank earlier so meh knob could be a bit cheesy. No that she'll fuckin notice. She pulls oot meh knob an looks up at me smilin before puttin it in her mooth. Eh feel a bit sick when eh notice the broken teeth an the yellow mouldy stains on them. She gees it a wee suck but she's no very good at it. Eh pick her up an bend her over the sink. Eh lift her mini skirt right up over her waist an pull doon her knickers re-vealin a fuckin lovely toned arse. Eh slide meh knob in an it feels like it's no even touchin the sides. Eh'm bangin awa but eh stop ti tak her knickers right aff so that eh could open her legs a bit mare. Eh slide them doon ti her ankles an as she steps oot o them eh notice the thick yellow stains. They re-mind me o curry sauce. Eh slide meh knob back in an as eh git meh rhythm back eh start ti think aboot diseases an realise eh dinna huv a condom on. This is a first fir me as it's never worried is before. Maybe cause it's the first time eh've shagged a burd we rotten teeth, breath like meh dogs farts...on a good day, airmpits that smell like onions, an a cunt that leaves mouldy stains on her knickers that resemble curry sauce. Then eh think...nah eh've hud worse.

There's nae point in worryin aboot it now, meh knobs ahready in. Eh feel that eh'm awa ti shoot meh load so eh grab her hair fae behind. This was ti make her groan a wee bit but ah it's done is put me aff eftir eh feel how greasy it is. Eh pull oot an start wankin. Eh shoot meh load right up her back an some drips doon her arse. Eh pull up meh jeans an git ti fuck oot o there as quick as eh could, no even turnin ti say cheerio. Eh run ti the car an drev aff feelin dirty as fuck...an no in a good wey.

11) Same jeans

E'm no lookin forward ti the night, Shane has nipped oor haed the hale week ti go ti some gig night at the Doghoose cause some burd he met asked him ti go. As lang as it's better than last Seturday eftir that run in he hud we Murdo. Eh ken he's no goin ti let that go. Eh've only seen Shane once this week an that was only ti drap aff some cash. Every time eh've phoned him he's been working. Eh jist hope he's no been seein that fuckin Lisa eftir ah the trouble she's caused. We meet up in the East View fir a few pints before headin ti the Doghoose an Jamie is on the end o the slaggin for shagging Emma. Every cunt kens now that Shane shagged her just oors before him. But as always it doesna last long we Jamie bein the smart arse that he is. The slaggin soon turns roond an now Shane is takin a bit o stick fir last week. Before we head aff eh eventually get Shane on he's ain ti enquire aboot Lisa but he swears he's no heard fae her since last week but he did mention somethin aboot he's car being damaged an thinks it was somethin ti dae we Dek Murdo. Eh telt him that it wasna his style, as Murdo wouldna be that sneaky he would probably dae it in front o him.

When we get ti the Doghoose there is a wee queue ti git in, which is very unusual as the first band has no even started yet. We struggle ti reach the bar as the place is packed. There is quite a young crowd aroond us but they soon move forward as the first band kicks aff. Eh stand at the bar we Kyle an Shane but Jamie, Mickey an Joey walk nearer the stage, which we ah agree is fir them ti get a better look at the wee lassies dancin aroond at the front. Shane looks distracted and eh see he's eye's scanin the whole pub.

"What's wrang mate, has she stood ye up?"

"What are you talking about?" He says we a straight face as if he doesna ken what eh mean.

"The burd wha telt ye ti come here, has she stood ye up?"

Eh look at Kyle an we baith laugh. Shane gets ah flustered an treys ti cheege the subject.

"There's the first band comin on."

We ah look up ti the stage ti see four wee hippy young guys pick up their guitars. Their called 'The View' an their average age is aboot seventeen, hence the wee lassies hangin aroond the stage. As soon as they blast oot their first tune eh'm hooked. Eh'm no even into ah that indie shite but eh can tell there a bit special...an that's withoot any drugs yet. They play a few sangs an lookin at the crowd jumpin aboot it makes is wish eh was a teenager again. Shane an Kyle are natterin ti themselves aboot how much they sound like this band or that sang sounds too much like that sang. Eh was never into that music ti ken what they're on aboot. Eh'm mare o a Hip Hop man, eh like artists that tell you how many bitches they've fucked or how many guns they huv. It's no that eh dinna like this type o music. Eh jist dinna listen ti it that much. Shane an Kyle have ripped into every sang that they've done. It starts annoyin me so eh hae ti say somethin.

"Look ye couple o cunts, eh think they're no bad. Fir one thing they're dein ah their ain sangs, which is unusual these days an so what if they sound like other bands. Every other fuckin group does it. An two they are onay fuckin seventeen or eighteen, eh'll bet Oasis or U2 wirna that good at that age. An three they can play better than any o you ever fuckin will."

The two o them look at is an then look at each other we a stupid expression before makin some childish noise in a high pitched tone "wooooooo."

Jamie, Joey an Mickey come over an they ah hae a funny

look on their pusses.

"What's the joke?" Eh say.

"Have you heard the sang that's on now? It's called 'Same Jeans.' It's aboot you Gaz. Eh've had the same jeans on fir four days now an em off inti the toon." Jamie tries ti sing we a stupid look on he's puss.

They ah laugh but eh soon turn it roond.

"Eh but what aboot the ain the singer says is called 'the don' that must be aboot you. A soft touch o a boy whah sits on he's ain while we are ah oot takin e's."

We ah laugh except Jamie as he turns ti the bar ti get another roond in before the next band comes on. When Jamie passes me a drink he asks is for a few e's an eh gee him a couple. Ahbody else is lookin on, so eh dish oot what's left between the rest o us. Eh obviously keep a few extra back fir mesel. Before the next band come on eh go ootside fir a quick joint we Shane an Kyle. While we are oot there eh notice that thirs loads o young people oot thir nut on e's. This is afay strange ti me as eh've nivir took e's in this kind o environment. It's always been at a rave like the Rumba or the Glam an sometimes the occasional trip ti Glesgay fir the Tunnel or the Arches. That was the time o Pete tong an the Judge dein the roonds before they became fuckin celebrity deejays. They kent how ti pick you up we the right tune when you were waitin on your hit kickin in. Now we jist swally a few an go ti Slim's but even that's no the same now. Different people, different atmospere, but we still go cause it's the only place left that still plays half decent tunes. Jist before we go back in eh see Shanes face light up as some wee dark haired lassie walks past.

"Hi remember me? You're taxi driver."

"Oh hi, so you made it then?"

"Yeah, I managed to persuade my friends to come."

Eh watch as Shane searches his mind for something else to say. It's only a few seconds but eh could tell he's stuck for words.

"I'll have to go and find my friends, I'll see you inside."

We ah watch her go in an when eh look at Shane he has this stupid smile on he's face.

"Is that it?"

"What?"

"Is that what you brought us ah here fir?"

"No I thought you'd like to see some bands"

Eh look at Kyle an we both make a face an laugh but Shane storms awa in the huff. We go back in an eh dinna ken if it was the joint but eh feel like the crowd has got mare aggressive. There's twa guys in front o is wah are definitely on e's but are swaggerin aboot like they are lookin ti start a fight we somebody, probably anybody. That's jist no what e's are aboot. It makes you wonder exactly what it is that they put in them nowadays.

When me an Shane first took them they lasted the hale night an the last thing that you felt like dein wis fightin we some cunt. Eh remember hearin once somebody describin thum as the love drug an judgin bey the wey they affected some people eh would certainly go alang we that. If you had took twa back then yeh were totally smashed, if you tak twa now yer lucky ti get a buzz. The names o the e's were cheenged we each different design they hud on them an this was happenin quite often, which usually meant that they gave yeh a different hit. They started ti get weaker ower time, which meant that ye needed mare an mare ti get a good hit, either that or oor systems were becomin immune ti thum. It got ti the point that we were takin between six an ten in one night an still no gettin the same buzz that we used ti git fae one o them. It started ruinin your night oot as we were mibbee at a perty an although there were plenty o good lookin lassies there, ah yeh could think aboot was gettin mare e's. When we should huv been havin a drink ti wind doon eftir a club an talkin shite ti lassies ti get in their knickers. Instaed we were phonin people treyin ti get oor hands on mare e's, lookin fir that good hit. When we eventually got oor hands on mare we were too fucked ti actually bather aboot the lassies. Eftir a lang night o frustration we would be at the pub fir it openin. Knock back a couple o pints an talk shite. For me it was easy as eh would head hame an hae a few joints, fah asleep an get up the next mornin feelin great. But Shane, Shane was different, he never really smoked much hash at that time so he would go hame an think aboot loads of shite. Ah these negative thoughts goin through he's haed. He's joab, he's life, ah felt worthless an would drev him nuts. Eh offered ti get him sleepin tablets but he refused. He says that's the first step on the wey ti bein a junkie…an he's probably right. Now he smokes hash when he's comin doon an he seems ahright.

Before the next band come on eh go ti the toilet an as eh'm takin a piss eh hear a few sniffs comin fae the cubicle. The door opens an twa young guys eh recognise walk oot.

"Aright Gaz, hows it goin?"

"No bad yersel?"

"Aye, eh'm aright, ye wanna line?"

"Eh sure why no?"

We go back into the cubicle and the young guy starts chappin is up a fair sized line on tap o the cistern.

"What's the crack we the music, bey the way?"

"What do ye mean?"

"Ah they young ains doon there oot there nut on e's an jumpin aboot ti rock music."

"You've got ti keep up we the times Gaz. We've ah moved on fae techno mate. Anywey have ye never heard o Hanney?"

"Nut how?"

"There the next band on, probably mare up your street mate."

Eh tak the line in one big sniff. This coke has probably

come fae the same stuff that eh drapped aff the other day. If anybody found oot eh would be banged up within the the week.

"So what are they like then? Eh've never heard o them."

"You're jokin. Ahh, there the business like."

He explains ti is that he kens the guys in the group. They are ah mates wah jist play the gither fir a laugh. Nothin serious but they are actually really good. They took their name fae a mate o theirs wah tragically killed hesel.

"Wee Bobby, he wis a great wee guy." He says as we head aff doon ti watch the band.

As the music kicks aff eh'm quite shocked ti find a girl on stage in front o the band dein some strange dance, the music is great. They sound a bit like faithless, a heavy bass dance beat, bit we guitars an a guy at the back on the decks, scratchin...this is meh type o music. It's got a bit o everythin. The crowd have obviously been waitin on this as they are ah on thir feet we thir airms in the air. Loads o the younger crowd have left, they must have only came fir The View an it seems ti be mare like ah the auld ravers thit are left. They must be good as even Kyle's feet are tapping awa, an it taks a lot ti get him goin. We ah stand noddin oor haeds an eh can see Shane lookin aboot again...obviously on the prowl fir that wee burd. Hanney's music cheenges we each tune, the last ain definitely had a Linkin Park influence but are now soundin mare like the Happy Mondays. It's really pickin me up now an eh start ti git a wee buzz fae they e's. It's jist enough ti get me goin, although the singer fae Hanney looks like he's had a few. He's aff the stage an into the crowd now, while still belting oot he's futba chantin lyrics an the crowd love it.

"What's he on?" Eh ask some guy wah is dancing awa next ti is.

"Wah?"

"The singer, eh'd like some o whatever he's hud."

"That's 'Bomber', he's always like that, 'Fuckin nutter.'"

"Dundee's ain Shaun Rider eh."

Eftir Hanney feenish the place clears oot a bit an eh could see Shane wanderin aboot lookin fir that burd again. As eh turn towards the bar eh see Dek Murdo an he's mates standin beside the door. Eh wonder what the fuck he's dein in here. Eh git the roond in as the next band comes on an introduce themselves. They look affay nervous as the singer says "Alright everyone, we are Killer Angels."

Eh'm expectin mare o the same o what eh've jist heard but eh'm wrang…affay wrang. The noise is deafenin, this is rock music at it's heaviest. There's a few people jumpin aboot ti their music but it's too much fir me. Eh turn ti look fir Shane when eh see ain o Murdo's mates squarin up ti him. Jist as eh go ti rush forward an stop it the cunt puts the haed on Shane. He steams right back but the rest o he's mates have ah jumped in. It must have been a set up. Eh see ain o them pickin up a stool an eh lift it right oot o he's hands before he gets a chance ti use it. Shane is doon an they are ah on tap o him layin in the boot. Eh start pullin them aff an the bouncers jist stand there watchin. Eh realise how when eh see Murdo standin next ti them.

"Dek what the fuck?" Eh shout across the pub ti him. He jist shrugs he's shidders an gees me a smug grin. He's obviously got something against Shane but we him bein oot on parole he canna get in any fights or he goes back ti feenish the time. We the help o Joey an Mickey we pull abody aff him an get him oot the side door.

"Are you aright?"

"What the fuck happened there?" Shane says.

He goes ti walk back in but we ah grab him back.

"Dinna be stupid Shane."

"What was all that about? Did I do something?"

"Nah the guy was jist bein wide."

"I'm going to fucking smash him when I get a hold of

him."

"Come on lets head ti Slims they dinna get in there any-wey."

12) That's what mates are for

On the wey ti Slims Shane decides ti go hame instaed an waves doon a taxi.

"You better no go back there."

"What? On my own, I don't think so."

"They ah gee him the usual shit o treyin ti persuade him ti stey oot bit when Shane makes up he's mind there's nae cheengin it. Eh dinna open meh mooth as he's ahready pulled is aside on the wey doon the road an telt is ti come up eftir Slims. Eh canna git us ti the front the night cause the bouncer that eh ken isna working. While we are in the queue eh feel a good buzz comin on an eh start ti git a tingle doon meh spine an this sets aff the happy mood an eh start chattin ti a group o lassies that are behind us in the queue. Eh ken that eh'm talkin a load o shite bit the buzz eh'm gittin is great an they ah seem nice enough. Jamie is helpin is oot we keepin the banter goin bit Joey, Mickey and Kyle are jist talkin shit between themselves. We ah head ti the bar as soon as we get in an Mickey shouts the roond up. As we wait fir the drinks eh scan the club lookin ti see wah eh recognise then Kyle shouts "Gaz, over there" an nods in the direction o the other bar. It's Lisa, wah is lookin quite smug standin we some new guy. Eh canna believe that last week she wis brakin her hert, stalkin an pesterin Shane, now this week she's moved on an found some other mug.

"It's a good thing that Shane went hame, eh." Kyle says as he passes me a drink.

"She obviously thought Shane wis gonna be here the night an start some shite we her new lad."

Eh wander aroond the club fir a while an find mesel in a conversation we some jumped up schemie. It's like they are a tryin ti impress ye bey goin on aboot kickin the shite oot o some pair cunt, wah jist happened ti be in the wrang place at the wrang time. These guys never seem ti get in a fight when they're on their ain, it's always when it's three or four onti one. If they do happen ti get themselves involved in a scuffle that's too much fir thum, that's when the bottles start gettin used or in other cases, knives. They probably tell the same story aboot ten times a night ti anybody wah will listen addin things each time they tell it. Pumped full o steroids, chist stickin oot an talkin as if they are hard as fuck. Eh'm in half a mind ti tell them exactly what eh think o them but eh ken what it will lead ti an eh think, do eh really want ti get banned fir these cunts. Eh'm really flyin right now an the bass fae the music is flowin through meh body, Eh make meh excuses fae thum an head ti the danceflare whare eh see ain o the lassies fae the queue. She pulls meh airm so that eh'm dancin closer ti her. Eh think she looks stunnin but that could be an effect fae the amount o drugs that eh've consumed an makin is think that she's stunnin. Eh see Joey dancin no far fae is an eh feel like askin him if she's ahright as Joey would have had less drugs than me. But then what if he says she's tidy so that eh go and shag her but she turns oot ti be a total horror an every cunt taks the piss oot o is fir it. Then Joey could have had mare e's than me an actually does think she's tidy but she really is a total horror...ah fuck it wah cares, eh'm oot meh nut an she canna be any worse than what eh've shagged before. While she's dancin she comes up an gees is a wee snog.

"Do ye want ti go ti a perty eftir Slims?"

"Eh, but can eh bring meh mate?"

"Sure."

Shane, you are getting woke up big time. Eh leave Slims before the end so that eh could head up ti Shane's withoot anybody folloyin us. Eh buzz up an as we walk in Shane is on the couch rollin a joint. Now that eh see him in the light eh can see a few marks on he's face.

"Have a good night then did we?" He says sarcastically.

Eh offer the girls a drink an they folly is ti the kitchen. We start talkin an end up in a very deep conversation but eh dinna ken what the fuck we are talkin aboot. Every now an again ah eh hear is 'Ken wot eh mean' an it's starting ti annoy is a bit. Eh ken thit eh speak dundonian bit these burds are orray as fuck. When e'm smashed eh wouldna normally notice how common a lassy talks but they must be bad cause it is doin meh nut in. Shane comes through we the joint but he doesna say much, he has a few puffs an passes it to me.

"I'm away to my bed, don't put the music too loud."

"Hey, nae probs mate."

Eh wonder what's up we him. Eh've brought back twa lovely burds wah are up fir their hole an he fucks off ti he's bed. The lassies feenish their drinks an eh go ti the kitchen fir mare. Ain o the lassies follay's is through an starts neckin we is.

"Do ye want ti go ti the bedroom?"

"What aboot meh mate?"

"Go an send her through ti see Shane."

The lassie goes through ti speak ti her mate while eh fix mare drinks. When eh go back she's sittin on her ain.

"Is she awa through?"

The lassie nods an smiles an eh put the drinks on the table. We start gettin it on, on the couch an she mentions something aboot condoms…but she gits telt straight.

"Fuck that, it's like haein a bath we yer socks on."

Eh dinna ken whare eh got that sayin fae, eh jist remember hearin it years ago. Eh'm on tap o her an she's makin these wee squeekin noises, which eh find is quite funny. Were at it fir a wee while when eh start ti think aboot what eh said aboot condoms an now eh'm imaginin exactly what it would be like ti actually huv a bath we yer socks on. Eh trey hard ti concentrate as eh'm desperate ti shoot meh load. Eh speed up a wee bit an go a wee bit harder an eh could feel the sweat runnin doon meh face. Eh look up an see Shane standin there watchin is.

"Carry on, don't mind me, I just came through for a drink."

He walks past inti the kitchen an eh trey ti keep goin but every time eh look up Shane is poppin he's haed aroond the corner an makin stupid faces, he's puttin he's airms up an showin is he's muscles. The cunt is puttin is aff meh stride. The cunts been there, he kens it's hard enough treyin ti come on e's without somebody distractin ye. He goes awa back inti the bedroom an eh trey ti git back inti it but eh keep picturing him makin they faces. Eh mak meh excuses an go ti the toilet. When eh git there eh canna pee but eh find mesel haein a wank. Jist as eh feel it buildin up eh start thinking aboot something else an it doesna happen…fuck. Eh go back ti the livin room and the other burd that eh thought wis we Shane has come back an the ain eh wis we has got ah her claithes back on.

"What's wrang?"

"Nothin, we hae ti go."

"Eh'm goin awa ti skin up, dae ye no want ti stey fir a smoke?"

"Nah we'll jist go."

They phone a taxi an bey the time it comes eh decide ti go we them. Eh go hame an git biscuit then go back ti Shane's. Eh stop aff at the shop fir some munchies an then walk around ti he's flat. He must ken it's me as he doesna even speak on the intercom he jist presses the buzzer ti let is in.

"What the fuck were you thinking bringing two mingers like that up to my flat?" He says as eh walk in the door.

"What are you on aboot?"

"What am I on about? The fucking mouldy orange that you sent through to my room that's what I am fucking on about."

He says walking inti he's bedroom an puttin the light on.

"Look at that." He says pointin ti a big patch o brown an orange stains on his pillay case. Eh burst oot laughin.

"Come on Shane ye ken me. She wis gropin meh bahs on the dance flair, eh jist saw the tanned legs an short skirt. Ye ken when eh'm full o it eh dinna look that far up.

13) Customer No. 724
Dirty weekend

Bank holiday weekend and all the taxis are out in force trying to make as much money as they can. I certainly wont be working any extra hours that's for sure. More than likely it will be less, but it really depends on what state I get in tonight. I know as soon as I go into the pub tonight someone will say, why are you not working? It must be busy as fuck this weekend. They will be told the same as everyone else, I work enough to pay my bills and get out on the piss. I don't understand some of those drivers who sometimes work from ten in the morning until four the next morning. They must either be in a mountain of debt or are just absolute greedy bastards. What kind of life is that? Most of all it's fucking dangerous. Knowing my luck it's one of those drivers that will pick me up when I crawl out of a nightclub in the early hours and fall asleep at the wheel. Actually, come to think of it, there's really not much chance of that when I think of all the abuse I give them.

My next job is to St. Mary's where I pick up two women carrying holdalls. One has the blonde bimbo hair with the streak of dark roots quite visible down the middle and the other has dark hair but has huge tits.

"So where are you two ladies off to then?"

"The train station." Blondie says.

"No, I mean from there."

"Oh sorry. Manchester."

"Shopping." They both say and start laughing.

"Nah it's really a weekend on the piss but we nip aroond

the market fir a couple o oors before we git the train hame."
Blondie says.

"We bey loads o shite but the trick is ti mak sure ye git loads o different bags so thit yer man thinks yev been busy." Big tits says.

"Eh busy pullin." Blondie says as they both laugh.

"We used ti go ti Newcastle bit we bumped inti too many people we kent fae Dundee an it wis gittin too risky."

"Remember that time we nearly got caught fae your cousin …"

They proceed to tell me some story about pulling a couple of blokes back to their hotel and kicking them out in the morning only to find that one of their mans cousins was staying at the same hotel. They went down for breakfast to find him with his family and he actually made a comment about one of the guests making some noise while getting their hole.

"Ken aye, he says somebody wis makin too much noise, it must huv been you cause the guy eh wis we wisna big enough ti mak me scream except ti laugh it the size o it."

That's a long way to go to get your hole, all that distance and hassle just to get fucked and they're not even guaranteed a good one.

Spiked

All of my customers have been in a rush today and all they've talked about is that it's a bank holiday and how good the weather is. One of them has actually mentioned that we are in for a heat wave this summer. I'm actually sweating sitting in this car and that's with the sunroof open and all the windows down. I'll be finishing shortly and it will be a quick shower, change of clothes, grab something to eat and up to the East View. I know it will be busy on the Taxi's this weekend, but fuck that, I work all week…it's party time.

I get to the East View and feel dehydrated due to the heat and it takes the first pint just to quench my thirst, the second flows down quite easily too. I head to the toilet and find Gaz in there getting his weekly supply of drugs from some shady looking fucker. I wait until the guy heads out before I say something to him.

"Gaz are you fucking stupid, I could have been anybody walking in here, you better watch what the fuck you're doing."

"Eh ken, it's usually a quick swap bit eh hud ti git extra this weekend, yeh ken what it's like…bank holiday. Ah they cunts are wantin stuff, so the guy hud ti git oot some mare fir is."

"What? You couldn't go into the cubicle."

Just as I say this, we hear a sniffing sound coming from in-side the cubicle. The door opens and Kyle pops his head out.

"Alright. You want a line?"

Gaz can't get in there quick enough. Kyle hands Gaz a credit card and he quickly goes to work chapping up a few lines. I snort half up one nostril and half up the other. My face cringes as the horrible taste goes down the back of my throat.

"While yer at it ye can pop ain o these doon ye tae." Gaz says as he passes the bag of e's with a big smile on his face before bending down to take his line of coke. We all take an e and then head back to the bar. After several more drinks Kyle phones a couple of taxis for us to go into the town. I head to the toilet again and when I come out I see Dek Murdo swaggering through the door. I put my head down and wait to see who he is with. Two of his mates walk in behind him and I recognise one of them immediately as the guy who nutted me last week. I run across the pub and throw a hook punch at him with everything I've got. It lands on the side of his jaw and he hit's the deck spark out. I look up to see

Murdo swinging at me and I can't get out of the way quick enough. He hit's the top of my head and I step back. He puts his hand in his pocket and goes to come forward but so many people jump in between us that he can't get near me.

"EH'M GONNA SMASH YOU YE LITTLE PRICK." He shouts at me.

"COME ON THEN, WHAT YOU THINK YOU'RE A BIG MAN DAMAGING SOMEBODY'S CAR. I'M NOT AFRAID OF YOU, LET'S GO." I manage to shout back before being pushed out the door.

I turn back to see a confused look on his face as he shrugs his shoulders. The hand in the pocket is obviously a threat as I know he wouldn't pull a blade in front of so many people in the pub and if he does have the bottle to do that it certainly won't be for buttering me a slice of bread that's for sure.

I get outside and am pushed straight into the taxi with Gaz, Mickey and Jamie. Joey and Kyle get into the other one.

"WHAT THE FUCK HAPPENED THERE?" Gaz shouts at me.

"What? It's just a little friendly banter that's all."

Still shouting Gaz says "ARE YOU AFF YOU'RE FUCKIN HAED?, HE'LL KILL YOU."

Then Mickey says "Did you see him goin in he's pocket?"

I see the driver looking in the mirror at us and I realise he is hearing all this so I make a face at Mickey and nod in the drivers direction. Nobody says a word until we get out of the taxi. We end up in a pub in the city centre, which is a total shit-hole and Kyle gets the round in while we find an empty corner. After several more drinks and discussing how stupid I am, they all change the conversation and it soon turns to shagging again in which they all take the piss out of Gaz for last week. We head off to Slims and I suddenly feel a little strange, like I am pissed but I'm not pissed. The queue for Slims is huge and it goes around the building and down the street, Gaz's mate is working tonight so he gets us to the front. While in Slims I still feel a little strange, like something is just not right. We are all standing at our usual place near the top bar on the second level and I make a comment that music seems to be better than usual. Gaz and Kyle look at each other and smile, which makes me a little paranoid and I feel I've missed the joke or that I've said something stupid. Slims is starting to fill up and every girl that walks past I feel as if they are staring at me. The deejay puts on an oldie which starts off slow and I now feel myself tapping my feet, my body feels all tingly like it's away to explode. Then I look at Gaz who I've just noticed has that stupid grin on his face.

"You've spiked me, haven't you?, you cunt."

"Me, now would eh dae a thing like that" he says all sarcastically then starts laughing.

The song breaks into a harder beat and then...whoosh. I get a rush that starts from my feet, comes up my body shooting through my spine until it reaches my head, now I'm buzzing. I'm on the dance floor and I have my arms in the air. The beat in the song slows down and every time it bursts in I get little rushes up my neck. I stay on the dance floor for a couple more tunes and Gaz comes over.

"Enjoying yersel are ye?" He says as he hands me a bottle.

"I can't believe you did that to me. Where did you get these ones they are really strong."

"Nah, it wasna an e, it was MDMA."

"What's it feel like?"

"Great."

"When did you do that?"

"After the run in we Murdo, ye were startin ti piss everybody aff goin on aboot it so we thought we would help ye oot a we bit."

It's only been half an hour and the rushes have now stopped. Immediately I am on the look out for more but Gaz says he only had a little bit of it. I've never taken that stuff in years and now I can see why we were all fucked every weekend. I leave the dance floor to go up to the bar while thinking about the hit I just had. It reminds me on the hit we used to get from just one e many years ago. When you were stressed out all week in your dead end job it meant that all you thought about was the weekend. Where you took a couple of good recreational drugs and escaped into a world where everything was great, you forgot about all your everyday petty problems and hum drum Monday to Friday existence. There was nothing better than going out at the weekend, popping some pills and getting wasted. It was all harmless fun. When you got up for work on the Monday morning bright and fresh ready to face another hard week of angry bosses and miserable work colleagues. You faced them with a smile because you knew you had something on your mind to get you through your day that the other workers didn't have and would probably never experience. Mortgages, bills and household tasks meant nothing if you couldn't go out and have fun at the weekend. Some of the people that you met and got to know through drugs came from a well to do family but they still had the same reasons for going out and getting involved in the party scene. They still wanted an escape from whatever boring life they had at home. If some of these peoples family knew what they got up to at the weekend they would disown them. Somehow I don't think their mothers would have approved.

I finish my bottle and get another round in for everyone, who all look at me with a stupid grin as I pass them their bottle, the cunts, they were obviously all in on it. The feeling has worn off very quickly but I pull up Gaz who slips me more e's while still wearing that smug grin. I know however many I take I'll never get that kind of hit I just had but it's better than nothing I suppose. I end up back on the dance floor and the hit is just enough to make me want to dance but before I know it the music stops and the lights go on. The time has passed very quickly and I feel I have only been in here for about an hour. I was given a strip of chewing gum from a girl on the dance floor some time ago and it now has no taste left but I am still chewing like mad. I stand there wiping the sweat from my head as Gaz comes over.

"So are we going up to yours then?"

"Yeah sure." I say without even thinking about it.

I end up in a taxi with Jamie and two young girls whom I have never seen before in my life and although I feel like talking I can't get a word in for these girls. I don't know what they are talking about but Jamie is taking the piss by repeating what they say. I don't think Jamie realises but he actually talks like that too.

"Ken wot eh mean, dinna hink so, aye."

The girls take offence and let Jamie know by telling him "Shit yer puss you."

When we get to mine it's a case of, music on, joints rolled and drinks poured. Gaz appears, and as usual goes straight to the stereo to change the music. He just looks up and says "You've got ti hae the right tunes on, man."

We all sarcastically repeat "Man."

I head off to the balcony for a smoke, Jamie appears and is shocked to find me out of my nut as he never really hung around with us at the time when the good e's were going around. There are a few girls in the flat sitting around chatting and I end up in deep conversation with one of them for what seems like minutes but before I know it most people are heading home as daylight is starting to creep through. The flat starts to empty and it's only Kyle and Jamie left, then the buzzer goes, it's Gaz who fucked off to go and get Biscuit, the cunt. I never even noticed he had left. He knows I don't like him bringing him up here, as soon as he comes in he jumps all over my bed with his dirty paws.

"Biscuit get to fuck." The little shit.

Later that day I manage to get some sleep but I am woken

by Biscuit, pawing at me to let it under the covers.

"Fuck off." I shout, as if it's going to understand me.

I go through to the living room to find it is a total pig sty with bottles and glasses lying about. Jamie is slouched on the chair and Gaz is lying across the sofa. The place is stinking of grass as they pass the joint between each other.

"What have I told you cunts about smoking grass in here?, go onto the fucking balcony."

As I say this Biscuit comes running through and jumps up on the sofa.

"And what have I told you about bringing that fucking dog up here?" The both of them start laughing.

"You're both sniggering like a couple of poofs."

Gaz the smart arse pouts his lips and makes a smooching sound.

"Do that again and you're fucking lips will be staying that size."

"Look jist cause you went ti go ahead we Murdo dinna start actin the hard man we us." He says as they both start sniggering again.

It sinks in exactly what I did last night and I know I've got trouble ahead, big trouble. If he was a stand up guy I wouldn't give a shit, but he's a sneaky blade man who wouldn't think twice about cutting me up.

"Don't you fucking start, spiking my drink, you better not do that again you cunt."

"Does that mean if eh got some mare you would be up for it again the night?"

I pause for a few seconds before answering "Yeah probably."

"Well what the fuck are you moanin aboot, let's get some mare an git on it."

14) Sunday, the day after the night before

I open the curtain that looks onto the balcony and am blinded by the light from the scorching sun as it shines into the living room. Although I'm feeling like shit today, seeing the sun does actually cheer me up a little. Its unusual for Scotland to get such good weather as I am used to opening the curtains to a miserable day with the rain pissing down. Gaz has to take Biscuit for a walk so I decide to go with him to get out of the flat for a while. We have to buy more alcohol so we head to the off license. As soon as we step outside the heat from the sun hits us and it gives me good feeling that we are in for a good summer. On the way back from the shop my good feeling is soon drained from me as I notice that my car has two flat tyres. As I get closer I become aware of another scrape that goes from one end to the other.

"For fuck sake." I walk over and straight away I can see the slash about three inches long going around the tyre.

"I'm going to fucking kill him."

"Who?"

"Murdo."

"What aboot the scratch alang the other side?"

"That was last week, I'm going to have to start parking it somewhere else now."

"Eh canna believe that we were ah in the flat an he's come an done this. It's no like him ti go an dae somethin like this. If anythin eh thought he would chap your door an trey ti smash ye. He's a bit auld fir goin aboot dein things like that. If he has a problem we ye, yer goin ti have ti git it sorted oot cause this is never gonna stop." Gaz says.

"Exactly, he's real tough slashing someone's tyres and key-ing their car, just wait until I catch up with him, we'll soon know how tough he is."

"The worse thing is it wouldna huv even been him as he'll hae sent ain o he's fuckin mates ti dae it. He mibbe was up at yer door but heard ye had a hoose full so decided against it."

"I'm gonna get the cunt." I say as I look at Gaz with my temper really starting to boil.

"Look dinna go daein anythin stupid mate, ye ken he's no afraid ti stick a blade in ye. Eh'll phone a few people wah ken him an trey ti sort this oot, see if he'll back aff." Gaz says this but I think this is his way of trying to calm me down so that I don't go looking for him.

"Do you know how much this will cost me to fix. This is a fucking re-spray job, not a fucking touch up."

When we get back in the flat Joey, Kyle and Mickey have turned up while we were out.

"You'd better pass that joint ti Shane when you've finished, as eh think he's ready ti explode." Gaz says to Kyle, who is busy skinning up.

"How, what's up?" Jamie asks.

"Nothing, just that I'm going to smash Dek fuckin Murdo when I see him. He's done my car again."

"Again, what do you mean again?"

"He keyed it last week down one side and sometime this morning while we were all in here he's slashed two of my tyres and keyed it down the other side."

"Fuck, eh canna believe he was up here while we were ah in the flat. Eh wonder what would have happened if ain o us had went oot an caught him."

"What's actually bothering me is who told the cunt where I lived."

"Mibbe he followed ye eftir Slims last night."

"But it was keyed last week as well."

"He mibbe followed ye some other night then."

We spend the rest of the afternoon getting stoned and drinking and this soon puts the thoughts of Dek Murdo out of my head for the time being. The banter is flowing fast and it puts me in a happy mood again.

"I take it everyone's out tonight again?"

"Yeah but onay if we get a chance ti spike ye again."

Everyone has a laugh and I smile with them but at the back of my mind all I'm really thinking about is going after Dek Murdo. Half of my mind is all for finding him and kicking the shit out of him but I know if I go after someone like that I would have to do it properly as he's the type who will just come back again and again until I end up dead. I think I would be best waiting to see if Gaz can sort it out first before it goes down that road.

We sit on the balcony drinking and talking shit until the sun starts to go down and then we head off down the Perth Road for a couple of drinks. We have to head off to Slims early as on a bank holiday weekend the queues for nightclubs are always very long. Before I finish my last drink Gaz hands me a couple of e's in which I stupidly swallow them both at once.

"Did you jist tak baith o them."

"Yeah I want to get the same buzz as last night."

"Fuck it." Gaz says and does the same.

On reaching Slims the queue is much longer than we thought it was going to be as it continues around the corner and down the street. Jamie makes a quick decision on seeing the queue and decides to go to the Mardi.

"Yer ah mare than welcome ti join is." He says as he walks away.

"Fuck it, e'm goin as well." Mickey says.

Then Gaz and Joey follow them leaving me and Kyle on our own to wait in this extra long queue. As I stand listening to Kyle talking the biggest load of shit I start thinking maybe I should have went with them but I get a horrible feeling that I am away to get my hit and have horrible thoughts of standing in the Mardi on an e...no thank you, I'll wait. I'm getting all tingly down my body but I don't want it to happen just now, I don't want my hit until I get in the club and I'm trying to fight it. It's like when you are having sex and you are about to shoot your load but the sex is so good you don't want to shoot your load at that moment. You want it to last a while longer, but you can't stop it and you come. The whole feeling is ruined by trying to hold back. By the time I get to the front door I'm totally flying and the buzz is being ruined by having to act straight in front of the bouncers. Once we are passed the entrance and in the club the rushes start to fade. I'm still enjoying the buzz but I feel its been ruined by fighting it to act straight. I find myself at the bar and the tables have turned as it's now Kyle who is listening to me talking a load of shit. I'm obviously wasted and don't realise this until Kyle starts taking the piss, that's when i know it's bad.

"Shane, check her out, to your left."

I turn discretely to see two girls next to me at the bar waiting to be served. One of them is tall, blonde and has a low cut top with a large chest that I feel is staring at me. I know this is what Kyle was wanting me to check out, but I've seen something better, much better. It's the girl from my taxi. I stand and stare at her for a few seconds and realise she is the total opposite to what I usually go for. She turns her head and I lock eyes with her and can't look away. Kyle doesn't remember her from that gig night at the doghouse and I am too wasted to let him know.

"Hi, how are you?"

"Fine."

"Did you enjoy the bands the other night."

"Yeah, they were really good."

"I was only there for a little while, something came up and I had to leave."

That'll be why I wandered around the place and couldn't find her. If she left then she obviously didn't see the trouble with me and Murdo's mates. I have waited ages to meet this girl again and just my luck it happens when I've took too many e's and feel too wasted to talk.

I want to start up conversation with her but for the first time I am stuck for words. Kyle is a little disappointed as I usually take the lead and he would follow up with the small talk, but not this time.

"What's wrong with you?"

"Nothing."

"Why aren't you firing in then?"

I shrug my shoulder and smile.

"Oh for fuck sake, your wasted man."

The girls receive their drinks but they don't move from the bar.

"Shane there not moving from the bar, come on, go and talk to them."

I turn to look at her again and she smiles back but I am still stuck for words. I look back at Kyle again and smile. I must look really fucked because Kyle slides past me and moves in closer to the tall blonde and introduces us. He makes me think of a slithery snake they way he moves. I try to keep this thought in my head so that I can call him that from now on...the slithery snake...Kyle the wee slithery snake...slithery snake Kyle.

"Hi, I'm Kelly." She says to me. Kyle introduces me to the blonde who's name is Sarah and then turns his back on me leaving me to stand with the girl I now know is called Kelly. Kyle looks back at me and lifts his eyebrows then leans over to my ear.

"If you're not fast you're last eh?"

Obviously he's referring to himself firing-in to the tall blonde and me getting left with the mate this time. I want to tell him I wasn't interested in the blonde but I cant find the words and have to let it go. While Kyle is chatting away to the blonde, who's name I've have now forgotten due to the state of my brain at this moment in time. I start to get a little paranoid as I'm standing next to this stunning girl and I can't even make conversation with her. To my relief she leans over to my ear and says

"You're wasted aren't you?"

I look at her and don't know what to say. If she's not into drugs and I say yes, I've blown it. If I say no she'll think I'm some weirdo acting like this while not on drugs so I can't win. With a half smile I force out an answer.

"What do you mean?"

"It's okay, I just feel a little jealous, I haven't been wasted in so long."

Wow what a relief to know that she knows the score. I feel like telling her it's been a while for me too...a whole twenty four hours actually but the words won't come out. She finishes her drink and before I get a chance to offer her another one she says

"Would you like to dance?"

I cant answer but she looks at me for a few seconds, grabs my arm and says "you need to dance."

The e's I've taken are obviously very heavy and are making me look a bit drunk. All I want to do is sit down and chill out. But this girl drags me up to dance and this snaps me out of my little daydream. Once I start to move it changes my frame of mind making me want to dance all night. I could do with some real dance music like last night but Slims on a Sunday is hip hop and r and b so I guess it will have to do.

"What's your name again?" I say smiling.

She puts her hand to my face and brings her lips to my ear.

"Kelly." she says as she moves away.

I suddenly get a rush of happiness as I watch her dance around me. My feet feel like they are glued to the floor. She takes my hands and forces me to move in time with her and this gives me a feeling of being drawn to her, a closeness I've never felt before. I know the e's have something to do with it…well probably a lot to do with it but right now I don't give a shit. I want to pull her close and ask her if she wants to come back to mine but I don't want to sound too forward. What the fuck is happening to me? These e's have made me go soft. I would usually have a girl sized up in the first five minutes and have it worked out what type of shag she would be and what positions I would get her in…but not on these fucking drugs. I'm looking at this girl dancing around me, smiling and rubbing up against me and all I'm thinking is…I'd love to kiss her. After several tunes we head to the bar for more drinks and I find Kyle still with the blonde, slavering in her ear. Kelly asks "So do you feel a bit better now."

"Yeah." I say smiling at her.

"That's the best thing you can do when you are feeling like that or you end up sitting in a corner all night." She says this like I've never experienced this before and I want to tell her that I've been there too many times to remember but the last thing I want to do is start is a conversation about drugs.

The two girls talk for a few minutes and then Kelly tells me that her friend is leaving and Kyle is going with her. I feel really happy for Kyle as he never usually pulls so quick he must have been talking some serious shit for her to leave so early with him.

"Shane could I get the keys to your flat?" Kyle says to me and gives me a wink.

"Use the spare room, I don't want any stains in my bed."

He laughs and walks away all happy with himself that he's pulled before me.

"Come on, we'll go for a walk." Kelly says taking my hand. I watch her from behind as she leads the way, I'm oblivious to the people passing me as I stare at her lovely shaped legs. She has on a short skirt and cowboy boots and has a sexy walk that makes her hips wiggle slightly.

We wander around Slims and find a secluded corner with

two vacant seats. We talk for a while but the conversation keeps going back to drugs which in my state is not really a good thing.

We end up talking about Slims and the types of people that walk past us.

"A while back people like that wouldn't get past the front door." She says as she nods in the direction of some schemie who looks like he's dressed to go berry picking. After another drink we go back to the dance floor, I start to feel more normal again and I think the e's must be wearing off a little. Kelly comes up close to me and gives me a little kiss while running her hand up my back, this gives me a rush that goes shooting up to my head. She moves back and looks at me smiling.

"Are you feeling alright?" She says sarcastically.

"I take it you've done that before."

"That's an old trick."

I eventually find the courage to ask her if she wants to come back to mine, I've never felt nervous like this around a girl in years.

"No, but you can come back to mine if you want." She says to my amusement as we both laugh.

"But you're friend is up at my flat with my friend."

"Exactly, I don't want them to be there when we're shagging."

We both look at each other and laugh again then she comes closer and kisses me.

"Do want to go now?" She says while nodding towards the front door.

As I walk out of Slims holding Kelly's hand she tells me her flat isn't far so we decide to walk instead of getting a taxi. She takes my hand and leads me in my hazy state of mind up the Hawkhill Road towards her flat. We walk past a group of girls and I hear my name being mentioned. I turn to see a girl I know.

"Oh hi, Ashley."

"Is this yer latest bimbo then?" She says as she stands with some guy's arm draped around her shoulders.

"You've got a hard neck calling anybody a bimbo." I say.

The guy takes his arm from around her and gives me the wide-o look.

"Just leave it Shane, come on." Kelly says pulling me away.

"Go on listen to yer wee slapper." She says.

"Wait a minute Kelly." I whisper in her ear.

"Ashley, you've got two kids to two different guys. You live with someone else who is neither of their fathers. Occasionally you would come up the road and fuck me before sneaking off home to him…and you have the cheek to call her a slapper."

Her friends start laughing and the guy who was with her has taken a step back. I walk away and stumble on up the road with Kelly's arm hooked into mine leading the way.

We stop every now and again for a little snog until we get back to her flat which she shares with her friend Sarah, who Kyle took back to mine with and is now probably doing her arse over the end of my couch.

I follow her into her bedroom, take of my boots and lie on the bed. Kelly does the same after putting on some music. We start to snog and our hands are all over each other. My hands is up her skirt and is resting on her arse. Any other girl and I would have had her knickers off by now but I feel something is holding me back. I have my eyes closed and I can feel her moving to slide the covers over us. She starts stroking my face and I feel myself drifting off.

"Hey sleepy head, you getting up?" I hear a voice say.

I open my eyes to see the sunlight coming through the curtains and Kelly standing in front of me all fresh with different clothes on.

"What happened?"

"What do you mean? You don't remember? And you said it was the best sex you've ever had too."

I go to say something but stop to think for a few seconds then I see the sly grin on her face.

"I fell asleep."

"Yeah." She says with a big smile.

"Sarah is just back from your flat, she says that your other friends came up and disturbed them while they were eh, ehm, you know."

We both laugh at the thought of them getting caught but I know the picture in my head is entirely different from how she is imagining it.

"I don't know what kind of e's you had last night but that's the first time I've ever seen anyone fall asleep like that after taking them." She says.

"It's probably because I was out all weekend, it catches up with you." I explain.

"Or it could be the junk that they put I them nowadays." She says like I'm stupid and should already know this.

"Anyway." I say changing the subject.

"I'd better take off and see what state my flat is in after those idiots."

I get up and start to put on my boots and I realise this must be the first time in years that I have went home with someone and not shagged them on the first night.

"I could give you a lift if you like. I'm on my way to uni."

"Thanks, that would be great."

We get outside and walk towards two cars at the end of the street, one is a old piece of junk and the other is a girly look-ing sports car. I stop at the piece of junk.

"Next one." Kelly says as she walks towards the sports car.

"Oh." I say looking surprised.

"Yeah right." She says walking back to the heap of shit.

In the journey to mine I do ask if I can see her again.

"Well I do have loads of course work to complete over the

next month but I'm sure I can fit you in somewhere."

"Oh don't go out of you're way like." I say sarcastically.

Before I get out the car I lean over to kiss her and she puts her lips up to mine but I kiss her on the cheek instead.

"Morning breath and that, you know."

"Yeah, you'd better go and get some mouth-wash." She says waving her hand in front of her nose implying that my breath stinks.

"Well I WAS kissing you last night." I say, being my typical smart arse self, just to get the last word in.

We both smile as I shut the car door and I walk away feeling on top of the world. But this only last a few seconds and then come crashing back down to earth when I see my car again.

My life seems to go from one extreme to the other. With customers who, one minute have me laughing my head off to others, who have me ready to rip their head off. I'll get the tyres fixed and get myself back on the road but that paint job is going to be some work.

15) Customer No. 441
Fuckin hame

The hawthorn bar on the Hilltown for Ramsay. The rain is pouring down so I run from the car and walk into this dodgy looking place. When I open the door the waft of smoke and stale beer hits me full on. There are about ten people in the bar, all older men and all of them looking more shadier than the next. The place is silent and several of them look around at me and then look back at the bar.

I shout the name, no answer, I look around to get someone's attention but they all stare into their drinks or at the T.V. watching intently at the horseracing. I shout again, no answer, the barmaid looks over and nods in the direction of a man sitting directly in front of me. I shout one last time and the man who is about six feet away from me slouched on a stool at the bar turns his head slightly and grunts. Why the fuck did he not answer me the first time the cunt. The man is in his late fifty's and is clearly a bit pissed. I walk back out in the pissing rain and jump back into the car. I wait for what feels like a long time and the guy doesn't appear. I'm thinking that I should just go as I can tell he's going to be more bother than he's worth. I am about to drive off when the guy stumbles from the bar and opens the front passenger door. He basically falls into the seat and kicks the speaker on the way, cracking the plastic cover.

"For fucks sake, watch what you're doing." I shout, but try not to loose the head. He doesn't say a word, no apology, nothing.

"Right mate, where are you going?"

He slowly turns his head and looks at me through his slanted eyes and gritted teeth

"Fuckin hame."

I feel the hair's standing up on the back of my neck as the adrenalin rushes through my body. I keep telling myself 'be calm' and don't bite as he's just being wide.

"I need to know where you are going mate."

He turns his head again, but this time he leans over only inches from my face and I can see his smirk as he says again "Fuckin hame."

In a split second of these words coming out of his mouth I have nutted him catching his top lip. I get out the car and bolt around to the passenger door, opening it with one hand and reaching in with the other. I grab the cunt by the throat and drag him out onto the wet pavement. As he struggles to get up he says "Do ye ken wah eh am?"

I've heard this saying so many times when I was growing up but it was usually by some young teenager who thought he was some sort of hard man, but they were always found out. I never usually hear it from a fifty something old man.

He gets to his feet and tries to throw a punch but I move back slightly and throw one of my own into his already bloody face. As he hit's the deck with a thud I look around to see people across the street wondering whats going on. I suddenly realise how stupid this must look. It's just after one on a Tuesday afternoon, in the pissing rain and I have just nutted and punched some fifty odd year old wide-o drunk. I see the door of the pub opening so I quickly get back in to the car and drive off leaving the cunt lying on the pavement with his face covered in blood.

Customer No. 473
Snob wannabe

I know who my next customer is and exactly where she's
going. She is a snobby bitch with a big fancy house...well I
say snobby but I really mean a fucking snob wannabe. She
obviously came into a bit of money and bought the big fancy
house, now she thinks she's better than every cunt else. I
can't stand people like that. There is a big difference between
bettering yourself and thinking you are better than yourself.
She tries to talk polite but it just comes out all wrong. Some
people are naturally polite when they talk, they are brought
up like that. Then you get people like this stuck up bitch who
was brought up as a schemie and is trying to become something she is not by losing her Dundee twang. The thing is, it's
not hard to talk polite but still keep your Dundee accent. It
sounds a hundred times better than this stupid bitch's snobbish patter. Before I turn the corner I dig out a heavy rock
CD and put it on. A little annoying trick that I've learned.
The last time I had her in my car she moaned at me that my
music was too loud. I turned it down but she got annoyed because I kept sniggering at her. So what did the bitch do, she
phoned my office to complain, who in turn called me and basically got told to 'get to fuck.' The stupid cow didn't realise
that I was actually sniggering at her stupid snobbish accent
changing with every word she said. There was obviously certain words that she couldn't pronounce in her fake, polite,
newly acquired accent. When I pick up people like that now I
put the music to a level where it's not low but not loud
enough for her to complain. Some heavy rock with loud guitars or even hard techno with some strong bass or a high
pitched beat is good for this. If you are not into that type of
music I know it can be quite annoying.

I drive around to the side door of the shopping centre and I notice her face straight away due to the amount of make up that is caked on it. She is dressed as if she is about to go to a fucking wedding. Don't get me wrong I would rather have someone with clean clothes in my car than some of the smelly minks I usually pick up. She has plenty of shopping bags with all the top high street labels on them, she wouldn't be seen with one of the discount clothing bags in her hands. I get out and shout her name and as soon as she sees me I can tell she's pissed off that I've been sent for her. I open the boot and usually I would take the bags from people and put them in myself…but not today, as she is not most people. She looks at me to help but I take a step back and look away so that she has no option but to do it herself…if looks could kill. She gets in the back and just as I am wondering if she'll have anything to moan about today she says "Could you put that window up please."

The front passenger window is open about six inches, it's quite warm today and this bitch asks me to close the window.

"Yeah sure." I say as I push the button to put the passengers window up and at the same time my window comes down. I can see her looking at me in the mirror with pure hatred and I'm fucking loving it.

I arrive outside her house and park at the start of her driveway. I drove here quite slow so that the music would start to get really annoying.

"That's four pounds sixty please." I say with a smarmy grin.

She hands me the fiver and waits on her forty pence change, which I knew she would. I go to the boot and take out her bags, dumping them on the ground at her feet. If it was any other customer I would have taken them to their door…but fuck her.

"Cheerio." I say as I walk back towards my car door.

She doesn't answer but looks at me in total disgust. She picks up her bags and I watch as she struggles with them up her driveway.

Customer No. 526
Lazy tattooed man

As I pull up to Asda I see several people waiting in the taxi rank and out of all the people there, I can tell which customer will be mine. Although there is a nice looking blonde girl who could possibly be going a good distance, I know it's going to be the smelly one that's only going around the corner. I shout the name and this very rough looking woman, dressed in clothes that are either too big or have been stretched in a tug-o-war competition. Her face has the distinguished features that you can tell she has had a hard life...but that's not to say she chose it.

Her trolley is overloaded and as I struggle to fit it all in my boot. I notice it is packed with junk food and alcohol. I was correct, her destination is less than a mile away. I pull up outside her house and can see this tiny little man watching her from the living room window. I think he's been waiting to help her with the shopping. I couldn't be more wrong. As I start taking the shopping up the front path this pathetic little man opens the front door. He has a dirty white vest on that shows off his ugly man breasts and loads of pointless home-made tattoo's all down his arms. He stands in the doorway with a tin of cheap lager in his hand and an expression on his face that looks like he's trying to squeeze a shit out of his arse. Judging by the stench from him I think he's actually done one in his pants.

"Alright" I say.

He doesn't answer but grunts back at me.

"Whare huv ye been?" He shouts to his missus.

She ignores him and looks at me. I can see fear in her eyes as she walks past him into the house with some of the shopping bags.

"Eh asked ye. Whare huv ye been? An hows meh dinner no

ready?" He shouts back into the house.

She goes to walk past him to get back out of the house and he says to her

"Jist tak them fae there, the drevir can bring them ti the door."

I have never wanted to smash somebody so much in such a long time. There is a vast amount of bags, which means I have to make several trips back to the car. All the time this little runt of a man stands at his top step staring at me. Each time I return to the door I have visions of hitting this cunt. Just one word, one little comment, please, you know you want to, just give me the slightest excuse and I will fucking dance on your head you miserable little bastard.

I drop the last of the bags at the door as his missus walks back out to pick them up. He shouts more abuse at her telling her she had better have got this or she had better have got that. He walks back into the house and stares at me from the living room window while shouting at his missus to hurry up and get his dinner on. I stay there for a few minutes looking at him and at what I would have done if he had gave me any lip. I think he is the type of person that if I hit him, I wouldn't stop. I drive off thinking to myself, what the fuck have I just witnessed there?

Customer No. 594
Pirate movies

The Cutty. This pub used to have one of the most feared reputations in Dundee. On my computer that has given me the job it says do not send car 15, 27, 45, 81, 124, 129. These numbers are taxis that are refusing to pick customers up from here. The few years that I have been working on the taxis I have had several calls here every week. Out of all those times

I have never had or even seen one bit of trouble in the place. Don't get me wrong I know it's full of guys…and women might I add, that don't take any shit from anyone. This pub has had a violent past including shootings, stabbings and many serious fights. The people I pick up from here always go out of their way to make conversation with me no matter how short the journey is. I never get any attitude from them and they always leave me a good tip with a 'cheers' or 'thanks' as they get out.

I open the door to the pub and a few hard faces look around but most of them nod in my direction and turn back to their pint. I am about to shout the name when I recognise my customer sitting at the end of the bar looking quite pissed. He's the movie man, who sells all the pirate DVD's and CD's.

"Did you phone for a taxi?"

"What? Oh, eh, cheers." He says as he picks up his holdall and follows me out.

He gets in the car and I ask him what he's got today, which happens to be the latest cinema blockbuster. I saw an advert the other day about pirate DVD's and the quality being shit and the sound a bit dodgy but every time I have bought a film from this guy, you could not fault it. He always says he wouldn't sell them if they weren't good quality as nobody would buy them again from him. The same advert went onto say that the money you spend on them is going into the hands of drug dealers and smugglers, basically you are funding the underworld. But people are obviously going to buy a product at a fraction of the price rather than the high street stores no matter where the money goes. The government spends thousands of our money from tax on adverts telling us that we are lining the pockets of criminals. What about them? They put so much tax on everything we buy, for what? So that politicians can line their pockets or spend our money on giving free drugs to junkies. To go to the cinema to watch the same film would cost a fiver or more. If you go with your partner, that's more than a tenner plus food and drinks. This guy sells the same film for three pound and you can watch it in the comfort of your own home. You don't have to put up with people munching crisps and sweets all the way through it and at least if you need to go to the toilet you can pause it instead of having someone squeeze past you halfway through the movie.

I drop the guy off in his usual destination in the city centre and instead of paying the fare I take a couple of movies from him. My intensions are for one to watch with the guys when we are all getting stoned and one for curling up with Kelly for either before or after I have had my hole.

Customer No. 833
Wee wide-o

Dundonald Street for Anderson. I drive along slowly as I look at the numbers on the vandalised tenement block doors. There is a group of young people hanging around up ahead and just my luck they are right outside the number I am look-ing for. One of the young guys in the group walks over and leans his elbow on my car. I roll down the window and shout

"OH, OFF THE CAR PLEASE."

"SHIT YER PUSS, EH'LL LEAN ON IT IF EH FUCKIN WANT." He shouts back and kicks his heel on the passenger door. I get out to confront him and clock the others as I walk around the car. There are three guys and two girls and all of them are in their late teens.

"Who do you think you are? You wee prick." I say as I in-spect the damage.

His hands drop to his sides and he puffs out his chest giv-ing me the hard man look.

"Wah are you callin a wee prick?" He says squaring up to

me and pushing his arms out wider and his chest out further.

"What, do think you're some sort of a hard man?"

"Eh ken eh'm a hard man." He says as he comes close and is now in my face. I can smell the alcohol off him and this is obviously the reason behind his hard man act

"Get out of my face." I say as I shove him back towards his friends.

"Do ye ken wah eh am?"

Oh fuck, here we go again.

"I couldn't give a fuck who you are?"

He takes a run at me with a punch that is swung from far behind him. I move out of the way and due to the momentum of the swing, he falls forward towards me. I step past him and push the back of his shoulder making him fall to the ground. I see one of his friends go to step towards me when my customer comes out.

"Is this my taxi?" He says.

"For Anderson?" I say. He nods and we both get in the car but before I drive off one of the group kicks the back of my car as they all shout abuse. I don't stop but speed off before anything else happens.

"Bit of trouble there was it?" My customer says.

"Nah, it's just somebody that's had too much to drink."

I play it down and make small talk but as soon as my customer is out of the car I am speeding back up to the same street looking for the little wide-o bastard. I see the group not far from where they were standing. I keep my distance and park up, waiting patiently for the right opportunity. After twenty minutes of watching him swagger about shouting abuse at anyone walking past he decides to brake away from the group. I watch him walk up a small alleyway in between two other tenement blocks. I get out of the car and run as fast as I can towards the alley. I cross the road and slow down to a jog, keeping my head down as I pass his group of friends who don't even notice me. I enter the pitch black alley and have slowed down to a fast walk as I hear him zip up. I see the swagger a few feet in front of me and without saying a word I launch forward with a barrage of punches to his head. As he falls to his knees in front of me I grab his hair at the back of his head and throw several more punches to his face. I swing my leg back and bring my knee forward to his face. I let go off his hair and watch his shadow fall back into his own piss. I walk back out of the alley and jog past his friends again. Once I cross the road I slow down to a walk and get my breathing back to normal.

I can only imagine him tomorrow when he has sobered up telling his exaggerated story of how he managed to sustain a black eye and possible broken nose. 'Eh got jumped fae fev guys' 'It was fir fuck all tae'. I would like to say that I taught the little wide-o cunt a lesson but I can tell he's the type who will be back out doing the same thing next week with more drink on him and a bigger chip on his shoulder. He'll be back in the same place giving abuse to anyone who happens to be in his way, a Murdo in the making.

16) Falling big time

Over the next few weeks I met up with Kelly several times. She was near the end of her course at university and was always busy finishing her course work or studying for exams. I would sometimes receive a phone call late at night from her saying that she had been studying for hours and wanted to talk as she was stressed out and needed a break. We would talk on the phone for a long time and eventually she would ask if I wanted her to come up for a while. Of course I did but I would obviously play it cool and answer 'If you want' as if It didn't put me up nor down if I saw her.

With the amount of shit I listened to from people all day it was actually good to meet someone who never really complained about anything. It was strange meeting a girl who didn't bitch about everybody and everything...she must be a rare breed. For a girl who is really good looking she is definitely not a 'Look at me.'

On the odd occasion I would be in my bed and she would come up unexpectedly. She just stripped down to her underwear and jumped in next to me. We would lie there and cuddle in but after a little touchy feely I would have a throbbing hard on. I was desperate for a shag but I held back and never pushed it. I always let her make the first move, in which most of the time she did. There were two things I hadn't done in years, one was wait for a girl to make the first move and the other was actually talk and get to know someone. Well the second thing was only in part as we although we talked for hours I never really got to know that much about Kelly. I never asked many personal questions about her unless she

mentioned them first but if a subject came up she would
sometimes work her way around it or just change the subject
altogether.

She was very strange as she wouldn't come out to meet any
of my friends, although Kyle and Gaz have seen her they can
hardly remember what she looked like. If I was in the East
View and she was picking me up to go somewhere with her,
she wouldn't come into the pub to get me. She would wait
outside in the car and give me a one ringer on my mobile to
let me know she was there. Nothing was ever planned, it was
always a last minute phone call to ask if I wanted to meet up.
It didn't bother me that much but it did bother the life out of
Gaz. If we were out on the piss and I received a phone call
from Kelly I would be off like a shot to go and meet her. I
never saw her regularly so by the time she phoned I was anxious to see her. I was sitting in the East View having a few
drinks not long after I met her, and she phoned me to ask if I
would like to go to a U2 concert that night as her friend had
pulled out. Of course I said yeah. I was never a big fan of U2
but as soon as I announced this Kyle and Mickey were calling me a lucky bastard, but not Gaz. He started this big spiel
about how he wouldn't go to a U2 concert if you paid him.

'Bono, treyin ti save the fuckin world cause he canna cut it
we the new bands nowadays. Oh eh, he still sells millions o
albums bit that's onay cause o ah he's loyal fans fae years
back. But if ye asked any o them aboot ah he's politics maist
o them would say that they couldna gee a fuck. The onay
time ye hear o the cunt is when he's aboot ti release a record.
While other bands are oot on the toon pullin burds an getting
pissed ti git themselves in the papers. He goes an gees some
speech aboot savin the fuckin world. An that cunt, Sir…' Gaz
spits and continues.

"Geldof, does he really think the average person gees a
fuck aboot people goin hungry in a country thousands o
miles awa…no. But what they do gee a fuck aboot is if they

hae enough cheege left fir that last pint o lager before they head hame, or if they'll hae enough tae pey their electric bill it the end o the week before it gits cut aff, or if they hae enough tae feed their ain bairns cause they've jist pit the co-oncil tax up again. Even mare important is if their team will win the league or on the ither hand git relegated. The average person doesna live like him we ah he's millions in the bank an royalty cheques every year ti depend on. Wha the fuck gees him the right ti ask people ti go on a march. What is he on? Does he no ken maist folk hae joabs ti go ti. Is he gonna pey thir wages or employ thum if they git sacked fir takin the day aff. Cunts like Bono and Geldof should concentrate on fuckin rock n roll music an livin like a real rock star, fuckin champagne socialists. Look at the Stones or even mare up tae date Oasis, you nivir see them on T.V. pleadin ti put money inti this charity or that charity. That's cause they sell oot their gigs without ah that shite. The fans respect them fir what they are, no fir goin roond pretendin ti be be something thir no an bein up thir ain arse. Real bands are busy shaggin an getting oot thir nut, like us. If onay we could play or sing we would mak better rock stars than they cunts."

"Thanks for putting a downer on going, I'll just phone her back and cancel, saying that due to Bono's politics I'm refusing to use the sixty pound ticket that I'm getting for fuck all." I said as Gaz finished his big speech and we all laughed except Gaz who now confirms what he has just said by me telling him how much the ticket cost. Although when I was at the concert I was more happy that I was out with Kelly than I was being at the U2 concert. I did find out that Gaz was right about Bono as he did a speech in between each song which made me think, that the people here paid sixty pound or more to hear you sing not fucking lecture about world politics, but I guess that's just what he's all about now and his fans obviously respect him for that as they cheer at his every word.

She phoned another time when I was in Slims and Gaz had

assumed I was having people back to mine but I left and went up to Kelly's flat without telling him. It happened to be a night he pulled a stunner and had nowhere to go with her when he got out of the club.

I assumed this would all change once she finished university but things started to get even more strange. If we met up in a pub in town for dinner she would always be looking around and couldn't relax, it felt like she didn't want to be there. I was starting to get a little paranoid that it was something to do with me then I would start to think that maybe she was hiding something. It did cross my mind that she had another boyfriend as she would disappear for a few days but then I would get a phone call from her from Spain as her father run a club or something out there and we would talk for hours, with her telling me she was missing me.

She hardly ever went out at night in Dundee and when she was with me it was like she didn't want anybody to see me with her. I sometimes asked what was wrong but she would just change the subject. We were always having a great laugh as she appeared to have a cheeky sense of humour like mine and when we were together that I didn't want to ruin it. Although I always had the feeling that everything was going too good and that there was something bad around the corner waiting to happen as that's just the way my life has always been.

We were now in the middle of a the heat wave that people had talked about for the past few months. We hadn't had a good summer in years and I was starting to believe what people had said about my flat before I bought it. There were several different styles in the one block on offer and two of the more expensive ones had balconies. Most people had told me that I was stupid for paying all that extra money for a balcony that I would only use a few days a year. It's always pissing down here and I wouldn't even make much more money on it when I go to sell it either. This advice was from people who had rented their homes all their lives. I started off with a flat that cost fifteen grand and am now living in one that is worth a hundred and fifty grand…and they are giving me advice. The way I looked at it is that, it was better to have something and not need it than to need something and not have it.

With this heat I would waken early and go to work but due to the bright sunny days people chose to walk more and I would sit for a while between jobs. If I received a phone call from Kelly it didn't take much persuasion for me to finish work and meet up with her. We would go for a drive in her heap of shit and for someone who didn't like a lot of attention she would have the windows down and the music up. As soon as we went somewhere outside Dundee she became so relaxed and appeared so much more happy. I knew i liked Kelly from the first night I met her, which was maybe the reason that it took me weeks to eventually shag her. It was a Saturday night and I was in Slims, out of my face wasted on e's as usual. I had already discussed with Gaz through my altered state of mind that we were going back to mine for a party when the club finished. I was sitting down in the chill out area next to a girl I knew who appeared to be in the same frame of mind as myself. We were in the middle of a deep meaningful conversation about something that I have no clue about whatsoever when I felt this tingling sensation in my balls. It reminded me of when I was a kid and I was on a carnival ride, like the waltzers. When someone pushed it from behind and it spun around really fast. I remember getting the same feeling and not wanting it to stop. Although this tingling sensation only lasted for a few seconds and then it would stop for a few seconds, it did this several times and then it would stop for about a minute and then it started all over again. The conversation with this girl started to sound even better as the tingling continued. This appeared to go on for quite some time until I reached over to the table in front of me for my drink and the tingling moved to my leg. I then realised that it was my phone vibrating in my pocket. The feeling was actually very good so I sat back in my comfortable position and carried on talking shit with this girl. I was hoping that the phone call was really important as whoever it was would continue to call me, thus keeping the tingling sensation going in my balls. I finished my drink and the girl offered to go to the bar and get more drinks in…with my money of course.

I went to the toilet while she was waiting to get served and I took out my phone to investigate and I found that it was Kelly calling me. I answered but it was very hard to make out what she was saying. I did decipher that she had been phoning for the past half an hour but I think I already knew that. She had not had a good night and wanted to see me.

I knew she was going to a party with her friends that night but she said she would either see me in Slims or meet me after it. That's why I didn't answer the phone as I thought it was just someone asking if I was having a party. I walked over to the bar where the girl I was talking to had just been served, I picked up the bottle next to her on the bar. She handed me the change and I then proceeded to tell her a big fat lie of how I would meet up with her at the end and we would go back to mine but right now I had to go and find my friends. She gave me a kiss on the cheek and I quickly walked off in the direction of the front door, downing the bottle as I went. I didn't even bother to look around for Gaz or anybody else to explain that the party was off. I flagged down the first taxi I saw and headed straight to Kelly's flat. As soon as I got to the door she opened it and put her arms around me.

"What's wrong?" I asked, returning the hug.

"I saw someone I didn't want to see tonight." She said, knowing full well that I was going to ask who.

"Well…are you going to tell me."

"It was my ex boyfriend, he turned up at the party."

"And what happened?" I asked. Not knowing if I wanted to hear the answer. I was expecting her to say that she went off with him or something, but she I guess she wouldn't have called me up to her flat if she did.

"Look, he's caused so much trouble for me in the past it was a bit of a shock seeing him tonight"

"What happened? Did he say anything to you?" I asked her, as I got ready to give the hard man speech that I would go and sort him out and that he'll not harm you while I'm with you.

"No I left before he saw me, well I hope he didn't see me."

I could tell that she was scared so I held the speech back for the right time and put my arms tighter around her. I had the thought of some young prick giving her shit and taking advantage of her and it made me feel angry. I had only known Kelly for a couple of weeks but I had picked up that she didn't like violence in the slightest, so for me to have acted all tough, would have been a big mistake.
"Do you want to talk about this?"

"Not really."
"Good, because I was having a good time until now and I was coming up here for it to continue."

"Oh you were, were you?" She said as she took my hand and lead me to her bedroom.

I had seen Kelly a few times and although being with her had got quite heavy on occasions it never really went to the stage of shagging. With everything going really good with her I was I bit worried about shagging her as It wouldn't have been the first time that I had really liked a girl, and once I had shot my load up them the feelings disappeared as quick as me running out the door. I was beginning to get a little paranoid by thinking that if I didn't try to shag her soon she would start thinking that I was some sort of a nonce.

Kelly pulled up the covers and climbed into bed with her

clothes on, I went to do the same.

"No, no, yours has to come off." She said with a smile then pulled the covers up to her eyes and peered out over the top.

"Oh they do, do they." I said smiling back at her.

I kicked off my boots and pulled up my t- shirt, but when it came to my jeans I started opening the buttons very slowly and she started making silly noises. I was down to my boxers and she opened the covers to let me jump in beside her. Our arms were wrapped around each other. Then she got out of bed and gave me a show by taking her own clothes off but she only went down to her knickers and bra and tried to get in the bed.

"No, no, carry on." I said keeping a tight grip of the covers.

"Let me in." She said grabbing a pillow and hitting me over the head. I through back the covers and she climbed into bed with me. After a quick hug and a little touchy feely we were nearly ripping the rest of our clothes off. I hadn't had sex in weeks and I was hoping that the few wanks I'd had in that time would have done the trick as I didn't want her thinking I was some sort of a two minute wonder. I then re- alised that I had taken several e's that night and the chances of me coming quick were slim and none. The sex was good, very intense, there were no fancy positions and it didn't go on for hours. It felt different from the sex I'd had recently and I couldn't tell if this was because I really like this girl or that I've just had too many drugs that night. We lay together in each others arms for a while and I thought to myself that anyone who says that the high from drugs is better than sex is obviously not doing it properly...or I'm not taking the right drugs. All I can say is that the only thing better than having sex and taking drugs is doing both together.

Back in the East View the next day Gaz grilled me for doing a bunk out of Slims and not even telling them I was going.

"So where did you fuck off to last night?"

"Kelly's. She had a bit of bother."

"Thanks for letting us ken like. We hung aboot fir ages waitin on ye."

"Fuck, sorry man. Where did you end up anyway?"

"We went back to ain o Jamie's mates hooses. What a laugh. As soon as eh walked in the hoose people were askin me for e's. Do eh look like a drug dealer or somethin?" Gaz said as we both laughed.

"Eh had a couple on is an eh wisna awa ti jist hand them ower so eh decided ti raffle ain o them. Made mesel twenty quid aff one e. Eh had a competition fir the other ain."

"What kind of competition?"

"Well eh had a we look in the kitchen an saw a box o Weetabix, so eh telt them ah that if anybody can eat a hale drey Weetabix they could hae the last e for free."

"You're sick…Did any of them go for it?"

"Every ain o them. You wouldna believe what some people would dae fir a free e. They were ah bokin but still treyin ti force this Weetabix doon their throat. Their was only one person that feenished it so eh gave him the e. He was walkin aboot the perty like he was the fuckin world champion or something."

17) T in the Park

T in the park is Scotland's largest music festival whare people pey way over the odds for a ticket ti gather in a field oot in the middle o naewhare ti watch their favourite bands play. This is no a rock concert as there are bands fae every different type o music performin. Fir me it means a weekend o drinkin, smokin an takin as many drugs as possible. We hae a mini bus that taks us there an brings us back baith days. There are thousands wah camp ah weekend an eh huv tred it in the past but, eh like meh hame comforts. Especially when eh've been on it ah day an night. The last thing eh need is ti go lookin fir a tent in the pitch dark, in a field we thousands o other tents. It's onay a short journey on the bus an eh'm hame in the comfort o meh ain bed curled up we Biscuit. Eh waken up ti meh granny's cooked breakfast as she makes sure eh hae a good meal in is before eh go an dae it ah ower again.

Eh hear her shoutin on is ti git up, she's mental meh gran. Eh telt her the bus was leavin at eleven so waken is at ten but eh ken it's onay nine thirty. This is her wey o makin me hae enough time ti get a shower an eat meh breakfast, bless er, she means well. She kens ah the shite eh git up ti, well no the specifics but she kens eh'm always up ti nae good. She lets me smoke grass aroond the hoose, she sometimes moans aboot the smell but secretly eh think she pinches some o it fir her an meh granda. That doesna bather her but if eh brought back a lassy ti stey fir the night she would go aff her fuckin nut. Eh always tak care o her an meh granda as they've ah eh've got, well except fir Biscuit. Meh mother died when eh was really young, eh nivir new meh dad. Eh've asked Danny meh granda aboot him ower the years when eh wis growin up but he didna really ken much aboot him either. They've always made sure eh nivir wanted fir anythin, eh wisna spoiled though an they taught me right fae wrang. But the past few years eh've got inti a lifestyle that eh ken if eh got caught they would be so disappointed, no ti mention eh would be locked up fir a very lang time.

Eh get oot the shower an can smell the bacon cookin, Eh rush doon the stairs ti a plate o sausage, eggs, bacon, tomatoes an twa slices o toast. Meh gran pours is a cup o coffee as she pours hersel ain an sits next ti is. Biscuit comes in the front door an rushes inti the kitchen, although he is waggin he's tail an looks happy ti see is, it's actually onay cause he smells the food. He doesna bark or pant, he hovers aroond ye hopin ti git somethin, the wee grubber. The smell o the bacon an sausages cookin has probably been drevin him nuts. Meh granda informs is thit he has been ti the shops an got is meh carry oot fir the bus. Plenty o cans o lager an twa half bottles o vodka. One bottle fir each day ti slip doon the jeans, if eh git caught treyin ti sneak thum in they'll onay tak them aff is. Fir the low price o ah fevir, it's worth the risk.
Jamie turns up at the door an we are too early so the tins o lager git started on, meh granda joins us an eh'm tempted ti ask if he wants ti come we us but eh dinna even say it as a joke cause the auld cunt would tak is up on the offer. We head ti the East View an wait on the mini bus an there are a number o faces eh've nivir seen before bit they are ah mates o mates an bey the end o the day, once the drugs kick in an the gibberin starts, eh'll probably ken them ah quite well.

While we are waitin fir the bus Shane phones an says he's runnin a bit late. Some cunt has damaged he's car again, he starts rantin an ravin doon the phone aboot Murdo but eh hing up on him as eh feel like he's pittin a downer on is. We are ah on the bus an ready ti go when this rust bucket o ah car pulls up. Shane gits oot an he's burd leans oot ti gee him a kiss an eh ken eh seen her that night at the doghoose bit eh'me sure eh recognise her face fae some place else. Shane gits on the bus an is still goin on aboot he's car bein damaged. He's bein a bit loud an mentions Murdo's name again. Eh tell him ti shut he's puss as he disna ken wah could be on the bus listenin. Eh hand him a can o lager an a few e's .

"There, sit on yer arse an git them doon ye. You'll no be gein a fuck aboot yer car in half an oor."

It's onay a forty fev meenit journey ti Kinross fae Dundee bit once we are there it taks aboot another half an oor fir oor coach ti actually reach the field whare the festival is held due ti the amount o traffic. As we approach the site aff the main road we can see the field o coloured tents an in the distance the big wheel is goin roond. As eh look aroond the bus eh notice abody gitting a bit excited, either that or they are ah bursting fir a piss. Shane appears ti huv cheered up an is blabbin awa in somebody's ear in between puffs on a joint that eh passed him. The e's eh gave him are obviously takin effect. There is a massive queue ti git through the gates inti the park so a group o us fae the bus find a space on the grass an sit in the sun until it goes doon a wee bit. We ah hae several cans left so they are knocked back while we bake in the melting sun. Shane mentions something aboot e's so eh hand him another few.

We go through the main gates an head straight fir the main stage whare we find the rest o the people wah were on oor bus. There is a good line-up here the day but there are loads o other acts that eh want ti see on some o the other stages. The onay problem is what state eh'll be in later ti actually go an see they other acts. There is a strong possibility eh winna be movin too far fae this spot. Weller is on stage two in aboot four oors, His new stuff isna meh cup o tea but the rest o them huv said that he always plays a few Jam numbers, which I'll dae fir me...He is the Modfather eftir ah. Four oors is no the problem as eh could tak it easy til then. The problem is that stage two is in a tent, which means that we'll hae ti go there really early if we want ti get in. If we go in good time, like an oor early. We'll hae ti tak a couple o drinks in we us as there's nae bar. But the worse thing is havin ti stand an suffer whatever shite act is on previous ti him.

The Arctic's are playing the main stage jist now an they've really got the crowd goin. Shane is lookin smashed an eh'm wonderin jist how much he's took ti git in that state. Eh hope he's no took ah they other ain's in one go. Eh warned him thit they were really strong ain's. Eh'd better keep meh eye on him fir a while. He's sittin on the grass in oor big group fae the bus, an he's gibbering a load o shite ti some lassie wah appears ti be treyin ti speak but canna git a word in. She was on oor bus we her lad but eh think he's buggered aff an left her in Shane's capable hands. Eh canna believe the state Shane is in. Eh partly feel responsible as eh gave him the e's in the first place. There is an act on the NME stage that eh want ti go an see but eh canna tak Shane we is while he's in that state. Eh overhear Joey mention that he's aboot ti go an watch The Streets that'll dae fir me, eh'm aff we him. Eh pull him aside an tell him that eh'm goin we him but to keep it quiet likes as eh dinna want Shane ti come. It'll be like babysitting if we bring him. We sneak awa an go ti the beer tent on the wey. Eh still hae loads o e's on is but eh dinna want ti tak anymare jist now. Eh'm jealous as fuck o the hit Shane has hud as eh've no hud ain like that fir years but eh'm jist wonderin how many he's took ti git in that state.

We git ti the N.M.E. stage an there's a fairly large crowd ah standin aboot in the sun waitin on them ti come on. We find a space deep in amongst the crowd bit no too near the front. Oor drinks are placed at oor feet as we struggle ti skin up withoot makin it look too obvious. The band come on an the crowd in front o us go wild. We picked a spot far enough back so as we are no shoved aboot. There are lassies on top o peoples shidders we jist their bras on. Eh wouldna mind if they took them aff an flashed their tit's a bit but eh guess that's jist meh dirty mind at work again. The band are only half wey through thir set when eh feel eh'm going ti explode as meh bladder is aboot ti burst. Eh tak meh tap aff an tie it aroond meh waist, leaving the knot hangin specifically at the front. Joey huds meh drink as eh pick up an empty cup. The cups that you git your drinks in are made o paper but they're big enough ti hud a pint. Eh stand we one hand hudin the cup an we the other eh casually open a few buttons an pish in the cup. Naebody bats an eyelid as eh fill the cup an place it back on the groond. eh button mesel back up an Joey goes ti hand is back meh drink.

"Hud on." Eh say we a sly grin.

"Nah Gaz, ye canna dae that." Joey says, obviously kenin what's on meh mind.

Eh pick up the cup o piss an pour some o it oot so thit it is onay half full. This is so that eh can fold the tap o the cup the gither withoot it spillin over is. Eh tak a sweeng an launch the cup upwards towards the stage. This sprays the crowd we meh piss until it lands on some pair cunt wah ends up soaked as the cup opens up when it hits them. Joey hands me meh drink an we watch The Streets storm through the last o their set. On the wey back ti whare the others are sittin, Joey stops some lassie we a programme an asks if he could hae a quick look at it. As he chats awa ti her eh flick through the pages until eh see that The Modfather. He is on Stage two in an oor. That'll dae fir me. Eh ken eh'm mare into rap an hip hop now but eh used ti be right inti the Jam when eh wis growin up. If the cunt plays some o that eh'll be happy as fuck. Eh hand back the programme an tell the lassie thanks as eh grab Joey an drag him awa before he ends up sneakin awa we her.

"Fuck sake Gaz eh wis in there."

"Wir ye fuck, she wis onay aboot fifteen anywey ye fuckin

beast."

We go ti the bar fir mare drinks before headin ti the main stage ti find Shane when eh spot him staggering past us.

"Oh, whare are ye goin?" Eh shout ti him.

"Alright mate" Shane says lookin at us we eyes that he can hardly keep open. Jamie is no far behind an makes a face at us when Shane isna lookin. It's ain o them looks that ye can tell he's pissed aff we Shane. Shane treys ti pit he's airms roond meh shidder an eh end up drappin ain o the drinks.

"Shane. Git a grip."

"Sorry mate, I'll get you another one."

"Git yersel ain. It wis fir you anywey."

He goes ti the bar an while he's gittin served Jamie tells us that he's been babysittin since we left them. He took him fir a walk ti trey an straighten him oot a bit.

"We're goin ti see Weller. Ye comin we us?" Joey says.

"Yeah sure there's naebody on the main stage in the next while that eh want ti see anywey. What aboot Shane?"

"Jist keep an eye on him, at least if he's we us he winna get inti any bather." Eh say ti them but eh ken this is wishful thinkin. How things cheenge. It used ti be me that got that wasted an Shane used ti hae ti look eftir me. We look aroond an Shane turns fae the bar we twa drinks an is struggling no ti spill them. He hands one ti Jamie an we walk aff ti Stage two.

There's a queue ti get inti the tent when we turn up an there's a band ahready on. But we ah ken that maist people are no here ti see them they are just gittin in early ti make sure they see Weller. We eventually get in an eh swally twa e's at once, eh've ahready hud a few but eh've no felt anythin. Eh should git a good hit bey the time Weller comes on though. We ah stick the gether in the tent an work oor wey ti get closer ti the front. The crowd starts ti get tighter so we stop ti feenish oor drinks before we end up wearin them. The band that wis on feenish their set an surprise surprise, hardly anybody moves. That means maist people are here ti watch Weller. He should huv been on the main stage.

"Whare's Shane?" Joey says lookin aroond.

"Ah whare the fuck has he went ti?" Eh say as if it's meh fault.

We ah look aroond but the tent's too dark an crowded ti find anybody.

"He kens whare we ah stand at the main stage an if it comes ti it, he kens whare the bus picks us up." Eh say thinkin to mesel that eh'm no awa ti spend the rest o the day lookin fir him.

We feenish oor drinks an squeeze oor wey through the crowd until we canna go any further. We are onay aboot four or fev rows fae the front which isna too bad. The lights on the stage go on an before Weller actually appears the crowd erupts. Weller walks on ti a thunderous noise. The sways in the crowd kick right aff. This is what eh wis hopin fir as it means eh can work meh wey closer ti the front. Eh look back ti see Joey an Jamie far aff ti meh left but they are still pushin forward. Eh ken Jamie will get ti the front as he would shove past he's ain granny ti dae it the evil wee cunt. As the crowd sways eh notice Shane ti meh right an he's closer to the front than me. He's we some lassie wah looks ti be in the same state as him. Eh work meh wey closer ti him an am jist aboot ti slap him ti get he's attention then eh notice he has he's hands on her hips an is rubbin up against her arse. So much fir him being loved up we he's new burd. Eh'm aboot twa fut awa fae him an huv just realised the lassie wah he has he's hands on actually has her hands on the guy in front o her. Eh'm aboot ti reach over an drag him awa but eh stop as eh think ti mesel that eh'll jist watch an see what happens. He's hands work their wey aroond ti the front o her jeans an end up inside them. Her man in front is turnin he's head ti kiss her then when he turns he's head back to face the stage she's turnin aroond an kissin Shane. The dirty bitch. Shane's airm is reachin further. Hmm eh wonder what he's dein...her face says it ah really. She's now reachin back we her hand an is gropin Shane's bahs...Oh oh, she's openin he's buttons now. Eh dinna ken what's happenin on stage or what tune Weller is playin as eh'm too busy pervin at this spacer. She has her hand in he's fly an is obviously wankin him aff. Oh fuck, her man has just turned aroond an noticed what's goin on.

"What the fuck are you dein?" He says in he's weedgie accent as he throws a crackin punch fae a fist full o sovereigns catchin Shane's forehaed an burstin it open.

The blood is tricklin doon he's face an the weedgie goes ti throw another ain bit Shane grabs he's wrist. He throws the other fist an Shane grabs this ain tae. Shane now has baith the guys wrists an eh'm waitin fir the haed ti git stuck on him an lay the weedgie cunt oot but it doesna happen. Shane is still full o it an is treyin ti talk ti the guy tellin him ti calm doon. Eh wid step in if Shane wis gettin a hidin bit it's one on one an it looks as though he's handlin it ah bey hesel. The e's huv made him ah mellow an he's nae anger in him ti fight back. Shane lets him go an the guy shouts at him ti get ti fuck. He turns towards the stage we he's burd in front o him this time. It looks as though it's ah over an eh go ti grab a hud o Shane but he's obviously still got the horn an is hingin aboot treying ti git the lassies attention when the guys no lookin. He taps the guy on the shidder an eh move in behind him but eh still dinna let on that eh'm there.

"Here mate what was all that about?" Shane says lookin quite confused.

The guy looks at Shane an in a complete rage he turns aroond an shouts "Are you still here?" An lays into Shane we he's fists flyin.

Eh grab the guy bey the throat, squeezin hard an he's attack suddenly stops. He looks at is an eh nut him in the bridge o he's nose. He puts he's hands up coverin he's face an crouches doon. Eh could huv hit him again but eh grab Shane an drag him awa fae there as quick as eh could. Shane keeps stoppin an turnin roond an eh canna tell if this is cause he wants ti go back an hit the guy or go get the guys burd. Eh find a place further back whare the crowd is no so tight an eh smile ti mesel when eh see the state o Shane's haed. He has a bump stickin oot o he's forehaed we a cut in the middle an blood tricklin doon he's face. Eh look at the state he's still in an eh'm wonderin how eh huvna hud a hit yet. Eh've took mare e's than Shane now includin two at once before eh came in this tent an eh'm still feelin straight. Noel Gallagher has just walked on stage an this has lifted the crowd again. They day twa sangs an feenish we 'That's entertainment' which fir me it certainly wis. They walk aff stage an the tent clears.

We head ti the bar fir a drink whare we catch up we Joey an Jamie wah are shocked ti find Shane we a bump that has now swelled ti the size o a half a golf bah. His recollection o how it happened is somewhat different ti how eh remember seein it.

"The guy just hit me for nothing." He says.

"What, an you didna hit him back?" Jamie says ah serious.

"Ehh, no."

"What does he look like? We'll go get the cunt." Jamie says keepin his serious face ti Shane but gees me an Joey the sneaky grin.

"I cant remember." Shane says lookin quite confused but is missin the point thit treyin ti find somebody in the middle o a field we forty thousand other people is the joke. Eh'm tempted ti tell them exactly what happened but eh'll save it fir a rainy day.

We go back an find the others ah sittin aroond on the grass catchin the last o the sun. We dinna get weather like this up in Scotland too often so every second is soaked up we ah the sun worshipers. Eh lie back on the grass haein a smoke an feenish meh drink. Razorlight have just come on stage an maist o the crowd are standin up now. Bit me, eh think eh'm goin ti stey here a bit langer. Eh close meh eyes fir a while an eh guess eh must huv dosed aff, either that or Razorlight huv onay done three sangs an are onto their finale. Eh waken up ti somebody trippin over is an eh stand up ti catch the last sang 'America'. The band sing the chorus an the music stops so that the crowd huv ti sing it back ti them. Hearin thousands o people sing a chorus in tune back ti the stage sends the shivers doon meh spine, an it's nothin ti dae we drugs. The closin band on the main stage the day is the Strokes but as much as they are probably a top act they are jist no meh cup o tea. Eh huv ti finish the day at the N.M.E. stage. New Order are closing the show there the day an eh dinna care if eh huv ti go on meh ain that's whare eh'm headin. Eh announce this ti see if any cunt wants ti join is bit it's onay Jamie wah taks is on. Eh look over at Shane wah has a drink in each hand an it looks as though the e's have finally worn aff.

Eh head ti the bar on the wey ti the N.M.E. an while eh'm bein served Jamie gets chattin ti a couple o lassies wah eh can make oot are wedgies judgin bey thir strong accent. Eh hand him twa drinks an as we head aff he offers them ti come we us, which ti meh annoyance they oblige. The band have no started yet so eh work my wey doon the side wah until eh find a good space ti sit doon. Eh put meh drinks ti one side o is an git mesel ah comfy on the groond. Eh start skinnin up while Jamie is next ti is in serious chit chat we the wedgies. Eh spark up an feel content we meh back against the wah an meh drink ti one side as eh tak long slow puffs on meh joint. Eh ken there's an unwritten rule aboot the twa puffs an pass it...fuck, it's usually me that enforces it, bit no this time. An it's no cause eh'm bein greedy or thit eh'm runnin low on grass, it's cause eh grudge passin ti a couple o hingers on, especially a couple o Glesgay mingers. As eh sit an listen ti thir conversation eh cringe at some o Jamie's comments ti them.

Ain o these weedgies is quite slim but has a face like she's been chasin parked cars, the other has a nice face but is fuckin enormous, the layers o fat are hingin ower the sides o her jeans an her stretch marks look as though some cunt has drew them on we a fluorescent permanent marker. Eh catch Jamie passin them a couple o e's an eh'm thinking, what the fuck are you dein? Eh eventually pass the joint eftir Jamie geein is a funny look an just as eh guessed he taks a quick puff an passes it straight ti them. They are campin oot here an have asked Jamie if we want, we can sleep in their tent the night…hmm eh wonder why?

"Are you up fir it Gaz?"

"What?"

"Steyin in thir tent."

"We dinna hae campin bands."

"That's ahright, they'll sort it."

Eh really dinna fancy sleepin in some smelly tent we a couple o weedgies when eh can jump on the bus an be curled up in a comfy bed in less than an oor bit eh wouldna leave Jamie in the lurch as eh ken he wouldna dae it ti me.

"Gaz, they said they hae loads o drink in their tent an baith are up fir a shag." Jamie says still treyin ti convince is ti go fir it.

"Eh'll even tak the fat ain." He says as he puts his bottom lip oot we a sad expression on he's face.

These lassies are onay aboot seventeen which doesna sound bad fir Jamie as he's onay nineteen bit eh'm twenty fev… this doesna look good fir me. Eh nod an tell him thit eh canna really leave him on he's ain so eh'll hae ti stey. He gees me a big cheesy grin then says "Eh kent that you wid be up fir it if eh mentioned you would get yer hole, ye dirty cunt."

"If we get caught sneakin in the campsite we'll hae ti run like fuck ti catch oor bus hame." Eh tell him.

"Dinna worry aboot it. Eh'll pey fir a taxi."

18) The campsite

We get ti the campsite gates an the security is checkin fir the wristbands as they let people through. The twa weedgies go through first an the fat ain snaps her wristband an the skinny ain comes back oot we it. She puts it roond Jamie's wrist an taks the chewny oot o her mooth an puts it on the ends o the wristband hudin it the gither. She taks Jamie's hand an they wak through...nae bather. She then comes back an does the same we me...weedgies, they ken every trick in the book.

We wak aroond the campsite fir a while as the lassies canna find thir tent. Eh pass a few people thit eh ken wah offer me ti stey an hae a beer. As much as eh would like ti stop an stey we them meh hand is tugged bey the skinny ugly lassie as we struggle ti keep up we Jamie an the skinny lassie. We eventually find their tent an as soon as eh sit doon eh'm passed a plastic cup.

"What the fuck is this?" Eh say as eh tak a sip.

"Fuck. This is cider. Di ye no hae any beer?"

"Naw, that's aw we've got."

Eh'm now thinkin that mibbe eh should go an find some cunt we beer bit mibbe eh'll stey an hae a smoke first, then eh'll go lookin fir that bloke that offered me ain on the wey here. Eh sit in the corner o the tent rollin a joint when meh phone goes.

"Hello."

"Gaz, where the fuck are you?"

"Ahright Kyle, eh'm in the campsite we Jamie."

"That's good. The bus is only been waiting here for half an

hour on you two."

"Sorry mate eh forgot ah aboot it. We are gonna stey here the night. We'll see ye the morn."

"Yeah, see you."

"That wis Kyle. He sounds a bit pissed aff that we didna tell him."

"Fuck him. If he had the offer he would be here tae." Jamie says treyin ti justify the bus waitin on us.

Eh light up an hae a few puffs before passin it ti Jamie wah is leyin curled up ti the fat lassie. Eh down the cider an ask fir mare. Eh'm hopin they've nane jist so eh could use the excuse ti escape. The skinny lassie pulls oot a three litre bottle an comes over next ti is an pours some inti the plastic cup eh hae. Eh'm no goin anywhare. She pours hersel another ain an moves in closer ti is.

"Hey Gaz have you got any e's left?" Jamie asks.

"Yeah a few bit they're fir the morn."

"Goin gee is a couple an eh'll phone Kyle in the mornin ti bring some mare."

Eh pull oot meh stash an realise eh hae aboot ten left bit eh dinna let on ti Jamie as eh ken the cunt will nip meh haed til they're ah feenished an he'll probably onay dish them oot ti these mingers. Eh hand him twa an he puts baith o them in he's mooth at once an swallys them we a moothful o cider.

"Fuck it." Eh say an dae the same.

As soon as eh swally it eh canna help but think that was a waste as eh huvna hud a proper hit ah day. Eh think eh must be gittin immune ti them or somethin. Eh think eftir this weekend eh should hae a break fae these, especially eftir seein the hit Shane hud fae them the day. Eh'll mibbe jist stick ti the coke fir a while. We sit aroond fir a while as we down cup eftir cup o this pishy cider. Jamie an the fat lassie are now in the same sleepin bag an are whispering in each others ear so eh guess they are geein each other a bit o foreplay. As eh'm talkin ti the skinny lassie she reaches over an starts kissin me, but eh think this is just so eh will shut meh puss as they twa e's must be makin is gibber shite ti her. Everywhare she touches is eh feel ah tingly an eh start gittin turned on. Eh keep thinkin thit this is ah wrang as this lassie is so young. Before eh ken it she has meh jeans open an she's wankin is aff. Eh open her jeans an put meh hand in her knickers. Eh trey ti slide meh fingers further doon but am findin it hard as she has the hairiest fanny eh huv ever came across.

"Eh think you need yer bikini line done hen." Eh whisper in her ear.

She sniggers so eh guess she thinks eh'm jokin. Eh eventually manage ti slide meh fingers doon an slide ain in her, then anither ain. This gets her goin a bit. She pushes up meh tap so eh tak meh hand oot o her knickers an tak meh tap aff an she dis the same. Eh put meh hands on her sides an she is that skinny eh feel her bones. She must be ain o they anorexic lassies, either that or eh'm just used ti the big fat burds. Eh dinna say anythin an we carry on takin the rest o oor claithes aff. We her knickers aff an her legs open, eh climb on tap o her an am bangin awa. Jist meh luck...a screamer.

Eh'm in a tent, in the middle o a field at T in the park an am shaggin a screamer, but no jist any screamer, a wee gadgie Glesgay screamer. Eh look ti the right o is an through the dark eh can see Jamie's shadow. He's oot o the sleepin bag an kneelin ower the fat lassie.

"Suck it then." He says in a low voice.

Eh snigger as eh heard it loud an clear. The skinny lassie is still groanin an screamin every time eh thrust inti her. Eh can hear a loud cheer in the distance we each scream that she makes an eh'm now gigglin awa ti mesel.

"Ye huv ti keep suckin till it goes hard." Jamie says in his low voice again. He obviously canna git a hard on an is gittin stressed oot.

"How do ye no just hum meh bahs instaed?" He says a bit louder.

"What?" The fat lassie says as eh trey ti stop mesel fae burstin oot laughin.

"What do you mean?"

"Eh mean just pit yer mooth aroond meh bahs an huuum." Jamie says as he drags the word hum oot a bit.

Eh start ti loose meh rhythm as eh struggle ti concentrate on what eh'm dein bey listenin ti this an hudin in meh laugh. Eh lift mesel aff the skinny lassie an tell her ti turn ower.

"Your no putting it up my arse." She says in her weedgie accent.

Eh laugh at this an say "Dinna be daft of course eh'm no gonna pit it up yer arse."
She turns ower an eh lift her boney hips so her arse is stickin up in the air. Eh'm back in an bangin awa feelin like eh'm the fuckin man. Eh can see Jamie's grin in the dark an he's makin faces at me. Eh start makin porn star noises an we baith burst oot laughin.

"Keep humming, dinna stop." Jamie says.

But the lassie does stop an says "Ah don't want tae dae this anymore. Ah want you tae shag me like he's shagging her."

"Just shut it an keep hummin, mibbe if you werena so fat an ugly eh wid hae a hard on, an eh wid be shaggin you like that."

The smile is drained fae meh face as eh canna believe thit Jamie has said that ti her. Eh feel sorry fir the lassie as eh think Jamie was a bit oot o order sayin that. But the lassie has a mooth on her an fires right back at him.

"If you were any sort o man your dick would be in me making me scream like her anyway." She says we a bit o attitude in her voice now.

"Oh ho, she's got ye there Jamie." Eh say laughin. At this point eh stop an sit back

"What's wrong?" The skinny ain turns ti is an says.

"Nothin, eh jist need a drink."

Eh sit back an pour mesel a cup o this pishy cider as meh hard on settles doon ti a semi. The fat lassie isna slow as she blurts oot "Are we swappin over then."

Eh ignore what she says an ask Jamie ti hud the phone near is so eh can use the light ti skin up.

The lassies are at one end o the tent drinkin an whisperin ti themselves an we are at the other drinkin an passin the joint between oorsels.

"Eh hud nae intension o shaggin her." Jamie whispers in meh ear.

"Eh onay said that ti persuade ye ti stey."

"What do you mean? If you said eh wis on the fat ain eh wid huv steyed anywey."

Eh say as we baith laugh like a couple o bairns.

"Well you can shag her now then cause she's no gonna let me near her."

"Wis that the plan then, wis it?" Eh say but dinna git a reply.

Eh hae one last puff an then pass it ti the lassies wah are pourin themselves mare cider.

"How do we go aboot this Jamie?"

"Eh'll show ye." He says movin towards the lassies side o the tent.

"Right, fatty you're now we Gaz an you. You're now we me." Jamie says as he taks he's tap aff an moves towards the skinny lassie.

Eh finish meh cup o cider an move towards the fat lassie wah is leyin doon. Although she's quite fat she does hae a nice face so eh start kissin her. Eh'm still naked an hae meh hands up her tap an she has her hands on meh arse. She works her wey aroond an it's no lang before eh'm hard again. Eh help her tak aff her tap ti reveal her big saggy tits but eh dinna ken what ti dae next as eh slide meh hand doon her waist onti the layers o fat folding ower her jeans. Eh'm aboot ti trey an open her tap button that is buried in her stomach but she moves meh hand an does it hersel...phew. She taks aff her jeans ti reveal her big granny pants an when eh help her tak these aff they feel like a pair o they lycra runnin shorts. Eh guess that's ti help hud in some o the fat ti make her appear thinner...Nae chance. She must be really turned on as eh pit meh fingers doon she feels afay wet...either that or she's pissed hersel. Eh slide a finger up one eftir another until eh hae three up nae problem withoot her even makin a noise...fuck. Am eh in trouble or what? The sayin when eh wis growin up comes ti mind 'It's like throwin a mars bar up a closey." Eh pull them oot an climb on tap o her an as eh dae this eh hae a wee sneaky smell o meh fingers...ahh. The lovely smell o a sweaty stinky fanny. She grabs meh willy an rams it in but she still doesna make a sound. Eh've heard the sayin fir years aboot no even touchin the sides an eh hud visions o this but it doesna appear ti be the case. She still doesna move or even mak a noise, an as eh thrust harder an harder she lies there like a sack o tatties. Eh lift up one o her legs so that eh can reach her arse cheek. This is no so that eh can grope her fat wrinkly arse but eh do hae an ulterior motive. Meh middle finger finds it's wey through the layers o fat an eh play aboot bey rubbin the tip o meh finger a aroond her wee browner. She starts ti groan a bit an this encourages me ti keep goin. Eh rub her fanny again which is drippin wet an eh squeeze meh finger in ti moisten it an then go back ti her arse. Eh circle aroond it then jist ram it up. This results in a much louder groan fae her...still nae movement bit at least it lets is ken she's still alev. Eh'm thrustin meh hips hard an wigglin meh finger up her arse an jist as eh start ti get the feelin eh'm aboot ti shoot meh load meh mind wanders an eh start thinkin aboot some weird shit...they fucking e's. Eh start ti think thit eh've been kissin that lassie eftir she wis hummin Jamie's bahs an eh start ti feel a bit sick. Eh forget whare eh am fir a bit as the sweat runs doon meh face. Eh jist start ti git inti it again when eh hear Jamie maonin at the skinny lassie cause she winna gee him a blow job. It starts ti git a bit aggressive an then in the dark eh see Jamie shove the lassie across the other side o the tent near me. The lassie shouts at him an eh see Jamie's airm go back as if he's awa ti hit her. Eh stop what eh'm dein an reach over an gee Jamie a hard slap in the puss.

"Dinna you fuckin dare." Eh say, ready ti gee him another ain.

"What the fuck are you dein?" He says.

"Dinna you ever lift yer hands ti a woman."

Eh'm aboot ti git aff an tell the fat lassie ti forget it bit eh think this wee cunt is no spoilin it fir me. Eh struggle ti git goin again an think ti mesel eh'll gee her it fae behind but then eh think o the size o her arse an think better o that idea. Eh git goin again an feel mesel buildin up an am aboot ti shoot meh load but eh dinna come up her. Eh pull oot at the last meenit an wank til eh shoot meh load ah over her.

"Oh thanks and how am I supposed to clean myself."

"What do ye mean? Yer a weedgie. You lot dinna wash anywey."

Eh hear Jamie laughin at this an eh reach ower puttin the finger eh hud up the fat lassies arse under Jamie's nose an rub it hard above he's lip. This is kent as a tangy porker. We used ti dae this type o thing when we were at skale. Eh guess some people jist nivir grow up.

"What are ye dein?…Ooh what the fuck is that?" He says sittin up ti wipe he's face.

Eh sit back in the corner an canna stop laughin as Jamie storms aboot the tent tryin ti get the smell o shit fae he's nose. Eh pick up the first thing at hand that happens ti be the fat lassies tap an eh gee meh finger a good rub ti clean it. Eh pit on meh claithes an start ti pour mesel a cup o cider. Jamie opens the zip on the tent an taks aff he's condom throwin it oot in the distance. As usual eh nivir even bathered we ain, an nane o these lassies asked is ti pit ain on...What dae ye expect fae Glesgay mingers.

"Eh'm gonna git you back fir that Gaz." Jamie says.

"That's fir startin on the wee lassie ye fuckin bully." Eh say pushin him lightly. He doesna say anythin back. We hae a few cups o cider an Jamie opens another bottle. Eh fuckin hate cider but that's ah they hae so eh guess beggars canna be choosers. Me an Jamie polish aff another bottle ti we'resels an the lassies start moanin an gettin nippy we us.

"Eh think it's time fir us ti find a new tent ti crash in as eh really dinna want ti waken up here in the morning. It's ahready stinkin o stale smoke, drink, sweat, spunk, an now shit fae your face Jamie."

"Ha ha dead funny. Ye prick."

Eh pull up the zip on the tent an throw oot ain o the full bottles o cider withoot the lassies kenin an without even sayin cheerio. We git ti fuck oot o there we nae intension o returnin. We stretch oor legs as we look aboot in the dark wondering which wey ti go. There are several lit areas whare we can hear groups o people talkin an we decide just ti trey an find somebody we ken, which shouldna be too hard. Eh pick up the bottle o cider as we go.

"Eh thought ye didna like cider?"

"Oh that's no for us, that's for barganin we."

Eftir walkin aroond in the dark fir a few meenits we hear some distinguished Dundee accents. We dinna ken them bit eftir a trade o some grass an a bottle o cider for a few tins o lager we are welcomed inti their company. Two tins o lager, a good smoke an eh'm comatose in a clean tent feelin safe in the company o some real Dundee schemies.

19) T in the park - day 2

I waken up as Kelly walks in and opens the curtains.

"Come on sleepy head, get up."

She passes me a cup of coffee and by the looks of it she's been up for ages as she looks fresh and ready to go.

"I have as surprise for you later."

"Oh you do, do you?" I say smiling at her.

"You were in some state last night." She says.

"Was I." I reply while trying to actually remember yesterday.

"At least the bump on your head has went down." She says nodding to my forehead.

I put my hand up to my head and feel a slight bump sticking out. I get a flash back of some guy punching me, but cannot remember why. I vaguely remember trying to push my way to the front for Weller coming on so I guess he wasn't happy about it. I wonder why I didn't hit him back.

"Come on, get in the shower and we'll go somewhere for breakfast."

I finish my coffee then quickly jump in the shower and the whole time I'm still trying to remember most of what happened yesterday. It's been a long time since I got myself in such a state where I can't remember the day before. I get changed and we head downstairs to Kelly's car. She points in the direction of my car, which has been fixed.

"Was that you?"

"Who else would go and sort your car?"

"You didn't have to do that."

She smiles and says "I just wanted to help you out."

"Thanks."

Kelly asked me yesterday when she dropped me of at the bus if I knew who was doing it but I didn't tell her. The last thing I want to do is let her know I have someone like Dek Murdo on my case. She takes me into the town and we go to a café for some breakfast. I don't feel hungry in the slightest but she is making such an effort I don't want to tell her. I play safe and order a bacon roll and Kelly orders the same. I mention we will have to be quick as I have to catch the bus shortly.

"Don't worry about it." She says with a big smile, which makes me think she wants me to miss the bus so I won't go.

"I can't believe the state of your head." She says, changing the subject.

"Don't worry about it."

"What if you see the guy again today, I hope you wont start fighting with him."

"Kelly there is forty thousand people a day at the park, not to mention that I can't remember what the guy looks like, so the chances of that happening are quite slim. Anyway the bus leaves in twenty minutes so we had better make a move soon."

"That's alright I'll give you a lift."

"What do you mean?"

She looks at me and smiles and pulls out a Sunday ticket from her pocket and puts it in front of me.

"What, are you coming too?"

"A friend of mine offered me it last night, so I thought I would surprise you."

"Brilliant." I say leaning over and kissing her.

"But this means you will have to meet all of my friends, I hope you realise that."

"Oh I think I can handle it."

We take our time finishing our breakfast and I text Kyle to say that I'm getting a lift from Kelly and that I'll meet them later. Although I have explained to Kelly that there is no chance of seeing the guy that hit me she has warned me that if the situation occurs she will walk away and I would never see her again as she absolutely hates violence.

"I understand that but what if someone is about to attack me, or you for that matter, I will have to fight to protect you, would you still walk away."

"That's different, and you know fine well what I mean."

"I know, I was just testing you." I say smiling at her but thinking the total opposite as in my mind if I saw the cunt again I would fucking smash him.

***

Meanwhile...back at camp

"Jamie that's Kyle just phoned, they're on their wey but Shane's no on the bus. Apparently he's phoned ti say he's gettin a lift fae he's burd an he'll meet us when he gits here. Huv you met her yet?"

"Nut, how?"

"Eh'm just wonderin how he nivir brings her oot ti meet us, it's like he doesna want us ti see her. Are we no good enough ti meet he's new burd or something."

"That's no what's batherin you, it's the fact that when he's we her you hae naewhare ti go eftir a club for a perty."

"Nah that's nothin ti dae we it...well, mibbe a wee bit but if he's happy bein we her then good luck ti him. Eh would just like ti meet her once an see what she's like, that's ah."

"Eh right, like her fae the taxi office, ye were on he's case constantly fir seein her."

"Eh, bit she was a fuckin idiot."

"That's no the point, every time Shane gets ah serious aboot some burd you lot always tak the piss oot o him an he ends up dumpin them."

You obviously dinna ken your brother very well then.

"That's cause he always ends up gettin serious aboot lassies that are fuckin idiots…dae ye ken what? Eh bet it's some burd eh've shagged before an he doesna want us geein him stick fir it."

Jamie cheenges the subject an eh think ti mesel that in future eh'm no gonna say anythin ti Shane aboot the burds he meets an we'll soon see what fuckin trouble he gets inti.

***

It's not long after the park opens that we arrive and meet everyone from the bus. They are sitting on the grass in their usual place in front of the main stage. I introduce Kelly to everyone and Gaz makes a comment that he thinks he knows her from somewhere.

"So you're the ain that's keepin oor mate occupied." He says but Kelly doesn't answer she just smiles back at him.

"She's a right wee pumper is she?" Gaz says smiling at me.

There are two ways that you can take it when someone says your girl is wee pumper. I have already pre warned Kelly of what they mean as this has been an on going thing between me and Gaz for years. In one way it could be said by meaning that she's a wee slapper and she'll pump anything, hence 'wee pumper'. In another way it could mean she's a lovely looking girl and that you would like to pump her. Kelly laughs as Gaz says this knowing full well that he is winding me up that he would like to pump her…well I fucking hope that's how the cunt is meaning it.

"And you, you're looking a bit rough mate" he says to me as he inspects the bump on my head.

The banter is flowing fast of the stories from the past twenty fours hours. Someone mentions that they saw Gaz and Jamie with a couple of horrors yesterday but although they try to deny it. Jamie puts Gaz right in it by pulling out a pair of knickers from his pocket and holds them up to everyone's amusement. These knickers are the biggest I have ever seen so I can just imagine the size of the girl that was wearing them. Jamie proceeds to explain in great exaggerated detail about what Gaz got up to with this girl. Gaz stands and takes it as he knows he'll wait for the right moment and get him back again.

***

Shane's burd is a bit wee'er than him we short dark hair. She's no what eh remember her looking like fae that night at the Doghoose. Eh end up speakin ti them again an eh find oot that she is a really nice lassie bit eh suddenly realise whare eh remember her fae. If it's the same person wah eh think it is, Shane's in a lot o trouble. She's obviously no telt Shane aboot her past if it is the same lassie or he widna be standin there hudin her hand an paradin her aboot like that. Nae wonder she disna come oot often ti meet people. He walks awa ti talk ti the others still hudin Kelly's hand but if eh manage ti get him on he's ain he winna be dein that fir very lang.

Eh watch them walk aff the gither ti the bar kissin an cuddlin up ti each other an eh realise that Shane must really like her as he would nivir be that forward we a lassie in front o he's mates. The last time eh saw him dae anythin like that we were still at skale, but eftir a good slaggin fae us, fir some reason he nivir done it again. Eh git Shanes attention an tell him eh need a word we him but he's burd drags him awa. There awa ti see that Dundee band 'The View' on another stage. Eh canna believe that cunt. He stood in the Doghoose an ripped into every sang that they done an now he's awa we he's burd ti go an see them. Eh'll bide meh time an trey an git him on he's ain later before the wrang person sees him we her.

***

Next years headliners

"So do like this new band then?" Kelly says as she puts her arm into mine as we walk towards one of the smaller tents where the new up and coming bands get to play.

"Yeah, they're great, I didn't think much of them when I saw them at the doghouse that night that you asked me to go to but I was pretty wasted. I was handed a copy of their demo C.D. from Mickey and play it all the time when I am working. It's not until you actually listen to the lyrics that you understand what they are all about."

As we enter the packed tent the band are on stage just about to start and for a new band who haven't even released a song they have quite a number of fans. They kick off and their young, mad army of followers go wild. I stand with Kelly further back as the drinks start to get thrown about. I stand looking at this band and I have so much respect for their attitude. Their song lyrics are superb, they make me think about the way we live by trying to fit in with society. Wearing the correct clothes with the correct labels, even where we live or what area we grew up in determining how people look at us and judge us. This young band have the crowd going more than some of the headliners and are up on this small stage ripping into all that shit with their powerful tunes and lyrics. We end up squashed at the back of the tent halfway through their set due to the amount of people coming in to see them play.

"They should be on a bigger stage." Kelly says.

"I know but just wait, they'll be next year's headliners."

As they announce their last song, some of the fans end up on stage and are dancing away. Somehow I can't see that being allowed to happen on the main stage next year.

We walk back to find everyone still sitting around at our usual area near the main stage. Kelly has to go to the toilet and I am about to go with her when Gaz tags along as he is going to the bar. We reach the toilets first and the queue is very long.

"I could be a while so why don't you two go to the bar and I'll meet you back here?" Kelly says as she gives me a kiss on the cheek before walking off to join the queue.

I order a couple of drinks and we stand around watching the main stage from a distance. Gaz is being a bit funny and I ask him what's up, thinking he's away to take the piss about yesterday.

"Shane, eh, ah…Kelly's dad wouldna happen ti own a nightclub would he?"

"Yeah, in Spain, why? Do you know him?"

"No but if your burd is wah eh think she is, then your in a lot o fuckin trouble."

"What are you talking about?" I say smiling.

"Shane, eh think Murdo could be on yer case cause o Kelly."

"What do you mean?"

"Eh think Kelly could be Murdo's ex burd."

"Fuck off." I say and start laughing as I think this is Gaz trying to wind me up.

He doesn't say anything but his smile drops and he looks at me all serious.

"You're taking the piss...right."

"Come on Shane, you ken eh wouldna wind you up aboot somethin like that."

"Yeah right. Get real Gaz, he's old enough to be her father and anyway Murdo's been in the jail for the past four years and Kelly's only twenty-one, which would make her about seventeen if he did happen to go out with her."

"Actually eh think she was onay sixteen when he went oot we her."

"Gaz, what are you talking about?"

"Shane, do you remember the nightclub a good few years ago called Velvet. It shut doon an it's now a day centre fir junkies or somethin."

"Yeah, it was a shit hole."

"Kelly's old man used ti own that."

"And what?"

"Look Shane, Murdo used ti be her dad's mate an wis the haed bouncer on the door there."

"Yeah I remember him, he wasn't actually allowed to work the door because of his criminal record so they gave him a different title but everybody knew he was in charge. If any trouble kicked off he stepped forward and sorted it out."

"Aye well, eh used ti end up there sometimes when eh wis oot we a few dodgy characters. Eh think you were busy dein up you're flats at the time. Well eh remember Kelly, she hud long blonde hair an always wore ah the tight short claithes. Eh dinna ken the full story bit the four years Murdo has just done, wis fir stabbin her cousin."

"Are you sure it's the same person Gaz?"

"Eh hope eh'm wrang mate, bit if it is her, jist watch what

you say. Eh ken her an her femily hud a hard time. Murdo was ain o they jealous people an didna like her talkin ti other guys. That's what started the fight we her cousin, the pair cunt was actually beatin Murdo until he pulled the blade an chibbed him a few times. Kelly an her auld man hud ti go up in court against him, it was ah on video but the sick cunt pleaded 'not guilty' jist so they wid huv ti testify. Apparently the footage on the video looked as though Murdo wis jist punchin him until he pulled he's hand back an there he was standin we this big blade in he's hand. Her old man hud ti eventually sell up an move due ti the amount o trouble he hud eftir that."

"That's why she doesn't go anywhere" I say to myself.

"This is what eh've tried ti explain ti ye every time you've mouthed aff at him. This is the type o person yer dealin we. He's been in jail twice for stabbin an it wis onay luck that he didna kill them."

"Well you know what they say, third time lucky." I joke but Gaz doesn't laugh.

"If that is her ex, what am I going to do?"

"Eh dinna ken mate. Eh could trey an hae a word bit Murdo's a nut job he's no gonna listen ti anybody."

I see Kelly coming back from the toilet and I make a face at Gaz who quickly turns around and gives her a big smile.

"Those toilets are disgusting." Kelly says.
"Ye should huv used the guys urinals" Gaz says as he smiles at her and we head to the bar for more drinks before we head back to find the others.

If this all turns out to be true and I keep seeing Kelly there could be some serious trouble ahead. I know Gaz will back me up all the way as I've lost count the amount of times I've had to step in for him but I just hope it doesn't come to that.

Back at the main stage it's starting to get really crowded as the final act is due to come on. Gaz mentions he's away to head to the N.M.E. stage as Primal Scream are closing it and he makes a sharp exit through the heavy crowd. I stand with Kelly as we wait for Faithless to come on and close the show on the main stage. I actually feel like asking her about all this now but I've had a good day and really don't want to spoil it. I've liked Faithless for years and never had a chance to see them live...I am not disappointed. They kick off while the sky is still bright but after a few songs the sun goes down. This makes the stage look great as it is all lit up in the dark. The lights and lasers move around in time with their music as the crowd cheer with each uplifting tune. They finish their set and received a massive cheer from the crowd.

As we walk back through the field we are treated to a fire-work show and although everyone's face lights up as each rocket shoots up into the sky you can tell they are disap-pointed that it's all over for another year, especially me who has had one of the best weekends ever...until next year.

20) Truth or dare

The long walk out of the park to Kelly's car gives me time to think about what Gaz told me. I have to find out if it's true but how I am going to bring this up.

"Are you alright?" Kelly says gripping my hand tighter.

"Yeah, of course, why?"

"You've hardly said a word all the way out."

"Sorry, I'm just thinking about something Gaz said, that's all."

Kelly smiles at me and I smile back but I'm actually looking at her thinking how could she have been with a prick like him. I am actually picturing the two of them together and it's making me feel sick. I'll wait until tomorrow when both of our heads are clear. The queues of traffic are locked and we sit in the car park for nearly an hour before it starts to move. We eventually get onto the main road and Kelly asks me again what's wrong.

"I've never seen you so quiet."

"Sorry, I just have something on my mind, that's all."

"Must be important."

"Eh, nah, well."

Ah fuck it

"Kelly can I ask you something?"

"Sounds a bit serious, I suppose it depends on what it is?"

"Did your dad used to own a club in Dundee?"

"Yeah, why?"

"Eh'm, it's just something Gaz told me."

"Why, what did he tell you?"

"He says your ex is Dek Murdo."

I don't get a reply and there is silence in the car for what seems like a long time.

"Well, is he?"

Kelly pulls the car over to the side of the road and brushes her hands up her forehead and through her hair letting out a long sigh at the same time.

"Yes, yes he is."

This is obviously something that she didn't want me to know so I try to reassure her.

"Look Kelly, I'm not bothered about your past." I say as I put my arm around her.

She leans over and puts her head into me and both her arms around me. This lasts for several minutes then we break off.

"So what else did Gaz tell you?"

She listens to me as I tell her exactly what Gaz told me earlier. When I finish she doesn't say anything.

"Well is it true?" I ask, knowing what the answer will be but wishing I am wrong.

"Yes." She says in a very soft voice.

"But there is a lot more to it than that."

"Look you don't have to explain it to me, I'm just disappointed you didn't tell me sooner before I found out from a mate."

"Look I need to explain so you know what really happened. Yes I did have long blonde hair and dressed in the tight clothes but I was sixteen and i didn't know any better. I got a lot of attention and most of it was from Dek. He was a friend of my dad's and he was always nice to me. I knew his reputation but when you are young and naïve you can be attracted to that. My dad went nuts but that encouraged me even more. Until it started to go wrong. He started to get jealous and it got to the point that I couldn't even talk to anyone, even girls. He would march over to me asking what I was saying to them. If I had a skirt on he would be constantly on my case and shout at people that he thought were looking at me."

"Why didn't you just leave him?" I ask getting myself worked up thinking about this beast with her.

"Believe me I tried, but he came up and smashed up my dads house threatening me that if he saw me with anyone he would kill them."

"Did he ever hit you?"

"No but he put a knife to my throat once."

"WHAT?" I shout.

"It was after he stabbed my cousin and he was out on bail. Do you believe it, my cousin was in hospital on a life support machine and he gets out on bail. Anyway he kept coming up to the house to try and speak to me. You know, bringing flowers saying he was sorry and sending stupid gifts. I just ignored him but he started following me around. I would go into a pub to meet up with friends, all females by the way, then he would appear and accuse me of meeting other guys and make a big scene."

"But you weren't seeing him anyway."

"I know, but that didn't register with him. I told him to leave me alone and he would try to drag me out of the pub. The other bouncers wouldn't go near him as they were all shit scared. One night I was out and there was a large group of us. My friends boyfriend was talking to me and Dek appeared and started ranting and raving that I was seeing him. It got so bad that I had to persuade Dek to leave with me before he hit my friends boyfriend. I didn't think for one minute he would do anything to me. Yeah he would hit guys and smash things but I never thought for a minute that he would harm me. I got outside the pub and phoned my dad to pick me up but there was no answer so I started walking towards the taxi rank. He dragged me into an alleyway by the hair and I was shouting and screaming to let me go then he pulled out a knife and put it to my throat telling me to shut up. He said if he couldn't have me then no one could and that if he ever saw me with anyone this is what they would get and so would I."

Kelly now has tears in her eyes and I pull her close to me to comfort her but comforting someone is the last thing I feel like doing right now.

"That's why you wouldn't go anywhere with me?"

"Yeah, that's right." She says looking straight at me.

"You don't have to worry about me Kelly, I can look after myself." I say trying to sound hard.

"But it's not just him it's his mates, if he snaps his fingers they go running. That's why we had to move away. After he put a knife to my throat I went to the police as there were conditions with him getting bail that he was not allowed to approach me or any of my family. I had plenty of witnesses to say he was harassing me so he was put back in until the trial. That's when it stated getting really bad for my dad. If it wasn't the house being broken into and our cars being smashed up it was the club. My dad couldn't get bouncers to work the door as Dek knew them all and they refused to work for him."

"You're dad must have known some other firm to work it."

"He did, he brought in a Glasgow firm but this caused more trouble as the fighting got worse. It played right into Dek's hands as he was locked up with all these gangsters and he obviously had a word with whoever run the Glasgow firm and they pulled out. The club was losing customers every week and eventually my dad had enough and sold it. The trial was creeping up so he decided to move abroad."

"Why didn't you go?"

"I did, but I missed my friends and I wanted to go to uni. After Dek got sentenced my Dad opened another club abroad. We both thought it would be safe enough for me to go back. I thought I would be finished uni by the time he got out."

"And then what? Hurry on back to Spain before he finds you."

"Something like that."

"I can't picture you two together, well I can but it doesn't seem right."

"Believe me if I could change it I would, but remember I wasn't the same person back then, I was just a very naive young girl. I didn't even look the same."

"So what happens now?"

"I don't know, my intensions were to move back to Spain and work for my dad, but I've met you and I don't know what to do. I really like you Shane but I can't live here. You could always come with me."

"Yeah right." I say as I laugh at this suggestion.

There is a long silence and Kelly starts the car and drives off. From the side of her face I can see the tears in her eyes. This makes me feel really sad seeing her unhappy, but at this moment I cannot think of anything to say to her. We arrive at my flat and I go to get out of her car.

"Do you want me to come up?"

"What do you mean? Of course I want you to come up?"

I get into the flat and head to the kitchen and put the kettle on.

"Do you want one?" I say as I pick up two cups.

Kelly nods.

"Please."

I put sugar and tea bags in the cups and as we wait on the kettle boiling she puts her arms around me tightly.

"Kelly can I ask you something?"

"Of course, what?"

"Are you still intending on leaving? I mean, you finished uni a while ago and you are still here."

"I had to wait on my exam results and one thing led to another so I decided I was going to hang on until my graduation."

"When were you going to tell me all this?"

"I don't know, I was always happy when I was with you

that I didn't want anything to spoil it. I always told you I was going to work for my dad anyway."

"Yeah, I know but I…"

"What?"

"Oh, nothing."

"You thought I would change my mind and stay here to be with you."

"Something like that."

"Me asking you to leave is the same as you expecting me to stay." Kelly says, now smiling at me and looking up into my face.

"Kelly, why don't you stay? He's been out for months now and he's not bothered you."

I now feel glad I have never mentioned the hassle I've been having with him or that when she fixed my car the other day that it was actually her ex boyfriend that done the damage.

"He hasn't seen me with you yet, actually since he's been out he hasn't even seen me yet."

I would love to tell her the truth that I think he's already seen us together.

"Stay Kelly? I'm not afraid of him."

"That's the problem Shane, neither was my cousin and look what happened to him."

"Look Kelly I can get someone to sort him out if you want and he'll never come near us."

As soon as I say this I realise how stupid it sounds. The someone I was thinking of was actually myself as I know nobody in Dundee would go near Dek Murdo as every hard case knows him and they certainly wouldn't tell him to back off for me.

"Shane don't you think my dad tried all that? He even offered him money to stay away from us."

There is a silence between us for a few minutes as my mind is going around in circles thinking of something to say that would make her change her mind.

"Look I really care about you, that's why I have to leave as I don't want anything to happen to you."

"Listen Kelly." I say holding her tighter.

"He's a coward, he won't do anything to me."

"It's not just him it's his mates too. They are just as bad. I don't want to get a phone call one night saying something's happened to you and I have to live with it."

"So that's it." I say, releasing my arms from around her gently.

"You are just going to leave and if I want us to continue I have to move to Spain."

"It's not like that Shane…look maybe I should just go now."

Kelly goes to walk past me but I grab her arm and pull her close to me.

"Look Kelly, this is a lot for me to take in, in one night. I would love to say I'll sell my flat and come with you but it's not as easy as that."

"I don't expect you to do that for me, but the fact is I can't stay here. Why don't you come for a few weeks and see what you think?"

"I can't just up and leave, I have my family and friends and my job. I also have this place which I have worked really hard for. What if it didn't work out? What if I didn't like it over there?"

"Shane you don't know until you try, you can rent your flat out for a few months. It will pay your mortgage and give you some extra income."

"You've got this all figured out don't you?"

Kelly hugs me again

"I don't expect you to do anything Shane but please just think about it."

Kelly takes my hand and leads me to the bedroom

"Come on, let's go to bed."

21) Smart move

I can't believe Kelly just left like that without saying anything. Three days after asking me to move to Spain and live with her. She packs her bags and leaves. I get a text saying she's away to her dad's as she needs some time to think and that she would be in touch. I went around to her flat and her friend let me in. All her stuff was gone. To top it all the next day my car gets paint stripper poured over it. I wonder who that was? I was ready to go after Mudro but Gaz calmed me down. He said he'd get someone to have a word with him first before I did anything stupid. It's not just the cost of the re-spray but it's the days off work that is more of a problem. By not working it's made me sit around thinking more about all this shit with Kelly and Dek Murdo.

I've been to the gym with Joey two days in a row as I thought a good work out would get it all out of me...no chance. Joey pushed me harder than ever but I don't think I worked out. I just worked myself up. I did phone the office and left a message for anyone who needs a driver for a couple of days but nobody got back to me. I hate working for other people and handing over half the money but at least it would have kept me occupied. Now I have to go out on the piss...downer.

I'm the first one in the pub so I get myself a drink and stand at the bar. I would go and sit down but I'll get a bit paranoid if anybody walks in and sees me sitting in the corner of the pub on my own. Gaz and Jamie walk in together and the rest of them follow. I can tell by the look on their faces as they walk past me that something is going on. I shout the round up then follow them to our usual corner and find them all sniggering between themselves.

"Right what's going on? What am I missing?" I say before I start to get pissed off.

"A few screws fae what eh hear." Jamie says.

"That's good comin fae you, your just as bad." Gaz says but I'm still not getting it.

"What do you mean? What's going on?" I ask, getting a little anxious as they all snigger to themselves.

"What did the guy hit ye fir at the park?" Jamie says.

"So this is why you lot are sniggering like a bunch of poofs, I've already told you I can't remember. But if you guys want to make up some shit and whisper it between yourselves like a bunch of wee lassies then that's up to you."

"So ye canna remember treyin to shag the guys burd?" Jamie says.

"What guys burd? What are you talking about?"

"The guy wah hit ye."

"Yeah right, who said I done that like?"

They all look at Gaz.

"Gaz." I say looking at him then turning back to Jamie.

"And you believed him?"

Gaz puts his hand on his heart and pleads.

"Ye did mate, eh swear. Eh stood an watched ye."

"You're full of shit."

I get up and head to the bar and when I come back with the drinks Gaz has now moved the discussion to Jamie who is now taking some stick due to his antics in the tent at T in the park with his gentle words and ways of foreplay.

We stay in the East View for several drinks before heading off to the city centre and into a disgusting hole of a pub. Gaz goes into the toilet and insists I follow him. He goes into the cubical and pulls out a small wrap of coke and asks for my credit card, something he has never had before. Actually I don't even think he's had a bank account in his life. He goes to work and starts chapping up a couple of lines with my card.

"Could you make mine a bit bigger?" I say, being sarcastic.

I have only ever taken coke with Gaz and the lines he's given me in the past are about a quarter of the size of the ones he is putting out now. He obviously knows they are big as all he does is turns and smiles at me.

"What's with the coke anyway? That's not really your thing Gaz."

"Eh ken bit eftir takin ah they e's last week at the park an hardly gettin a hit, eh thought eh had better tak a break fae them."

"What? And start on the coke...Smart move." I say sarcastically.

Gaz rolls up a tenner and snorts half a line up one nostril and changes to the next for the other half. He passes me the tenner and nods towards the cistern where there is another large line waiting on me.

"Bey the way Shane, ye wouldna happen ti hae left a message at the office sayin ye needed a car ti drev wid ye?"

"Yeah, it's just for a few days while mines is in getting a re-spray."

"Wully, the auld guy eh work fir. He kens thit eh ken you an telt is ti pass on a message. Somebody has started a rumour aroond the office sayin that you rip every cunt aff an thit ye drev thir cars like a maniac."

"What? No need to guess who that was...Lisa."

"Well, mibbe no, as he's also heard thit thir is a lot o talk aboot ye bangin Lisa an thit she wis sendin ye extra work. The directors are gonna be lookin inti it."

"Fucking hell, you wait until I've had a line before telling me this."

He knows once this coke kicks in none of this will bother me as all the bad thoughts will be pushed to the back of my mind. But tomorrow...tomorrow will be a different story as it will all come crashing back into my mind and I will feel ten times worse. But fuck it, I will just have to make sure I have a good night tonight to justify it. We start a little pub crawl around the city centre and realise why we drink up the West End. It's not really to do with the actual pubs but the people that drink in them...scheemies. These are the guys who are barred from all the clubs, sometimes just for wearing the wrong clothes, the stripy Lacoste or Henry Lloyd jumpers. The Burberry caps and the Timberlands with the laces open and the tongues hanging out. They now have a socially acceptable name...Chavs. It's those type of people that have given e's a bad name. Saying that, most of them have moved onto coke now anyway.

We eventually reach Slims a bit worse for wear. After several drinks and line after line of Gaz's coke, I am flying out my head. Everything that has happened to me in the past week is just a blur and I actually feel on top of the world. The time in the club goes so fast and before I know it I am in the back of a taxi with Gaz and Jamie heading to my flat for a party.

"Eh invited Emma an her mates up ti yer flat bey the way." Jamie says.

"Oh you did, well why didn't you just hand out flyers and invite the whole of fucking Slims up while you're at it. Did you not think of asking me first as I might not want them up to my flat." I say, winking at Gaz.

"Is that so that you can trey an git in Emma's knickers again jist remember an let Shane shag her first, like last time" Gaz says as we start laughing.

"Ah shit yer pusses." Jamie shouts from the front seat as me and Gaz sit in the back laughing our heads off. We take a detour on the way to my flat and stop at the twenty four hour garage.

"What are we stopping here for?" I ask.

"Emma's bringin up a bottle o vodka, an she asked me ti

git juice an also Gaz is needin skins."

"Ooh she's got ye right under her thumb ahreaddy, sendin ye fir juice." Gaz says as we both snigger and Jamie tells us to fuck off as he storms out the taxi and joins the queue outside the garage.

There are a lot of people around as all the clubs finish at the same time. A group of girls go past the car and a couple of them have very short skirts on but me and Gaz don't think anything of it as they look really young. The taxi drivers eyes light up.

"Look at them, I wouldn't mind getting one of them in the back of the car." He says in a strong Irish accent as he leers out the window.

"She's a bit young thought mate, even fir meh likin." Gaz says sounding a bit straight now.

The driver looks over his shoulder slightly with his face looking a little distorted and says. "The younger the better though eh."

"What are ye? Some sort o a paedophile." Gaz says very serious.

The driver laughs and then says "Don't tell me you guys weren't thinking the same thing when you saw them."

Me and Gaz look at each other and lift our eye brows and I'm thinking what is this guy all about?

"Well eh, no we didna actually, as girls wah look aboot fourteen dinna actually dae it for us." Gaz says gettin louder an soundin angry.

It must be the coke as I've never seen Gaz get worked up so quickly.

"Don't give me that, if you had the chance you would be off with them." The driver says. I am in shock as I don't think this guy realises what he's doing. Gaz looks at me and I can see the anger in his face. I shrug my shoulders and lift my hands up to let him know that I don't know what to say to him. Gaz has an answer. He launches forward as fast as I've seen anybody move and punches the guy in the side of the face. Gaz gets out the car and storms around to the drivers door. He pulls the handle but the driver has locked it from the inside...smart move. I get out and pull Gaz away thinking the Irish cunt will drive off and that will be it, all over...but no. the Irish cunt gets out the car and starts mouthing off. He appears to be a lot bigger now that he's out of the car.

"That's right, get that trouble making bastard out of here." He shouts at me.

"Why don't you get back in your car get and fuck off before both of us smash you, you fucking idiot." I shout back while still holding Gaz from getting near him.

Everyone is now staring over from the garage queue to see what's going on and the driver is still mouthing off.

"What because you have a drink on you, you think your some sort of a hard man." He says.

I am trying my best to stop Gaz from going over and he suddenly stops struggling to get away. I look around to find Jamie walking over. He puts the bottles of juice that he's just bought on the ground near the taxi and is walking up to the driver with his arms out wide and his hands up telling the driver to calm down but he starts ranting and raving at Jamie and is now in his face.

"What are you..." Before he finishes his sentence Jamie nuts him straight in the nose and the driver crumbles to the ground. He walks back and picks up the juice. The driver is out cold and I look at Gaz as we stand in shock.

"Eh tak it we're walkin up ti yours now." Jamie says.

22) Night night

The wak up ti Shane's flat didna actually look that far but eh feel fucked now that we're here. At least one good thing is that it has gave me time ti git that Irish cunt oot o meh haed. Eh canna wait tae get in, sit doon, hae a smoke an listen ti some tunes. The rest o them can go an dae whatever they fuckin like. Eh jist want ti sit back an git stoned. Shane's phone has been ringin a the wey up the road we people askin whare he is. First it was Kyle an then that daft burd Emma an now Joey. They are a standin the gither at the bottom o Shane's flat, yet they tak it in turns ti phone an ask whare he is.

"It's aboot time." Mickey says as we turn the corner ti Shane's block.

We ah pile inti the flat an it looks as though Shane has got ower he's burd as he sneaks awa inti the kitchen we that Stacey's hands on he's arse. Eh head straight fir the stereo an put on some good hip hop tunes that eh brought we is. Eh dinna fancy listenin ti ah that indie shite. Naebody likes meh taste in music, but fuck them. Eh find a space on the sofa an start skinnin up an eh look over ti see Kyle sittin ah comfy in the corner skinnin up tae…he obviously had the same idea as me.

"Gaz. Beer?" Joey shouts as he pops his haed through fae the kitchen.

"Ah, eh." Too fuckin right eh will. Eh ken theres are onay a few bottles o beer left so eh might as well git ain before there's onay vody thats left. Eh head oot ti the balcony we meh beer as eh spark up the joint, Don Juan in the kitchen there disna like the grass stinkin oot he's flat. Eh can just see him fae the balcony through the kitchen windee, whisperin sweet nothins in that Stacey burd's ear but good luck tae him. At least it taks he's mind aff Kelly for a while cause he's been moppin aboot fir ages now.

"Hey Gaz, how's it going?" Emma says as she steps oot on ti the balcony.

"Ahright."

What the fuck is this daft wee burd wantin? As if eh didna ken. Well she can wait cos it's jist been lit an Joeys wantin it eftir me. She starts talkin ti is an eh dinna ken what the fuck to say back as she is thick as shit an she's e'd oot er nut. The conversation is jist really stupid, Fuck eh hope eh dinna speak aboot shite like that when e'm on an e. Eh feel em noddin an agreein we everythin she is sayin but eh dinna ken what the fuck she's on aboot. Eh shout Joey through an pass him the joint thinkin this will be meh sharp exit, bit no. She involves Joey in on the conversation an ah he does is maks faces behind her back an the actions as though he's humpin her. Every time eh look at her legs Joey catches me an starts takin the piss...the cunt. He has a few puffs an passes it ti Emma, then sneaks back inti the livin room leavin me we her again. Eh keep lookin doon at her legs an they're makin me think aboot shaggin her. She has on a wee short skirt we the tanned legs an accordin ti Shane she's a good shag. Bit that's the problem, eh tak the piss oot o them cos they baith shagged her in the same night. How is it gonna look if eh go an shag her as well. The spunk bucket. Eh smile tae mesel as eh think aboot this. She must be wantin shagged as she's comin on ti is big time, nudgin me an laughin as eh mak meh smart arse comments aboot whatever the fuck it is she's treyin ti tell me. Does this daft burd no ken that ah eh'm interested in is smokin an shaggin. She has her airm aroond is an eh'm startin ti git a bit paranoid as this appears ti be too easy. Eh widna pit it past Shane an Jamie the wee shite ti tell her ti come on ti is, just ti see if eh wid go fir it. Then blow is aff in front o thum. That's their sense o humour the cunts…actually it's mibbe mair like something eh wid dae. She is now cuddlin up ti me an em now thinkin fuck it, e'll tak it as far as she'll go. We start neckin an eh hay meh hands on her arse. She has the maist loveliest tight wee bum eh have ever felt. Eh pull her closer ti me an eh kin feel mesel gittin a semi. She pulls awa an looks aroond like somebody is watchin us.

"It's ahright the curtains closed, naebody can see us." Eh say. Hopin this will be enough ti persuade her ti keep goin.

She's ahready shagged two o meh mates in this flat an she's worried aboot somebody seein us neckin. Eh go back inti the flat an head fir the kitchen while Emma wanders inti the livin room whare the banter is flowin an people are startin ti git louder bey the minute. Eh find Shane still in the kitchen talkin ti that Stacey bird an they go ah silent when eh walk in. Shane gees is a funny look behind her back as if she's doin he's haed in. Eh smile at him as a pour mesel a vody but its mare cause eh realise he's no set Emma up ti tak the piss. But em no countin oot Jamie though, he could've done it on he's ain. But the mair eh think aboot this the mair eh think the wee cunts no really got the brens ti think o a wind up like that. Eh pick up the gless an shift oot o there before Shane uses me as an excuse ti git awa fae Stacey. As eh go inti the livin room the onay place ti sit is right across fae Emma. Eh look over ti her an she tilts her haed in the direction o the door. She announces she has ti pee an heads aff ti the door geein me a look as if ti folly her. As she heads through the door Shane appears we Stacey an they walk past everybody an oot the door inti the bedroom withoot anybody battin an eyelid. Eh probably could've done the same thing we Emma bit that's jist like sayin ti every cunt in the room that we are awa fir a shag. No thit anybody here wid bather but eh just cannae dae that…guess eh'm just mair o a sneaky cunt. No lang eftir Shane an Stacey go through eh folly them bit eh stand ootside the toilet an Emma appears.

"What are you waiting on?" She says treyin ti be a smart arse.

"Eh'm just waitin ti use the toilet." Eh say, treyin ti coverin mesel in case it's still a wind up. She grabs me we baith hands an starts neckin we is. She treys ti pull me towards Shane's room but eh tell her that somebody's in so she pulls me inti the spare room. We end up leyin on the bed, still just neckin like, an she puts a hand doon an rubs meh wee semi. Fuck, this girls no shy man. Eh dinna ken what it is, if it's cause eh ken her a bit we goin back ti pertys or somethin but eh feel different we her than eh've felt we other burds. It's like, eh kind a like her a wee bit mare an eh dinna want ti jist shag her. Eh'm kind o happy jist leyin here we her an cuddlin in. Eh ken she's got a bit o a reputation an that, bit that disna bather me. Eh canna say anythin bad eftir some o the things eh've got up ti. It's ahright fir a guy ti go aboot shagging wahever he wants, an if he's got a burd an shags somethin behind her back he thinks he's the man. If a bird does anythin like that she would be called ah the slags an slappers under the sun. Emma has stopped rubbin me an is cuddlin in closer now. This is weird cause eh'm leyin here we a really sexy burd an eh'm deyin ti shag her bit eh canna move as eh dinna want ti spoil this. Eh slide meh hand doon under her wee skirt an eh stroke her leg right up ti her thong. Eh feel a few sprouters stickin ootside o her thong an eh always hud a mental picture o her havin a nicely wee trimmed or even shaved fanny…bit it's no ti be. She starts ti git inti it a wee bit an moves onti her back. Eh git on tap o her an start kissin her as eh work meh wey doon ti her skirt. Eh lift it up ti reveal her wee thong barely coverin her fanny. Eh kiss on tap o her thong an eh git a wee wiff. It's no that bad, it's jist a normal fanny smell but when eh pull her thong ti the side the stench hits is full on. It's like a cundie. Any other time it wouldna bather is. Meh tongue would be in aboot her but somehow the night eh jist canna dae it. Eh dinna want tae be rude and tell her that her fanny's stinkin, so eh kiss aroond it an work meh wey back up tae her face again. Eh feel disappointed that a girl as sexy as that widna clean her fanny a bit mair. Eh start kissin her again an we fumble aboot fir a wee while. Before eh ken it meh boxers are at meh ankles an she's on tap o is moanin an groanin. Eh feel thit eh'm awa ti shoot meh load an eh dinna want her ti think eh'm a two minute wonder but eh canna help it. It could be cause eh've no took any e's the night.

"Eh'm awa ti cum." Eh say.

"No...hold on." She says.

Too late..."ahhh."

She leys doon aside is an cuddles in but now eh've shot meh load eh canna really get inti it now. Meh mind is thinkin aboot the stench that has now filled the room fae her fanny bein fully exposed when she opened her legs. Eh'll hae ti remember an ask Shane aboot this. We ley fir a wee while then she starts ti snore a bit so eh slide mesel oot fae under her an put meh jeans back on. Eh hope she didna think eh wid dae a Jamie an fah asleep we her. Eh hae a wee look at her thong afore eh sneak oot the room, as eh had visions oh stains like curry sauce or even cottage cheese like that burd fae a while back, but eh'm relieved ti find they are ah clear. As eh come oot the bedroom, eh hear somebody at it in the toilet. They are obviously pissed an dinna realise eh can hear them. Eh thought that eh wid hear Shane an Stacey at it bit there wisna a peep fae his room. Eh walk through ti the livin room jist in meh jeans an eh git a wolf whistle fae Joey, the big poof. Eh sit across the room fae him but eh kin hear him speakin aboot is ti ane o they daft burds. He's talkin aboot meh build an meh six pack the fuckin weirdo. Em share he's been takin it up the arse workin in that gym we a they body builders. Studied fir a degree an thinks he kens it ah. Ah he ever talks

aboot is weights an trainin, an what ti eat an what no ti eat.
Eh eat whatever eh fuckin want an eh'm fitter than that poof
that's never oot o the fuckin gym. Eh skin up an head ti the
balcony fir a smoke when Mickey appears sayin that eh beat
him to it, fir the spare bedroom.

"Ye should have asked Shane fir his, it didna sound like
there wis anythin goin on in there anywey." Eh say.

Eh go back inti the livin room an tell them thit eh'm headin
an Kyle starts laughin at is.

"What are you laughin at?"

"You, you do that every time, you get your hole from some
bird and then sneak off to leave Shane to get rid of them."

"Listen if eh meet a burd that is worth hangin aroond fir,
eh'll stey, but until that day comes...anywey eh'm comin
back."

"What, with Biscuit?"

"Ye ken me too well."

Eh'm aboot ti head oot the door when eh walk past the mirror in the lobby an notice meh hair ah stickin up, it must have
been fae shaggin. Eh grab Shane's baseball cap as eh go oot,
only ti be grabbed bey Jamie.

"An whare the fuck dae you think yer sneakin aff ti?"

"Ti get Biscuit, man."

"Tut tut, Shane winna be happy. Hud on eh'll come we ye.
Eh need some munchies fae the shop."

We get a taxi an the drevir taks us ower ti meh grans, he
stops ootside her hoose an eh tell Jamie ti wait in the taxi as
eh'll no be lang. Meh granda's obviously up as Biscuit is oot
in the gairden. He sees me an right awa he's tail is goin like a
wee helicopter ready ti tak aff...at least somebody is always
happy ti see is. Eh go in the hoose ti pick up he's lead.

"What ye up tae?" Meh granda says as he sits we he's cup
o coffee.

"Nothin much. Jist shagged some wee slapper an sneaked
awa ti pick up Biscuit. Eh've got Jamie we is in the taxi.

Eh'll be back later on."

"See ye son." Ma granda says. Eh'm obviously no he's son bit he's always said that since eh wis a bairn.

We dinna go straight ti Shane's. We stop at the shops doon the street so Jamie could get some munchies, plus it gees Biscuit a wee walk up the road. Eh stand ootside an can smell the fresh rolls as the door is opened we the paper boy's goin in an oot. They stroke Biscuit as they walk past an he's tail starts goin again…he loves ah the attention.

Jamie comes oot we a bag o rolls, bacon, juice, various bars o chocolate an mare skins. As we walk up the road ti Shane's flat, Biscuit is a good bit in front o us. There is a patch o spare groond at the back o the block whare he usually sniffs aboot so eh ken that's whare he's headin. Me an Jamie walk aroond the block slowly an eh could see him sniffin aroond a tree an liftin he's leg. We stand talkin shit for a few minutes bit my mind is actually thinkin aboot sittin back in Shane's flat an gettin served ain o they bacon rolls, mmm. Meh thoughts are suddenly interrupted when eh hear some-body behind is sayin "Ohh Shane you cunt."

"What, eh'm no Sh…"

Eh feel a sudden pain in meh lower back, like eh've been punched hard…very fuckin hard. Eh go ti turn an see wah it is but the next thing eh ken, eh'm on the deck strugglin fir a braeth. This feelin is strange, it's as if somebody is pinnin me doon an eh dinna hae the strength ti get them aff. Eh look up bit eh kin barely open meh eyes an eh kin see Jamie strugglin we somebody. Ah na, he's doon as well…meh eyes feel re-ally heavy like eh'm driftin aff tae sleep. It's like eh've took too many downer's or something. One good thing is the pain in meh back has went awa…Meh body just feels ah numb. Jamie is shoutin at is ti waken up but fuck him, naebody is interruptin this sleep. The wee cunt is slappin is now, if eh huv ti git up eh'm gonna boot he's bahs. Eh'll bet that wee cunt has spiked is we vally's, well if he has…they are fuckin good ains. He can slap me ah he wants, cos eh'm just gonna cosy up here an enjoy them…night night Jamie.

23) A really bad day

Everybody seems to have left at the same time. First Gaz and Jamie sneak off without saying a word to anybody then the rest of them phone taxis and leave me here on my own. I'm not complaining though as I usually can't get rid of them. I thought Gaz would have came back up with Biscuit, that's not like him. Well maybe I'll get to my bed now...fuck there's the buzzer, I guess it was wishful thinking.

"Yeah."

"Shane, help we've been stabbed." Jamie says in a faint voice.

"Yeah right, just hurry up and come in."

"Nah seriously, phone an ambulance, Gaz is in a bad wey."

I grab a t-shirt and put it on as I run down the stairs but all the time I'm thinking that if those cunts are taking the piss I'll fucking slap them. I open the front door to the flats and find Jamie only semi conscious and in a pool of blood.

"Where's Gaz? What's happened?" I shout while lifting his head up.

He doesn't answer but as I move him I go in his pocket and take out his mobile. I put him in the recovery position and dial 999 on his mobile, I then follow the trail of blood around the block until I find Gaz. He's lying there not moving, Biscuit is next to him licking his face and making whimpering noises. There is blood on him but it doesn't appear to be his own. I get through to emergency and ask for an ambulance. I tell them the situation and they give me some advice before I am cut off, it's always when you most need it the battery goes.

"Fuck."

"Gaz...waken up...Gaz" I shout as I slap him hard in the face.

I take his arm and feel his wrist for a pulse but I've never done this before so I don't really know where to find it, nothing. I look up and see one of my neighbours at the window obviously wondering what all the shouting is.

"HELP, MY BROTHER'S BEEN STABBED, HE'S AT THE FRONT DOOR, I'VE PHONED THE AMBU-LANCE."

I lift Gaz to put him on his side and as I do this thick blood comes out from underneath him. This is not the red blood you see when you cut your finger, it is a thick dark red almost burgundy. As I move him the amount of blood coming out is frightening. My neighbour, an older woman in her dressing gown comes rushing over with a pile of towels. She nudges me out of the way and puts her fingers on his neck. "He's doesn't have a pulse." She says as she puts a towel on the wound and slides him on his back. She gives him mouth to mouth as I stand back thinking I'm in some sort of nightmare. She get's on top of him and starts pushing his chest.

"Your friend around the corner, he has a pulse so go and keep pressure on his wounds, talk to him and try to keep him awake."

The ambulance finally arrives and as they take over I manage to get a hold of Biscuit and put him in the flat. I rush back down the stairs to find the police have arrived. Jamie and Gaz are in the ambulance and the police are trying to get me to stay behind to talk to them. Their attitude is disgusting and they are told where to go, which sees me being handcuffed and put into the back of the police car. My neighbour talks some sense into them and I am let out to travel in the ambulance. I enter to see them giving Gaz the shock treatment, which to my relief gets his pulse going. Jamie is unconscious but breathing. Although they eventually get a pulse from Gaz but it's the machine keeping him going. I take Gaz's phone from his pocket and the ambulance guy tells me I can't use it here, I ignore him and use it anyway. I call my mother and tell her what's happened. She rushes off to tell Gaz's gran. I also phone Kyle and tell him to get his arse up to my flat as quick as he can as I left without locking the door or even picking up my keys. If the police walk in I'm fucked, with all those drugs lying around.

"Don't worry about it, I'll take care of it, I'll see you up at the hospital." He says.

"Yeah Biscuit, he's at mine too."

"I'll take care of it, I'll be up as quick as I can."

"Okay, cheers." I say cutting him off.

As I sit in the waiting room a nurse brings me a blanket and a pair of these horrible plastic slip-ons with elastic around the ankles to wear. I only had on a pair of boxers and a t-shirt, which are covered in blood. I struggle to put them on as my hands are shaking so much, but this time it's not due to adrenaline or anger it's because I'm fucking scared. The nurse said she would try to find me something else to wear but I tell her it's alright I'll get someone to bring me up some clothes. I still have Gaz's mobile so I walk outside and phone Kyle again who is just arriving at my flat. He asks what happened but I don't know and at this moment it is the least of my worries as I wait on the news that both of them are going to be okay.

My mother arrives with Kate, Gaz's gran and their faces drop when they see me covered in blood.

"Are you okay?" My mother says as she rushes over.

"Where are they?" She adds but is cut off by Kate.

"What happened? How bad is it?" She says.

"WAH DONE IT?" Big Danny shouts in his deep voice as he storms through the hospital doors.

All these questions at once and as I struggle to answer them the only one that sinks in is the last one…who done it? My first thought is Murdo but then he has nothing against Gaz or Jamie. Although it is his style to creep about outside someone's house in the early hours waiting for you. My thoughts turn to the taxi driver, the Irish cunt from last night, nah it couldn't have been…could it.

We sit for a long time staring at the walls until a doctor appears. We all stand when he comes over to us as we listen for the good news that both will be fine, but it doesn't come.

"Jamie is stable, he had five puncture wounds but they missed any vital organs, although he has lost a considerable amount of blood."

"What about Gareth?" Kate says with a croaky voice and tears rolling down her face. It's only by Gaz's gran that I have ever heard him being called Gareth, even Big Danny only ever called him Gaz.

"Gareth was stabbed once but it punctured a lung. His heart had stopped by the time the paramedics arrived. Although they managed to resuscitate him we don't know how long his brain was starved of oxygen. We have to operate and only then will we know his condition. If he manages to breath on his own there could be a chance, but that doesn't rule out the possibility of brain damage."

The doctor says what he has to say and fucks off leaving us to let all the information sink in. Kyle, Mickey and Joey turn up and not before time, they hand me a bag of clean clothes.

"I've taken Biscuit to mine. I had a hard time from the police trying to get into your flat, but your neighbour persuaded them that I was your mate." Kyle says as he hands me the keys to the flat.

"What's happening?" Joey asks.

We sit down away from everyone as I tell them what happened and also what the doctor has just said.

"I can't believe we were all there not an hour before it happened." Kyle says.

"Any idea wah done it?" Joey says.

I pause for a few seconds before answering as the thought has been flashing through my mind constantly.

"I don't know, my first thought was Murdo, then the Irish taxi driver but I really don't know."

"Mare likely it was Murdo?" Mickey says.

I shrug my shoulders as I think of all the possibilities. It could have been something Gaz was involved in with his dealing but I can't mention any of that in front of them. We sit for what seems like hours then we are told that we can go and see Jamie. The police are still hanging around but I know Jamie won't tell them anything before he's talked to me. My mother and Jerry, Jamie's dad, who has just turned up after being called away from his job go in first. They are not in long before they come out with my mother sobbing in Jerry's arms. Me and Kyle go in to see Jamie wired up to machines and ventilators but his eyes are open slightly. I get the small talk out of the way then I ask the questions that have been going through my head constantly since I arrived here.

"What happened? Did you see who done it?" I say trying to sound as calm as possible but it still comes out in fast mumble. Jamie opens his mouth but I can hardly hear him. I put my face closer to his ear and he says "They thought Gaz was you."

I step back and look at him very confused.

"What do you mean? They thought Gaz was you."

Jamie opens his mouth so I move in closer again.

"He came fae behind an said yer name ti Gaz before stabbin him." He says in a weak voice.

I look at Kyle and we both stare at each other then he says "He had on yer baseball cap, they thought he wis you."

I sit down in the seat next to the bed in total shock that all this has happened when it was intended for me. The only vision I have now is Dek Murdo. I have a picture of his ugly distorted face in my head. I can't believe he's went this far because I was seeing Kelly. She was right all along. Jamie is back snoozing away before we leave the room and the machines are beeping away showing a strong pulse. I walk back to the waiting room and sit down. My mother tells me to go home.

"Eh'll phone ye if there's any news on Gaz."

"No mum, I'm staying here until I know he's going to be okay."

I go for a walk with Kyle, Joey and Mickey around the hospital to get some fresh air but the real reason is to have a joint. We pass it between ourselves as we talk about what happened. Joey mentions again whom it could have been and I give Kyle a stare as if to say don't mention anything about what Jamie said which he knows, goes without saying. As soon as I get the news that Gaz is okay I'm going straight for Murdo to get this sorted out. I'm not waiting around looking over my shoulder on him to get me. The joint relaxes me a little and when we get back to the waiting room I feel my eyes getting really heavy and I want to go to my bed. I nod off for a while when Joey nudges me awake.

"Shane, the doctors jist took Kate an Big Danny awa."

I jerk up feeling very groggy but that soon disappears when I hear a scream from around the corner, which can only mean one thing. It's the news we've all been dreading. Gaz is dead. Kate walks back into the waiting room with Big Danny's huge arms around her, consoling each other.

"They couldna save him." I hear Kate say through her tears.

We all stand there staring, speechless. A moment later the doctor comes back and asks if they would like to go and see him. Kate shakes her head but I ask them if I could go. Kate walks over to me and wipes the tears from my eyes, I hadn't even realised I was crying.

"Dinna you go doin anythin stupid now Shane. Eh dinna want ti be here we your mother fir the same reason that eh'm here the day."

I don't answer but big Danny puts his arm around me and walks me off to see Gaz. The nurse leads us to a room that is filled with equipment and the walls are full of charts and diagrams. I see Gaz lying on a table. He has a white sheet over him that has been dyed red with blood, it goes up to his chest leaving his tattoo on his shoulder exposed. It is one he had done recently of Biscuit. I walk over to the table and Big Danny walks around the other side. We both stare at him for a while half expecting him to open his eyes and start laughing or jumping up and calling me a big poof for crying…but I know that's not going to happen. I stare at him and can't help but think that it should be me lyning there instead.

"Hey Gaz, you don't have to worry about Biscuit I'm going to look after him. I know I used to moan when you brought him up to the flat but secretly we both knew I liked having him there. I'm really sorry Gaz, it should be me lying there." I feel a hand on my shoulder and I turn to see Big Danny, then I realise I am in floods of tears.

"Shane do you ken eh had to bury meh daughter when she was aboot the age Gaz was now. When she was deyin Gaz's dad wanted ti tak him awa but meh daughter telt him he would be better aff in oor care. Eh promised her eh would tak care o him. She trusted us that he would hae a better life than we the waster o a faither he had. Life sure has a sick sense o humour does it."

I have known Gaz nearly all my life and this is the first time I have ever heard Big Danny mention Gaz's dad. I think that was one of the things we had in common. We both had absent fathers. Of course I had Jamie's dad but he wasn't a father he was just some bullying bastard. I feel like a big kid sitting here with Big Danny as he was probably more of a father figure than the wanker I had to look up to. This brings back memories of when I used to run across to his house after Jamie's dad slapped me around. He would let me stay at his for a bit until it all calmed down. He was tempted to march across the road and slap him around but Kate always stopped him as it was none of his business. He never had to as it turned out. As a few years down the line I done it myself and it was nothing to do with him hitting me. I caught him lifting his hands to my mother, it apparently went on hidden for years. He still tries to order Jamie about but with the evil streak that Jamie has I can't see that lasting much longer.

For the size of Big Danny and how tough he is, the man in front of me looks like he is ready to crumble and fade away.

"Danny I know Kate said not to do anything about this and I always listen to you two, but you know I can't let this go. I'm going after whoever did this."

I am expecting him to go along with Kate and tell me not to be stupid as whatever I do is never going to bring him back or that I could be the next one lying there but I know Big Danny thinks like us.

"Eh thought ye would. If ye ever need meh help just let is ken." He says.

Through the tears and anger I smile to myself when I hear this as it's exactly what Gaz would say.

Kyle drives me to my flat and the first thing I notice is the incident box the police have now set up not far from my block. I guess it's now a murder enquiry. Kyle, Joey and Mickey offer to come up but I send them on their way as I feel I want to be on my own for a bit.

"Just gee us a phone if ye need anything mate." Mickey says.

I nod and turn towards my flat. The whole place is cornered off with tape but I am allowed through without any harassment. I walk around to the door to see the pools of blood and one of them that leads all the way up to my front steps from Jamie dragging himself to use my intercom.

I go straight to the shower and wash off the rest of the blood that is on me. I swallow two valium that was handed to me by my mother as I left the hospital. I stare at the television watching nothing in particular as I have a cup of tea and a joint with Biscuit curled up next to me. I eventually drop of to sleep with thoughts of the past twenty four hours and the many different ways that I would change it. I can't decide if I would like to be there just before it happened to stop it but also to see who it was that done it or have the whole night changed so that none of it happened but then the same thing could have happened on another night. My much needed sleep is broken several hours later when the buzzer sounds and wakens me.

"Hello this is D.C. Richmond, I'm looking for…"

I don't let him finish I just press the button to let him in. I rush over to the coffee table and hide the hash and empty the ashtray. I open the door and tell them to come in and have a seat. They have their notebooks at the ready but I feel like telling them not to bother. They introduce themselves and proceed to ask me details about the previous night. They appear to be a lot more civilized compared with the other arrogant cunts this morning, and I let them know this. Although they do apologise for their colleagues behaviour and give me an explanation with big words that mean absolutely fuck all to me. I can tell they are trying to be nice but they know, that I know, that they can't fucking stand me and I have very little if any respect for them or any of their colleagues. They leave disappointed with their notepads full of useless information and I shut the door after them. I watch them from the window talking between themselves as they walk into their incident box. I am soon back on the sofa having another joint but wide awake this time. I sit and think about Gaz for a while and it suddenly sinks in that I am never going to see him again. He's been my best friend since I moved here as a kid and now he's been killed because of me, because of some girl I was into. If I hadn't been seeing her maybe this wouldn't have happened. If this had been Kyle, Mickey or even Joey that had been killed I would be sitting here with Gaz planning on how to get the cunt back. I've always known he was a blade man but I always thought that it was just for show to build up his reputation to make people fear him. I've never feared him, but reality is setting in fast that I could be in a hospital bed next to Jamie or even next to Gaz in the morgue. At least now I know just what he is capable of and how cunning and violent he can be and that he's not going to stop until he's hurt or even killed me. Well I'm certainly not going to wait around on him coming for me, I'm going to get the cunt first. I know I'm usually a stand up and square go type of person but to beat him I will have to think like him and lower myself to his level. I don't have Gaz to help me out and the only other person I can really trust is Kyle. He's not much of a fighter to back me up but he has a lot of bottle. Mickey has too much of a big mouth and Joey I wouldn't trust as far as I could throw him.

24) Keeping busy

I am just not in the mood for working today but if I don't I
only have two options. One is go to the pub and the other is
to sit in the flat and get stoned. Both of these options will result in me getting wasted and doing something stupid. I have
to keep a clear head if I am serious about getting back at
Murdo because if something goes wrong then I am well and
truly fucked.

I went for a run this morning before going to the gym to try
and wear me out but all it done was got me fired up even
more. Joey was working and kept hanging around trying to
talk to me. He was asking loads of stupid questions and
telling me the gossip that he heard going around the gym.
One thing's for sure, whatever I end up doing to get Murdo
back, Joey will never get to know about it. He just can't keep
his mouth shut.

Customer No. 1162
Old gits

I receive a job to the Old Bank Bar pub where two old men
are waiting outside. They come over to the car and actually
struggle to get in due to them being too drunk. I don't have a
problem with that as I know I've probably been in the same
state before. What I do have a problem with is the damage
they do to my car when try to get in or out, the most annoying part is that they look you as if it's all you fault. These two

have kicked the seats, the doors and the one in the front has also managed to kick the panel under the dashboard.

"We're headin up the Lochee road Jim."

Jim my names not Jim. What is that all about? Why do these old gits insist on calling all taxi drivers Jim? The guy in the front is pissing me off already and I haven't even moved yet. He's trying to reach for the seat belt but he can't turn his body around for his fat gut to grab it. I'll bet if it was a pint of lager he would turn quick enough though. He pisses me off that much that when I stop at traffic lights I reach over and grab the thing myself, nearly choking the cunt in the process. Next thing he unwraps a boiled sweet and pops it in his mouth.

"Excuse me but there's no eating in the taxi" I say pointing to the sign on the dash in front of him.

'NO FOOD OR DRINK TO BE CONSUMED IN THE VE-HICLE'.

"Ach it's onay a wee sweetie." He says.

These signs are put up for the simple reason so that kids don't get a chance to leave sweets, crisps or chewing gum stuck to the floor or on the seats. The reason they are put up in my car are for my pet hate, people like this old cunt who has his mouth open letting everyone hear it clatter against his falsers. Then it gets worse, he starts sucking on it while talking to his friend in the back. All I hear is the sweet clunking around his mouth as he slurps and talks at the same time. They are having a conversation and both of them are talking at the same time about two totally different subjects.

I can't get to their destination quick enough but what makes it worse is that I don't know where they are going.

"Tak a left here, then at the tap o the road tak a right."

"Where is it you are actually going?" I ask.

"Left here."

"Yeah but where are you going?"

"LEFT." He shouts at me.

I'm starting to get really pissed off with this old cunt, why can't he just tell me the fucking street where he is going."

"Alang here an it's the fourth lamppost on the right" he says in between crunches on his sweet...or hopefully it's just the annoying cunts falsers fucking crumbling away. Instead of watching the road I am now trying to count fucking lampposts. A journey which at the start was to go up the lochee road has now ended in St. Mary's without me actually being told. Why the fuck didn't he just tell me he was going there instead of all these fucking lefts and rights? He pays me and turns to face the door.

"Eh canna fine the honl." He says.

"What?"

"Eh canna fine the honl."

"I don't know what your saying."

Is this cunt taking the piss.

"The honl, where's the honl?" He shouts at me as he swipes his hand up and down the inside of the door.

It eventually registers, he can't find the handle. I've heard it all now, a honl, a fucking honl. Where the fuck do they get these words from?

A job comes through the computer for Johnstone at The Highway Man. This used to be one of the roughest pubs on the Hilltown. It closed down several years ago and reopened as a day centre. It was intended as a community centre type of place but that only lasted a few weeks before the junkies took it over. I pull up outside and there is a small group of people gathered near the front door. They are all junkies and I recognise one of them from years ago. She was at school at the same time as me and I remember her having a really pretty face and a great body. Now she looks like she is riddled with every disease known to man.

"Is that taxi for Johnstone?" A tall, skeleton looking guy shouts over.

"Yeah."

He puts his index finger up to signal to me that he'll be there in a minute as he gets the last few puffs on his already beefed roll up. I look over at the girl I knew and feel quite shocked at they way she has turned out. It makes me wonder how she managed to get herself in such a mess.

"Eh'm goin to Greenbank Place mate." The skeleton guy says as he gets in the back of the car.

During the journey the guy talks the biggest load of shit and every time he opens his mouth a disgusting smell comes past his rotten teeth and fills the car. I drive into his street and he goes quiet and starts to fidget a bit in the back. I know what's coming.

"Eh'll just hae ti nip up fir the money." He says as he opens the car door and goes to take off. I grab his smelly shell suit top by the arm.

"You're going nowhere." I say.

He pulls his arm away and runs. Wrong time wrong day to try to pull that one on me. I am out of the car and only feet away as he runs behind a block of flats. I grab his top from behind and he turns to punch me. It lands on the side of my face. This just gets me even more angry and I throw one of my own. He stumbles back and I launch forward throwing punch after punch. He is on the deck with blood pouring from his nose. I grab him by the hair and as my grip tightens I can feel the greasy strands slide through my fingers. I step forward bringing my knee up to his face.

"You junkie bastard." I shout as I lay into him on the deck with a barrage of punches and kicks. I step back but before I walk away I run at him with one last kick to the head leaving him motionless on the ground. I get back into the car and speed off back to my flat.

After I wash the greasy smell from my hands I change my blood stained clothes and go for a walk with Biscuit to calm myself down. After a cup of coffee I am back to work as if nothing happened and make polite conversation with my next few customers and try putting all the violent thoughts to the back of my mind. After smashing that junkie it has given me a burning rage to go and get Murdo but I control it as I know I have to do it right as the least mistake could cost me my life.

Customer No. 1210
Women worse than men

I decide to work late to try and tire myself out and I find myself being sent to the bingo in Douglas. Before I arrive I am picturing my customer to be an old woman standing with a headscarf who has just gambled half her weekly pension but I couldn't be more wrong.

"Taxi for Bennett." I shout out of the window to large queue of people.

"That's us." I hear someone shout.

Two women stagger forward who look a little bit worse for wear. They are in their late thirty's and are dressed like teenagers…or hookers.

"Right drevir, we're goin ti the Bowbrig on the Hulltoon." One of them says as she climbs in the back.

"Oh look, it's a young drevir." The other one says as she puts her arm through the gap in the front seats and starts pawing at me.

"Excuse me, but could you not do that while I'm driving please."

"Oh he's gittin offended cause eh touched him."

"Mibbe he's gay?".

"Are ye gay? Di ye no like wimen touchin ye?"

"No it's because if I was drunk and touched you, you would be the first person to go running to the police and get me done."

"Eh you drevirs are ah the same, takin young lassies up ah they back roads late at night."

"I don't think so." I say getting a bit irritated by them now.

But I would like to take you up a back road and give you a good slap you fucking minger.

"It's no that when yous are makin rude comments to us an yaysin yer mirrors to look up oor skirts when we're drunk."

Fuck, these women must have been in Gaz's taxi before. I smile to myself as I think what Gaz would be saying to these women. My smile soon fades as I feel one of the women's hands touching my neck.

"Could you stop that please?"

She then slides her hand around and starts rubbing my leg.

"Could you move your hand please or I'll stop the car and put you out."

"What's yer problem? Ye should feel privileged that women as good lookin as us are touchin ye."

Their attitude starts to become quite aggressive and I know that most guys would probably think I am being stupid as they would love to get that kind of attention but I know if it was the other way around any man would be banged up for it. Maybe on another day I would just laugh this off but not today.

"Ye big poof." One of them says with her face looking quite angry at me.

"Look here missus, if you had got in this car and I turned around and touched your leg. I would be charged. Lose my licence and no doubt put on the sex offenders list for the rest of my life. Now you've got in my taxi and touched me and I'm supposed to just laugh and think nothing of it."

"Ah shit yer puss. Yer jist a big poof."

"Do you know what? Just get to fuck out" I say as I stop the car in the middle of a busy road.

"Fine, we fuckin will git oot."

They slam the doors shut and I drive off leaving them

walking along the side of the road.

I am about to switch off the computer and head home before I loose the plot. But I am sent another job and I reluctantly take it.

Customer No. 1241
The rainbow flag

I sit outside a tenement block in Fairbairn Street as I wait on my customer. Two guys walk out of the block and one of them is well over six foot wearing a long over coat. The other is quite small and is wearing a bomber jacket. I had one the same when I was a kid but back then they were known as N.F. jackets. This was due to skin headed thugs in the National Front that wore them. Somehow I don't think you could go around calling them that now. Back in those days none of us actually knew what any of that stood for. We were just young and they were in the fashion.

These two guys do have the skinheads and some of the worst growler looking faces I have ever encountered. They swagger towards the car like they are about to smash me, so naturally I am on the defensive. This is the reason I don't like working late at night, you never know what you are going to pick up. I get myself ready as I don't know what kind of shit they are about to give me. If they start, I am certainly not going to sit back and take it no matter how hard they think they are. Both of them get in the back and straight away I'm thinking that they are about to grab me from behind. I look in the mirror to see the tall one with the long coat putting his seat belt on. This I find to be strange as nobody does that unless they are about five years old.

"So where are you guys off to then?"

The reply I receive is not what shocks me but the way it is

said.

"The bus station please." The small guy with the N.F. jacket says in the most camp voice I have ever heard in my life.

Twenty seconds ago my heart was pounding as I prepared myself to take on these two scary looking psychopaths and now, I am smiling as I drive off with the now, two ugly poofs. As I drive off down the road I cant help thinking why they said they were going to the bus station as I know they are going to Liberty's, the gay nightclub across the road. I drop them off at the bus station and sure enough they cross over the road and walk into liberty's. I look up to see the rainbow flag outside. This reminds me of a trip we had down to Manchester for an Oasis gig. When it finished we headed into town to catch a few bars before closing. I found myself chatting to a couple of girls and a guy whom I thought was one of their boyfriends. Gaz and Jamie were just over from me standing at the bar and Kyle, Mickey and Joey had disappeared to another bar along the road. The girls invited me back to a party so I go back over to Gaz and Jamie to tell them. They found this really amusing.

"What's the joke? I don't get it."

"Have the girls asked you back to a party or has the guy asked you back to do your ass?" Gaz said with a big grin.

"What are you talking about?"

"Have a look, I think the girls have started without you."

I turned to see the girls kissing and the guy who was with them was nodding at me to come over. Then it hit me that we were in a fucking gay bar. The guy had been chatting me up...I felt violated.

Gaz clocked the guy nodding at me and put on a camp voice

"Come on now Shane, run along, your new boyfriend is waiting on you."

He then changed it to a deep rough sound and said "So he

can rip a new hole in your ass."

The both of them stood there pissing themselves laughing as I stood there mortified.

"How did you know it was a gay bar?"

"Jamie told me before we came in, the whole street is full of gay bars so it would be interesting to find out how the rest of them are getting on."

Back at the hotel I asked Jamie how he knew it was a gay bar and he tells us about the rainbow flags all the way along the street.

"How do you know they were gay flags?"

"Eh, eh'm I saw it on the Simpson's."

An hour after we got in Mickey, Joey and Kyle show up and were arguing about how they didn't know the girls were lesbians and were blaming each other for not knowing.

On the way home the next day I was waiting on the whined ups about being chatted up by the gay guy but they never came. It was all vented towards Jamie for knowing about the rainbow flag and using the feeble excuse that he saw it on the Simpson's.

Customer No. 1289
Wrong time wrong person

With these happy thoughts in my head I decide to drive home but on the way I am flagged down by two guys. They are in their mid thirty's and as I pull up they stagger towards me. One of the guys gets in the back and one gets in the front.

"We're going to Monifieth mate." The one in the front says.

The one in the back starts to give me shit before I even drive off.

"Look I'm not taking you guys anywhere."

"Nah nah, he's pissed mate, just ignore him." The guy in the front says.

"Aaron, shut it or he's not going to take us."

"Yeah he fucking will because we are paying customers so he has to take us." The guy in the back mumbles to himself.

"Do I fuck, now get to fuck out of the car I'm taking you nowhere."

"Ah look mate, he's drunk, I'll apologise for him."

I know I should just throw them out now but I stupidly decide to drive them. This is the wrong time and I am the wrong person for them to get wide with right now. I only drive about half a mile up the road and the mouth in the back starts again.

"Hey I've never been in a taxi like this before, it's a bit sporty looking to be a taxi. You taxi drivers must make some money with all they new cars on the road."

I ignore him but I feel myself getting agitated. I know at this point I should stop the car and ask them to leave but once again I let it go.

"That's a great tune." The guy in the front says as he reaches over and turns the volume up really loud.

"Do you fucking mind?" I say turning it back down.

Both of them start laughing and the guy in the back nudges his mate in the front and signals for him to do it again. Due to him being drunk he obviously thinks he's invisible to me in my mirrors. At this moment I feel I have just made the decision to sort these two out, but somewhere I think I subconsciously made that decision the minute they entered my car. I know of a small piece of wasteland up ahead and I start to speed up as my heart beats a little faster anticipating what lies ahead. The guy in front leans over and puts the volume up full blast. This time I leave it up. As they nod their heads to each other and laugh they don't realise I have left the main road and am now seconds away from the middle of nowhere.

The guy in the front is now pushing buttons on the stereo to change the tracks. I drive around the back of a derelict industrial unit and screech the car to a halt.

"Right you couple of cunts." I say as I get out and run around to the other side of the car. I open the rear door and drag the first drunken guy out by his shirt. I punch him to the ground as the front passenger door is opened. The guy in the front gets out and attempts to throw a punch. I land mine first. He doesn't go down but his body falls back onto the car. He lunges forward at me and grabs my shirt with both hands. I put me head back and launch forward nutting him in the mouth. He falls to his knees and puts his hands up to his face. I turn to see the other guy on his feet and watch as he stumbles towards me with both fists flailing. Not one of them land on me as I put my hands up to block them. I throw two straight punches to his head and he falls back on to his arse. I give him a kick to the head and he falls back. I turn back to the other guy who has his face in his hands which are covered in blood. I reach over him closing the passenger doors. Everything goes quiet as I realise the music from the stereo has been blasting out the whole time. I get in the car and speed off with the wheels skidding on the gravel. I switch off the computer and drive home as fast as I can. I walk into the flat to be met with a cute friendly face with his tail whizzing around ready to lick me.

25) Payback part 1

I've been trying to get a hold of Kyle all day but he won't answer his phone. He knows what it's about so maybe that's why he's not answering. I'll try Mickey.

"Hello."

"Is that you Mickey?"

"Yeah."

"Where are you?"

"Eh'm sittin in meh room we Kyle haein a smoke."

"What, Kyle's with you?"

"Yeah."

"I've been trying to get a hold of him all day."

"Yeah he's battery's dead."

"I'll be up in ten minutes."

His battery's dead, my arse, the cunts trying to avoid me. I know he agreed to help out but when I explained exactly what that involved I could see the fear in his eyes. I already told him if he doesn't want to do it, to tell me straight away.

"Alright guys how's it going? Your mum let me in Mickey."

"It's cool, here ye look like ye need this Shane." Mickey says as he goes to pass me the ashtray with the burning joint in it.

"Nah, I'll pass. I have too much on my mind and I don't want something to alter it"

Kyle stares at me as he knows why I'm here.

"Do ye no want ti sit doon?" Mickey gestures towards the edge of the bed.

The two of them sit and stare at me as I stand in the middle of the room tensed and serious.

"Mickey, I need to ask you something."

I look at Kyle thinking he might have already told him but I know Kyle is not like that.

"Sounds serious."

"Don't be afraid to say no, I'm away to do something really stupid and I need your help. If you say no I'll understand."

"Depends on what it is." He says smiling and looks at Kyle.

Kyle puts his head down and Mickey realises I am not fucking about. His eyes widen and he looks back at me.

"I can't tell you what it is. If you don't want involved it's better off you don't know what it is."

I gave the exact same speech to Kyle and I don't think he realised what he was agreeing to help me with. If you say something like that people are obviously more interested in what it is than what they are agreeing to do.

"Eh sure. Whatever it is, eh'm in." He says moving to the edge of the bed wanting to know more. I sit down to relax a little as I proceed to tell Mickey exactly what I need him to do.

"So all you have to do is drive my car around for a while with the computer on like your working."

"Eh dinna understand."

"Right the computer in the car is fitted with a device called a G.P.S. It is like a tracking system. It means when it is switched on, whatever area the car is in, It will send a signal to the main computer via satellite to the taxi office. This lets them know exactly where the car is. If a job comes up in that area it automatically sends it to the computer in the car."

"So what dae ye want me ti drev yer car aroond fir?"

I look at Kyle and he smiles and shakes his head.

"You're not too bright Mickey, are you? While you are driving my car around I will be elsewhere."

"Ahh, now eh git it. That's yer alibi."

"That's right."

"This wouldna happen ti be anything ti dae we Murdo would it?"

I don't answer but give Mickey a serious look again.

"Wait a minute, what if someone gets in the taxi?"

I look at Kyle again and realise why I picked him to do this, because if this goes wrong I would be in even more trouble if Mickey was with me.

"Don't worry about that I'll give you instructions when the time comes."

I might even get Joey involved by phoning up as a customer and letting Mickey drive him around for a while.

"Are you sure you know what you are doing Shane?" Kyle asks.

"Guys that fucker killed our best friend and the both of you know now that Gaz was mistaken for me. If I don't do something, I'm going to be next."

"When is this gonna be happenin?"

"Tomorrow night."

"The day before Gaz's funeral." Kyle mumbles to himself.

Both of them go quiet and I feel I've said what I came to say. I stand up to leave as Mickey starts skinning up again. I make a sharp exit before I end staying for that much needed smoke.

We meet up at my flat and I throw Mickey the keys to my car. I hand him a list of instructions, all written out of where to go and at what time. I decided not to involve Joey as he is too much of a big mouth and I just don't trust the cunt.

"The instructions are all there."

As Mickey heads out the door I go to the bedroom and start to change my clothes.

"What are you waiting on Kyle? Get changed man, we've only got so long to do this."

Kyle pulls out his old tattered clothes from a holdall that I asked him to bring along and he starts to get changed. Kyle makes a comment that I am supposed to be in my old scruffy clothes but look like I am dressed to hit a fucking nightclub. I pull out a black bin liner from under my bed and from this I take out a wooden baseball bat and a metal pole that has been shaped at both ends. One end has been shaped for gripping and the other is shaped with sharp edges that stick out for a purpose that I can only describe as to inflict as much damage as possible to the recipient.

"Which one do you want?" I say as I hold one in each hand.

"Neither. I'm taking your bread knife." He says smiling.

I smile back and hand him the metal pole with the evil looking shaped edges.

"You would be better with this."

He takes the pole and holds the gripped handle with both hands.

"It's not fucking Darth Vader you're about to take on." I say smiling.

He smiles back at me but I can tell it's more of a nervous smile as reality sets in as to what he could be about to do with that scary piece of weaponry.

"Hold it like this." I say taking the pole from him and putting one hand on the shaped edge and one half way up.

"You'll get more leverage to hit somebody if you hold it like this."

"Where did you get these from?"

"Jamie's wardrobe."

"Where did he get them?"

"I gave him the baseball bat. It was a holiday present from years ago. He made the pole himself when he was involved in all that gang fighting shit. Me and Gaz had a word with

223

him and told him to get rid of it. It was about the same time Gaz got him to start hanging around with us. I didn't mind at the time as it stopped him from getting the bloody jail."

"A bit ironic is it not?"

"Oh aren't you the smart arse."

"Well, you told him to get rid of it to keep him out of jail and now you have it and are about to risk going to jail."

"You're forgetting something."

"What?"

"I'm not about to use it…you are. I'm just away for a game of baseball." Shane says as he pulls a ball out of the bin liner and grins at me.

"Come on, we'd better go."

Kyle drives towards the Hilltown and on my instructions of lefts and rights he is now lost as he has never been down any of these streets before in his life.

"I can only guess why Murdo lives in a secluded area full of narrow streets and high walls." Kyle comments.

"Yeah well just think of his lifestyle and the amount of people waiting to smash him. Right, park here."

We stop in a one way street with high walls all around us.

"Do you see that gate we've just driven past?"

He nods as he looks in the mirror at a tall slim gate, the kind that if you blink you'll miss it.

"Behind that gate there is a path and some steps. The path leads to the lower house but there are no windows looking onto the path so no-one in the lower house can see us. The steps lead to the flat above, that's where Murdo lives.

"How do you know all this?"

"I'm a taxi driver, I know everything."

I reach in the back of the car and hand Kyle the pole.

"Look Kyle, I'm not asking you to do anything here, I'm going in there after Murdo, I want you to keep your distance behind me. If it gets out of hand I want you to run back here to the car and take off. You drive to end of this street take a left and you'll know where you are from there. Phone Big Danny and tell him what's happened, he'll know what to do."

"What do I have this pole for then?"

"To protect yourself. There could be five of his mates up there."

"What if they all jump on you. Would I not be better phoning the police?"

"And how do you explain what we were doing here? They're not going to be much fucking help when I'm nailed to the fucking floor are they?"

I check my watch, then from Kyle's mobile I call the taxi office and order a car in name of smith to the Swallow Hotel going to Broughty Ferry.

Leaving the car running, we casually walk up to the gates with the weapons by our sides. I know most people doing something like this would plan it late at night or the early hours of the morning. It's seven at night in the middle of summer and the sun is still cracking the pavements, which is probably the best time to catch him unaware, when he least expects it. I've already been here and checked his door, there is a Yale and a Mortise lock but there is more chance of it only being the Yale on at this time. We walk up the first flight of steps and I tell Kyle to wait while I crouch down and crawl up the next flight. There is a small window situated next to the door and I peer through for a few seconds. I see him lounging on his couch watching T.V. with his top off. A sudden rush of fear comes over me and for a split second I am ready to take off and forget the whole thing. Then I think about Gaz and Jamie and what he done to them. I picture him with Kelly and the fear is soon put aside as I look at this big, fat, ugly, bullying beast of a man and I know I have to end this now. I look through the keyhole of the Mortise lock and there is no key, I know nine out of ten people who lock it from the inside would leave the key in it. I go back down to Kyle.

"Right Kyle, I've just seen him, I think he's on his own."

"So what are you going to do then?"

"Look just try and stay out of sight but keep close enough to watch my back."

"Shane it's not to late to turn away. Are you sure you want to do this?"

"Kyle seeing him lying up there has encouraged me even more."

I smile at Kyle and then turn to bolt back up the second flight of steps two at a time. Once at the top there is a distance of nearly twelve feet to the front door. I look behind at Kyle who is standing with the pole in both hands the way I showed him. I turn back towards the door in a pure rage with gritted teeth I bolt forward, and using my momentum and with as much power as I can, I place a kick as near to the lock as possible. It bursts open and Murdo jumps to his feet. Before he gets a chance to do anything I strike him on the side of the head with the baseball bat. It splits his head open and the blood splatters across the room onto the walls. He falls to the floor and I drop the bat and dive on top of him throwing punch after punch to his face, which is now also covered in blood. I grab him by the throat and nut him several times.

"LOOK AT ME…LOOK AT ME" I shout, tightening my grip around his throat.

"WHY DID YOU DO IT?…WHY DID YOU KILL GAZ, EH?…ALL THIS OVER A FUCKING BURD."

"WHAT ARE YE ON ABOOT?…EH NIVIR KILLED GAZ." Murdo splutters back through broken teeth and a mouthful of blood.

"YOU KILLED HIM THINKING HE WAS ME."

"EH NIVIR KILLED GAZ, EH SWEAR."

I stand up and pick up the bat again and start smashing it into any part of Murdo's body that's exposed as he curls up trying to protect himself. He stops moving and I stand and stare at his limp body curled up on the floor. I turn to see Kyle standing in the doorway with the pole by his side shaking with fear. I see his eyes widen and as I turn back I catch Murdo taking a swing at my leg. He has a blade in his hand and it cuts through my jeans and slices my calf. Before I get a chance to raise the bat he is on his feet with the blade in his hand. I swing the bat hitting his wrist but he doesn't drop the blade. He comes forward and I have no option but to drop the bat and grab his wrist to stop the blade from going near me. There is a struggle as I try to get the blade out of his hand and we both end up on the floor. He is on top of me and I way underestimated his strength as I struggle to push him off while keeping the blade away from me. I eventually prize it from his fingers and it slides across the floor. He gets to the bat before I get a chance to get up and as he swings it clips the top of my head sending me back to the floor. I look up as he holds the bat above my head with his face like a horror movie and one eye shut .

"Eh could assure ye, eh had nothing ti dae we Gaz's muder. Ye should have looked mare in the direction o yer last wee slapper, the ain wah asked me ti do ye in fir er. An as fir ye seein Kelly. Well, ye had it comin." He says as he goes to bring the bat down over my head.

I am about to try and move out of the way when the bat stops in mid air and Murdo falls to the floor with the pole sticking out of his back. Kyle stands rigid in the middle of the room. I stand up and pull the pole out of his back and he makes a low whimpering noise which to Kyle's relief he knows he didn't kill him. I pick up the bat and grab Kyle's arm.

"Come on, we've got to get out of here." I say as I hobble away.

I reach the door and turn to see Kyle repeatedly kicking Mudro in the groin.

"Kyle that's enough, come on we've got to get out of here."

We get to the car and after wrapping the bat and pole back in to the bin liner Kyle gets into the passenger seat.

"I take it you want me to drive."

He doesn't answer but puts his trembling hands out in front of me. I drive off slowly back to my flat. once inside I turn on the shower and strip off. When I pull my jeans down the cut is still bleeding quite a lot. I tear up a towel into lengths and use one of them to cover the cut. I tie it tightly to stop the bleeding until I have a shower. After washing off Mudro's blood I come out and put a fresh length of the towel over the cut.

"I think that needs stitched mate."

"Yeah I know but I'll have to leave it for a few days. I can't exactly show up at the hospital just now can I?"

Kyle puts all the blood stained clothes in the bag with the weapons.

"I could really do with a smoke."

"I'll skin up now if you want." Kyle's says.

"No let's just get to yours and get this over with. Phone Mickey and tell him to meet us at yours."

I take the bag with us and also bring a cloth soaked in disinfectant . We get down to the car and I wipe all the places I've touched with Murdo's blood. When we get to Kyle's, Mickey is already waiting, he's full of questions but neither of us answer him. Kyle walks into his house with Mickey following. I hang back and swap the bag over to my car. I enter Kyle's house and watch as he tries to skin up with his hands still shaking.

"Give it here, I'll do it, you go put the kettle on."

Kyle gets up and goes through to the kitchen and Mickey keeps at me asking what happened.

"Look Mickey, the less you know the better, just leave it okay."

I spark up the joint and have a few puffs before passing it to Mickey. Kyle comes through with the tea and the joint is

228

passed again until it comes back to me. I have another smoke but I feel I can't relax with the evidence still in my car. I quickly drink my tea, make my excuses and leave. On the way home I drive by the docks and park up. I make sure no-one is around and take out the bag. I tie it tightly before throwing it as far as I can into the water.

26) Cum on feel the noise

I really don't want to go to this today. I hate funerals and try to avoid going to them at all costs. But this is different, this is my best mate whom I've known since I was a kid. Kate phoned me the other day and asked which song I would like played for him. There's not going to be any prayers or hymns or any of that shit as Gaz hated religion. I know everyone else will pick all the sad songs but that's not how he would want remembered. He was so full of life all the time so I told her I wanted 'Cum on feel the noise.' This actually made her laugh down the phone and she understood straight away why I chose it. Well he always said he never understood why they had a minutes silence for people that had died. If it was him he would want as much noise as possible for a whole minute. He once said he would want everybody clapping and cheering to celebrate his life rather than mourn it. She also asked if I wanted to say a few words at the funeral. But I didn't think I would be up to it.

If I sit too long thinking about it the guilt starts to get to me as I still feel it's all my fault that he's gone. I look at Biscuit and sometimes wonder if he knows why Gaz's not here. I know it should have been me instead of him but I know that Gaz wouldn't want me to feel guilty. 'It's meh fate' he would say. 'What's meant fir ye winna go past ye.' I smile as I think about him saying this. That's my buzzer. It must be Kyle, he's a bit early to pick me up though.

"Hello."

"Hi Shane."

Shit it's Kelly. What the fuck will I do?

"Oh, eh. Hi come in." I say as I push the button to open the door.

I walk out onto the landing and watch her coming up the stairs. She's all in black so I guess she's here for the funeral.

"I thought you were in Spain." I say as she gives me a smile. It's not a happy smile, it's one of those forced sympathetic ones.

"I thought you might need some company. Do you mind if I come with you?"

"Don't be daft. Of course not." I say as I put my arms around her.

"It's good to see you Shane."

We go back into the flat and Biscuit rushes over wagging his tail and lifts up his paws on to her. I am ready to jump in feet first with all the questions 'Why did you take off? Why did you not call me? But I am so happy to see her I don't want to scare her away.

"I'm sorry about Gaz."

"How did you find out?"

"A friend called me."

"Is that the only reason you're back?"

"I was intending to come back to see you. It's just a bit sooner than I had planned. I know we have a lot of things to talk about and you probably have a million questions for me but I think it's best we wait until after the funeral."

"Okay sure, but just so that you know. I am really happy to see you."

"I know. Now come on. Go and get changed and we'll get this over with."

"I was supposed to be getting picked up from Kyle as I'm taking Biscuit with me. Do you want to take us in your car instead."

"Yeah sure…wait, why are you taking Biscuit?"

"I think Gaz would appreciate it."

"Will he be allowed in?"

"I don't care, he's coming."

I phone Kyle and tell him not to pick me up but to meet me outside as I will need his help to sneak Biscuit in.

We arrive at the crematorium and there is a large queue outside. Kyle sees us and comes over with Mickey and Joey. Jamie is here too but is up at the front with my mother. He is still on some serious pain killers to help him move about. I pick Biscuit up and we all huddle together to hide him as we all walk towards the door. There are a few funny looks from people but I hear the whispers behind me commenting that it's Gaz's dog.

We find a space at the side to stand as all the seats are taken. Kate told me there would be a seat kept at the front for me with them but I told her I was sneaking in Biscuit so I would be best to stand at the side. She laughed and cried at this at the same time. We find a space in amongst the packed room and I put Biscuit down on the ground.

A strange looking guy stands up on the platform next to the microphone and explains to everyone that this is not a service but a gathering to celebrate the life of Gaz as he wasn't religious. Too fucking right he wasn't religious. If anyone brought up religion Gaz would be the first person to join in on the conversation and get himself all worked up. 'How can they justify sayin they are men o god when their ain priests use their position ti tamper we ah they wee alter boys. Every ither week there is a story aboot abuse or some sort o preacher embezzlin money fae some pair cunt. An what aboot the preacher in America wha set up cameras in he's neighbours hoose an wis watchin them an their bairns get the toilet an stuff. Then you've got ah they other religious cunts abroad blowin things up an killin hundreds o innocent people an they've got the hard neck ti say it's for god. What a load o shite. An dinna get me started on they fuckin Rangers an Celtic cunts wah sing ah they religious sangs at gems. They dinna even ken what they're on aboot. Gaz would go on for hours about all that. Kate would tell him stories about his great granny, who was brought up by the nuns and how wicked they were to her. These were people who were supposed to be doing the work of god but all they really did was use it as an excuse to bully and beat up kids that were in their care. These stories were obviously passed down through the years and Gaz would fill our heads with them.

The strange looking guy introduces Big Danny who says loads of funny things that give me a massive lump in my throat. He mentions his daughter dying really young which left him and Kate to bring up Gaz. No mention of his dad though, which makes me wonder if he's here. Big Danny introduces a song that he says reminds both him and Kate of Gaz. Perfect Day. The song kicks in for about thirty seconds and people are bursting into tears. I feel close to tears myself and am glad I chose not to go up and say anything as I don't think the words would come out. The song finishes and then the strange looking guy introduces me, Jamie, Kyle, Mickey and Joey.

"These people have been friends of Gaz for many years and have written something for me to read out to you."

I actually wrote it myself and read it to the guys before submitting it to Kate.

"If Gaz was here today to see us with tears in our eyes feeling sad that he's gone he would say 'look at you, greeetin like a big poof'."

The crowd laugh out loud at this as it sounds so funny hearing this scary looking guy say our speech.

"If anyone knew Gaz, they would know Biscuit and know how much he meant to him. It was his 'bairn' as he would put it and if anyone should remember anything about Gaz they should picture him with Biscuit. We want you to remember him as we have always known him, loud, funny and the most genuine person any friend could have. The song that we've picked sums up the way in which we want to remember him."

There is a short silence of a few seconds and Kelly looks at me with tears in her eyes until Slade's 'Come on feel the noise' kicks in. Her face breaks into a smile and she puts her arms around me. I look around me and can see a smile on so many people's faces.

Before the song finishes I head towards the exit door with Kelly's hand gripping mines tightly. There is another strange looking guy guarding the door but I nod in the direction of Biscuit and he quietly opens it and lets us out.

"Is everything okay?" Kelly says as we get out and walk towards her car.

"Yeah, I just don't like funerals and I know all the other songs that are about to be played, they are all sad and depressing. That's not how I want to remember Gaz."

Kelly comes closer and puts her arms around me.

"Who wrote the speech?"

"Me."

"I'm sure Gaz would have loved it."

I feel a lump in my throat again and the tears trickle down my cheek.

"Hey it's okay." Kelly says when she sees the tears and hugs me tighter.

"No. No it's not."

"What do you mean?"

"Gaz…Gaz was killed for me."

"I don't understand."

"Someone thought that Gaz was me. That why he was stabbed."

"Who? Why?"

"I don't know, look can we take off? I really don't want to see everyone when they come out of there."

"Yeah, of course."

I open the door to my flat and Biscuit goes rushing past me sniffing around the place. It makes me feel sad when I see him wagging his tail, he's obviously looking for Gaz and wondering what's going on. He jumps up on the sofa and makes himself at home. Kelly sits next to him, patting his head. I make us both a cup of coffee and we go out onto the balcony to catch the sun as it breaks through the clouds. We sit for a while as I try to explain what's happened the last few weeks that she's been away. I tell her about going after Dek but I leave out the part where it might not have been him after all.

"Oh my god, I can't believe all this. When I heard Gaz had been killed I never imagined it was to do with any of this. I thought it was a random fight, like he was in the wrong place at the wrong time or something. I hope you know this is never going to stop until one of you is killed."

"I know, I should have ended it last night when I had the chance."

"I'm glad you didn't."

"Why?"

"Because that would make you just as bad as him and I know you are better than that Shane."

I guess she doesn't know me at all. There is a long uncomfortable silence. One of those where no-matter what you want to say, you know it will be the wrong thing.

"I left here so that nothing would happen and nobody would get hurt, but he goes after you anyway. You're best friend is killed. You're brother is nearly killed and it's all my fault."

I take hold of Kelly's hands and look her into her eyes, which are now filling up with tears. I know straight away before I open my mouth that I am about to tell her a load of shit but...ah well, here goes.

"Kelly this has nothing to do with you, if it wasn't Gaz it would have been someone else."

"What do you mean?"

"Dek was a maniac. He is the type of person who looks for

excuses to cause trouble. I had a few run ins with him before I even met you. He's a nut job. It's not you're fault. This could have happened even if we never met."

She has her arms around me and is crying into my shoulder.

"Shane, I have something to tell you."

"What?"

"I'm pregnant."

Wow, I didn't see that coming. I move from her and again I feel one of those uncomfortable silences.

"Say something."

"How?…When did you?"

"I found out the first day that you were at the park."

"Why didn't you tell me the next day?"

"I was going to tell you when we got home but then all that came out about Dek, I was too upset and couldn't think straight so I took off to get my head sorted out."

"You could have told me before now."

"And what would you have done? I had to figure out for myself what I wanted. I was planning to come back in a few weeks to tell you but because of all this I thought I'd better do it now."

"I don't know what to say."

"Well I need to know if you want to be with me."

"Of course."

"I've thought about you non stop since you left."

"I was hoping you would feel like that, as there is something else."

"I'm listening."

"I want you to come and live with me in Spain, I don't want to bring my child up here."

"What? you're joking."

She doesn't answer but her expression says it all. There is another long silence, but there are so many thoughts going through my head right now the silence is welcomed so that I can let everything sink in.

"Do you know what you're asking me to do?"

"You could give it a try, if you don't like it you could always come back."

"But I have my friends and…"

"…I know, you told me all this before and I know it's asking a lot of you but I don't want my baby growing up here. You can rent your flat out for a while. It will be here if you decide to come back. Shane I don't want anything to happen to you, I don't want my baby growing up without a father."

"I know, it could turn out like me" I say smiling, my sick sense of humour trying to make fun of a serious situation.

"We would have our own place to live. My dad could give you a job. This is a great opportunity for you to get away from…"

"Okay." I say cutting her off before she finishes.

"Okay. I'll do it" I say smiling at her.

"You will."

"Yeah. Yeah I will."

"I thought it would have taken more persuasion than that."

"Yeah, you certainly picked the right time to ask me, didn't you."

I have never really thought about leaving Dundee before, I mean everybody dreams about moving abroad and living in the sun but how many people actually just get up and do it. I know when you are young and you have your two week holiday with your mates. You save up for months and the minute you arrive you are on the piss…well sometimes it's before you arrive. The first week is a blast. You go out and drink for Scotland and you meet all these knew people. There are maids cleaning up after you and barmen who laugh at your drunken abuse because your spending money in his pub and not forgetting you are getting your hole from all these young girls who are out for the same reason that you are. The idea comes into your head that you want to stay there and get a job…All in the space of a week. Then your money runs out, the barman doesn't laugh at you jokes anymore and he stops taking any of your shit. Your room is a tip because the maid hasn't been seen for a week and you can't stop scratching your balls because of some glesgay mink you slept with the first night you arrived. The same one that you've been buying her and her mates loads of drinks for the past week. The job situation doesn't look good either as it's touting to get punters into the pubs and clubs or selling drugs to pay for some shit hole of a one bedroom flat that is actually sleeping four. Yeah the moving abroad thing is very short lived…But somehow I think this is a bit different. During one of our many heavy smoking sessions, where Gaz liked to have his little rant now and again. Someone had mentioned about moving abroad and I remember him being really stoned and saying 'Eh wouldna leave Dundee in a mullion years. Eh think Dundee is a fuckin great place ti live. Eh always hear people moanin aboot how shite it is an how it's full o junkies an schemies an a that shite. Bit ye can go anywhare an ye'll get that. The onay thing bringin Dundee doon is they Labour cunts runnin the cooncil. If people open their eyes ti what they're ah aboot we could get them voted oot an mibbe the toon would hae a fightin chance. They Labour cunts must be loaded we ah they back handers they must git fae punters wantin planning permission an what huv ye. The onay back hander they would get fae me across the fuckin puss. An as fir that fuckin (spit) Lord Provost, the wee specky cunt. He would definitely git a good kickin, an any o his off spring afore they got any ideas ti replace him.

I laugh to myself as I think about Gaz when he was stoned. He would be talking about something random and it would always lead to him bumping his gums about some other shit and then forgetting what he was talking about in the first place. I think this was because he knew so much about everything that he had too many thoughts going around in his head at once.

"Shane. What are you smiling at?"

"What? Oh, I eh, was thinking about Gaz." I say being brought back to reality.

"Look I'm going to need a few weeks to get everything sorted out."

What I really mean is that I need time to get a hold of that fucking Lisa and find out what the hell is going on.

"Are you sure you want to do this?"

"Of course I'm sure, I've not stopped thinking about you since you left. Although I am still pissed off that you never even thought about phoning me." I say while making a face at her.

"Come on, lets go. I'll have to catch up with everyone after the funeral. I have to go and see Kate and Big Danny but please don't mention to anyone about what we've just talked about."

"Why? Don't you want them to know that you're running away with me?"

"No, and especially don't tell them you're pregnant."

We walk into the function suite where everyone has gathered after the funeral but I am only here to show face and make small talk. I introduce Kelly to my mother and leave them chatting as I go in search of Big Danny. I find him at the bar giving out some of his worldly advice.

"Hey old man." I say nudging him.

"Eh'll fuckin ald man ye."

"I need a word." I say nodding towards the front door.

"Eh, nae bather Shane." He says following me outside.

"What's up?" He says.

"I just need a word with you on your own." I say walking away from the door.

"Sounds serious."

"It's about Gaz."

"Eh'm listening."

"You know how Gaz was always up to dodgy shit."

"Uh huh."

"Well for years I've been helping him put some of his money away."

"Fuck is that ah? Jist keep it. He obviously trusted ye ti look eftir it. So he would have wanted ye ti keep it."

"You don't understand Danny. It's a lot of money."

"How much?"

"Thousands. I don't know exactly. I never counted it. I just kept putting it away."

"Is it fae sellin they fuckin drugs?"

"Eh'm, Gaz never actually sold them Danny."

"What do ye mean? He always hud them on him. Eh assumed that was whare he got ah he's money fae."

"Well yeah, but the stuff on him was never for sale that was just for us to take. The stuff he made money from he never really laid his hands on it."

"Eh dinna understand."

"Look no-one knew any of this except me. Gaz had a contact in Glasgow, a top guy. He also knew one of the top guys in Dundee, but he played them off each other for years. To the top guy in Glasgow, Gaz was the man and in Dundee he was just the go between. Most of the money he made he gave to me to put away for safe keeping."

"Whare is the money in some sort o bank account?"

"Come on Danny, you knew Gaz better than that."

"Whare is it?"

"A security box. I could get it to you by tomorrow."

"Eh dinna want it."

"Then what am I going to do with it?"

"Spend it."

"Yeah right, look I'll come up sometime tomorrow and I'll speak to you when your sober."

"Shane whatever ye dae. Dinna mention any o this ti Kate."

"Don't be stupid. Why do you think I pulled you out here?"

"You're a good lad Shane." He says as we walk back inside.

I work my way around the place and hear nearly the same sentence from everyone until I end up back to Kelly and my mother, who appears to be slightly more pissed than when I got here only twenty minutes ago. Kelly looks as thought she's enjoying herself listening to embarrassing stories about me. I clock Jamie trying to work his way over to me and I can tell he's pissed but I manage to make a sharp exit with Kelly before he reaches me.

"That was short and sweet." Kelly says as we head back to mine.

I spend the rest of the day chilling out with Kelly and we take Biscuit for a long walk, which keeps my mind off other things that are niggling away at me. This doesn't last long before I end up back at work and driving around trying to get a hold of Lisa. Late into the night as I sit in the taxi waiting on drunken customers, I end up in deep thought about everything that's happened. I start to feel sad as my thoughts move onto Gaz. This keeps me occupied as I stay on late until the shift change at the office but there is still no sign of her. I storm up to the office to make sure she's not there and I am met with a few blank faces staring up from the computer screens and phones. One guy who looks familiar sits back in his chair and doesn't take his eyes off me until I walk back out of the office.

Kelly is up before me this morning and serves me coffee in bed. She's off to her friends house to pick up her things and move them into mine. I gave her the spare key and told her to make herself at home, well for the time being anyway. At least she could keep Biscuit company so that I don't have to rush back form work to take him out.

Over the last few days I have been banging in the hours to get some extra money before taking off. I've arranged a solicitor to have the flat rented out for me while I am away. I have no mortgage so at least I will have some money coming in every month.

Saturday night and I'm working, this must be a first for years. The busiest night of the week means more dickheads out on the piss...and more hassle for me.

I have checked the office everyday now and still no sign of Lisa. I am desperate to find out the truth so I drive to her flat and when I look up there is a light on. I park up and take the wheel brace out of the boot. I walk up her foul smelling stairs to her flat and put my ear to the door. I lift up the letter box but I can't hear any voices or movement. I take a few steps back and launch forward to kick the door in. it takes a few attempts but the lock eventually gives way. I am not too worried about the noise as in this block or even this whole area you can scream fire at the top of your voice and still no-one will come out. I walk in the flat and quickly scan the rooms. Nothing looks any different since I was last here. I run back down the stairs to the car and speed off feeling even more anxious to talk to her.

Customer No...
Glasgow big shot

As I sit in the taxi on the Nethergate rank in the city centre ready to move down to the next space someone comes form behind and gets into the back of the car.

"Sorry mate, the car in front is next."

"Ah don't give a shit, ah want you tae drive me." The man says in his strong Glasgow accent. I recognise him straight away as I look in my mirror to see his heavily scarred face.

"Where do you want to go?"

"Ah don't care, just drive."

As I drive through the town he manoeuvres his position so that I can't see him in my mirror anymore. This makes me really edgy. I am ready to slam on the brakes and make a run for it.

"Ah'm an acquaintance aye your late friend." He says.

"Yeah I know."

"Look ah'm sorry tae hear about what happened, Ah know you two were really close."

"Yeah we were."

"He had a lot of respect for you. That 's why ah came tae see you."

"Thanks, but I'm sure you didn't drive eighty miles just to tell me that."

"Aye your right, an Gaz was right about you. No fuckin about. Straight tae the point. Right, well first of all just so that you know, Dek worked for me."

"Murdo?" I say sounding surprised.

"Aye, an ah know that it was you that smashed him. Don't worry ah know why, you think it was him that killed Gaz so ah understand. Bit ah've spoke tae Dek an ah could assure ye it was nothing tae dae we him. Aye he told me he had it in for ye aboot he's burd or something bit that doesna interest me. What ah'm here for is, now that Gaz is gone and Dek, well Dek's fucked. Ah don't hae anybody tae dae mah drop offs. Well ah no ah can get loads ay people tae dae them bit ah dinna hae anybody ah can trust." He says now moving so that I can see his scarred face in my mirror again.

"No chance." I say.

"You won't even consider it? It's a lot o money. I'll even negotiate a better price we ye."

"Sorry, I'm not interested."

"You would be in charge, an run the whole show. Ye wouldna even hae tae touch anything as ye could pay people tae dae it for ye....You would be the man."

Oh my god, this guy has watched far too many gangster movies. If this was some punter that was into all that hard man shit they would fall for this line in a second. But I have been around long enough to know that these weedgies talk like this all the time. I've heard their patter so much I can see right through it

"There's plenty of people out there that would do it for you."

"Ah don't trust them, ah trusted Gaz, an he trusted you, which basically means ah'm now puttin mah trust in tae you."

"Sorry but it's just not for me."

As I reach the end of Riverside Drive I turn around and head back towards the city centre.

"Ah'm sorry tae hear that. Ah can't say ah'm no disappointed. But if ye ever change yer mind just get in touch, ye know who ah ah'm now. Oh, an you don't hae tae worry aboot Dek. He's been warned that there's tae be nae retaliation fae him, out ay respect fir Gaz. No that he's capable ah doin anythin anyway."

I don't say anything as I drive back to the same rank from where this pointless journey started. As he gets out of the car he pats me on the shoulder.

"Take care." He says as he shuts the door and walks towards a shiny black car across the street with tinted windows. No retaliation, from Dek Murdo. I'm supposed to believe that from a jumped up drug dealing wee wide-o Glasgow gangster. He must think I'm zipped up the back. I'll be lucky if I don't end up with a bullet in my head for turning down his offer.

The set up

I've been sent from Charleston to Lochee and it's a phone box job. The chances of the customer still being there are very slim. Pentland, here we are. It must be the phone box at the top of the hill. There's a shock, the customer is still here. I can't see his face but he signals to me that he'll be out in a minute and he looks as though he's talking to someone on the phone.

I lean over to change tracks on the CD player when I hear a loud crash. At first I think someone has bumped into my car but it's actually a brick that has been thrown through my back window. I see a guy running towards me from the front with a large baton. I quickly put the car in reverse and as I look back and start to move down the hill at a fast speed another car tears up the hill and into the back of me. There's no place to go, I have to get out of the car. The guy with the baton is still running towards me. I turn to run the other way but there is someone coming from each direction. They have their faces covered with scarves. As the guy running at me from down the hill gets closer his baton looks much like the others but has nails through it, these guys mean business. The guy from the phone box who now has his face covered is also running towards me with a large blade out in front of him.

Before they all get too close and I am boxed in I make a quick decision to go for the blade man. If he is swaying it out in front of him he certainly doesn't know how to use it. I run towards him and he is now holding the blade like it's a sword or something. I lunge forward with my arm reaching passed the blade. I push his wrist away from him, which exposes his whole body. I keep travelling forward smacking the palm of my hand into his face. This pushes him back onto his heals making him off balance. As I charge forward my shoulder hits him, putting him down. I turn to see the others running towards me so I stamp on the blade mans face as I take off further up the hill with the others in pursuit. After about twenty metres I hear shouting behind me and I turn to find they have given up the chase. One of them pulls out a bottle and I'm thinking, yeah right as if they are going to reach me with that. But it's a petrol bomb. They light it and throw it in my car. Wow, I didn't see that coming.

I keep running up the hill which takes me to Balgay Park. I run through it until I get to the main road at the other side. I have no mobile as it was left in the car. I run until I reach the nearest shop and ask them to phone the police. Not that they'll be much fucking help, but I have to report it for insurance purposes otherwise I wouldn't even bother. I play the innocent victim and they tell me to stay where I am until they come for me. Give them there due, they turn up only minutes later and drive me back to my car…well what's left of it. The flames and smoke are shooting out from it. They tell me to wait in the back of the patrol car while they cordon off the area as there are crowds of people gathered to investigate what's going on. The fire brigade arrive shortly after and quickly put it out. I am taken down to Bell Street station where I give a statement of what happened but I also have to endure all the usual questions. Have you any idea who they were? Can you think of anyone who would want to do this? Blah blah blah. Just hurry up and give me a lift home you fucking tossers.

As soon as I am home I phone Kelly's mobile and she rushes back from her friends house. I hold back the details but I do tell her that I was set up. I am more confused now as to who is behind all this. Only hours ago I had a top Glasgow gangster in the back of my car asking me to be his drug courier, I turn him down and then this happens. At the back of my mind I still think it's something to do with Murdo then I think about Lisa the psycho bitch and that maybe she is in on it too. This gives Kelly more reasons for me to take off with her…as if I need any. She drives me up to the office as I explain that I'll have to inform them of what's happened. I know the police will have already been up there but the real reason is that I am about to confront Lisa and find out the truth. Someone had to know where I was at that exact time and it had to have been someone at the office. If I storm in there and pull her up in front of everyone I will be able to tell by her reaction.

Kelly pulls up outside the office and I tell her I won't be long. She smiles at me as I shut the door and my mind changes so quickly it's scary. One minute I am blowing kisses to Kelly the next I am running up the stairs at the office working myself up into a rage. This is soon diminished as I reach the top of the stairs and look around to find that Lisa's not working again. I was so sure that it was her who set me up. I receive a few dubious looks from the other office staff before the boss walks through from a side door.

"How are you? I've just had the police up here. They told me what happened."

"Yeah, I'm fine, just a little shaken up."

"We've checked the records on the computer and the call didn't come from the phone box it was a mobile."

"What does that mean?"

"Well it was either random. The guys who done it were just out for anybody or someone was following you around and waited for you to enter that area before calling, hoping you would get the job. A car rammed into the back of you didn't it?"

"Yeah"

"Well it must have been following you."

"Or someone from this office sent me there on purpose" I

say a bit louder as I look around at the faces trying to hide behind the screens.

"According to the computer your car was the second one to be sent to that phone box in the hour previous. The first was a no-job."

"A dry run for me?"

The boss shrugs his shoulders and says "It's possible."

"What car did you send there before me? And who was it that took the call?" I say very seriously as several pairs of eyes peer at me above the screens.

"There are five people working in this office, it doesn't matter which one took the call, every computer has access to where your car is allocated. Shane I know you've been through a lot the past few weeks." He says lowering his voice.

"But you can't come up here and start pointing the finger at anyone. Come up and see me tomorrow and I'll sort you out with another car to work. If you get your insurance sorted out and get another car on the road I'll see about getting you another computer fitted." He says as he ushers me out of the office.

I walk back down the stairs feeling very confused. I was sure that I was set up from Lisa. Kelly drives me back to the flat but I don't say much on the way as my head is going around in circles. I know some people would let something like this get to them and they would be thinking, what if those guys caught up with me? They could have killed me and they would probably be afraid to leave their house. I don't know why, I guess it's just my nature but all I want to do is find the fucker who is behind this and get them back. I feel more than ever now, that I should have finished off Murdo for good when I had the chance. Back in the flat I go to the kitchen to make a cup of tea when Kelly follows me in and hugs me really tight.

"Shane why don't we leave now?" She says with tears in

her eyes.

"We'll leave soon, I promise."

I hate seeing her upset. It makes me feel very bad and for her sake I want to just pack my bags and leave, but I feel I would be running away from a problem that is going to follow me around until I find out the truth. It doesn't matter where I go and for how long it will always keep niggling away at me.

"Lets just pack up and go."

"I just need a few more days to sort a few things out, is that okay."

"Not really, but there's nothing I can do about it."

She hugs me tight again and I think to myself that this is going to be a very busy few days.

28)

I go and see the old guy Wully that Gaz worked for and after a long discussion he agrees to give me his taxi for a few days. He told me to log on to the computer with his password. This will register that he is working and not me. That way, if it is someone at the office they wont know where I am. I also paid one of my neighbours from across the road from me to use their garage for a few days so that Kelly can hide her car.

I don't actually need to work the next few days as it's not as if I need the money. The flat will pull in extra cash every month and I'll now have the insurance money from my car to come as well. There is only one reason I am doing this and that is to try and find out who the hell is behind this.

Customer No. 1123
Toy soldiers

This is just my luck that I decide to work late tonight and it is so fucking slow. I join the Mardi rank and as I sit and watch the bouncers throw out a couple of drunken guys. I watch as they swagger their way across to the taxi. They look like brothers with the skinheads, broad shoulders and the same bad dress sense.

They are marines and are on their way back to Condor. Their base in Arbroath. It's a good fare but the company is not. I have to listen to them as they rant and rave about why the bouncer through them out of the club. The guy in the front is talking like he never did anything wrong but his friend is telling a different story. From what I have picked up it appears that the guy in the front was pestering some girl who happened to be with her boyfriend. The boyfriend apparently warned him but that wasn't a good enough rejection so he persisted until she had to physically push him away. He was not happy at this either so he decided to punch the boyfriend. The boyfriend retaliated by laying into him so his mate sitting in the back jumped in to help. Judging by the mess of their faces the boyfriend has given both of them a good go. Either that or it was the bouncer's gentle ways of persuasion to get them out of the club.

I try to make conversation as it's a long journey but it's like speaking to brick wall. These guys don't have an opinion on anything, when I ask them a question it's like they are waiting on someone answering for them. These two guys I have in the taxi are probably the pride of our nation, the ones who sign up willingly to fight for their country. They train all day in tactical warfare and are trusted with some of the most advanced weaponry known to man. These guys learn from day one how to follow rules and show respect. If they were ever captured they are trained to withstand brutal torture methods imposed on them. Some of them are sent into countries that they probably couldn't even spell and are ordered to kill people without even knowing why. These are brave men who are willing to go on the front line and have prepared themselves that there is a possibility they could be killed. Yet the minute they are let off their leash on the street the discipline and respect is thrown out of the window.

I feel sorry on these guys who the government prey on. They get them signed up when they are all young and stupid and full of life. They are so naïve that they are easily brainwashed into not asking questions. I can only imagine the conversation when they go to sign up.

'Why do you want to join the marines?'

'Eh, uh, to shoot guns.'

'Okay, you'll do.'

The ones that sign up that have any common sense are the ones who train in a certain field. They can't get an apprenticeship on the street so they do their time, learn a trade and get to fuck out. A few years down the line if they happen to be called up to go to war such as Iraqi, would they go? Would they fuck.

That is why the government preys on uneducated guys like these two numbskulls who are so gung ho they would never question orders. They would always obey and commit themselves to whatever they have been ordered to do, even if it meant taking the lives of hundreds of people. I drop off these couple of brainless twats and head back to Dundee.

What the...?

I drive around for a while and find myself in the city centre again after dropping off a couple of fat mingers out to pull some unfortunate guy. I join an unofficial rank with several other cars outside the Mardi nightclub. The other taxi drivers have gathered outside their cars to stand and chat...or moan. There is a car park opposite the rank, which is part of a cheap supermarket. This is where a number of car enthusiasts gather every night to inspect each others latest monstrosity that they have added to their heaps of shit. I sit in the car reading the local paper and try to comprehend the latest fuck ups Dundee Council has managed to achieve. I hear a lot of noise from the car park opposite as the young drivers wheel spin in and out of there. I watch as they lift their bonnets and inspect each others engines. At one point I think one of them is about to get his dick out and shoot his load as he gets a little over excited checking out someone's oversized shiny new alloys. Some of these cars have more patched up rust on them than paint and yet they spend more money on accessories than what the car is actually worth. By the sounds of it they purposefully drill holes in their exhausts to make them more noisy, I guess these guys have never moved on from the lollypop stick in their bicycle wheel. The police drive past several times and appear to leave them to it. They are more interested in what the taxi drivers are doing than some fucking idiots who are wheel spinning at dangerous speeds through the town during the night where drunks are falling about on the road. Now if I drive past them with a dodgy brake light I am stopped and put off the road for it.

The taxi driver two cars in front of me gets a fare so all the cars move up a space. The driver in front of me has no-one to talk to now but I see him get out of his car and hover over towards my window.

"Ahright mate, how's it goin?" He says.

What the fuck does this prick want?

"Not bad." I say with my fake smile as though I feel privileged that he has come over to talk to me. I really feel like saying, Fuck off and find someone else who wants to listen to your shite.

"What aboot they Mercedes cars eh." He says.

"What about them?" I say pleading ignorant. I know exactly where this is going. It's all these fucking drivers ever talk about. It's a new taxi company that's started up and they're not happy about it. With their competitive prices and top of the range cars they are gaining a lot of respective customers.

"They Private Hire Cabs. They were onay meant to be openin up as executive travel fir business men an the like but now they're pickin up anybody. As if it's no hard enough ti earn a livin withoot them."

He's obviously looking for me to be sympathetic but I really couldn't give a shit. I don't say anything and nod my head in agreement hoping he will say his piece and fuck off back to his car…but no he continues his little rant.

"Eh've heard that he's awa ti advertise fir drevirs in the paper an has put an advert up in the brew. He's actually offerin ti pit them through their taxi tests anah."

"Really, what's wrong with that? I think that's a great idea."

He looks at me like I have just called his mother a whore or something.

"Eh well you'll no be sayin that when they're takin ah the work an yer no makin any money." He says getting himself worked up.

"What is it with you cunts? You moan about people scrounging benefits and being idle but when someone comes up with a good idea to get people off their arses and back to work you're the first people to criticise it. As far as I am concerned there is enough work for everyone to go around. What your problem is, is that you guys have had it easy for to long and now you have a bit of competition you have to go out and work for your money."

This new firm that's started is run by a guy named Ray. I have heard his name many times when I was growing up. He has a hard reputation and the impression I get from drivers is that it's not the new firm that is the problem but that he is behind it. The company has a large fleet of brand new Mercedes saloon cars and the drivers are kitted out in shirts, ties and waistcoats. They look really professional compared to some scruffy smelly old man who has his large gut hanging out over his trousers and his 'bricky bum' on show.

"Thir drevirs are ah bloody scabs, takin ah oor jobs." He says. This statement sounds too well rehearsed, which makes me think he has said this too many times over the past while or he has heard so many other drivers say it and has waited on his chance to use it.

"Well I'll tell you what pal, if this firm had came along a few years earlier, I would have been working for them too. I used to work in a shit hole of a factory for minimum wage where I couldn't even go for a piss without some weedy little man, a bit like yourself I might add, shouting at me for taking to long. In the winter, I went in when it was dark and came out when it was dark. I only saw daylight at the weekend and by then I was too fucking tired to appreciate it . So if you are trying to turn me against these drivers, who in my opinion saw an opportunity to better themselves by driving people around all day in a brand new Mercedes, then you've got a long way to go."

The guy storms off with his head down marching towards his car.

"Hey don't go, I'm finished yet…you fucking we tosser." I shout out of the window.

I have heard so many rumours about this Ray and his new taxi firm and most of them are probably started by these stupid fucking drivers. If this Ray has any ambitions of taking over the taxi business in Dundee, good luck to him. It would definitely take someone with a lot of backing and a hell of a lot of brown envelopes placed into the pockets of the right councillors. Actually with the reputation of Dundee Council…I don't think it would take that many envelopes.

It's four in the morning and the town has cleared except from a few stragglers. I turn off the computer and head up to the office. I park in between two other cars where I have a good view of the office doors. I tilt the seat back and wait. I was at Lisa's flat several times tonight but there was still no answer. After the last time I didn't think it would be a good idea if I hung around too long. I shouted through the letter box that I only wanted to talk but she was either not in or she wasn't answering to me. I wouldn't care if Dek Murdo answered the door and he ran out and kicked the shit out of me, at least I would know he was behind it.

I know there is a shift change at this time and I am hoping to try and catch her if she's away to start. I have had to stay out until now because if I went home and came out again Kelly would know that I was up to something. I have only sat here for about ten minutes but it feels like an hour. Several people go in and out but still no Lisa. Another car rips past me and up to the office doors. I recognise the driver from somewhere but he was too fast and it was too dark to get a good look at him. Another guy from the office comes out, it's the same a big guy with the distinguished features who gives me the stare each time I go up there. He has a bony face and a kind of aggressive look about him that seems very familiar. He walks around to the passenger side and when he opens the door the interior light comes on...Macintosh. It's fucking Macintosh and his son. They go to drive off when another taxi comes in and blocks the road. Lisa gets out...fuck. I can't jump out with those cunts there. She walks past Macintosh's car and gives him a look of disgust. Shit...What the fuck is going on? The taxi reverses, giving Macintosh room to get out. He drives off...with me not far behind, my heart racing. I follow them at a distance all the way to Lochee until they turn into the Eastwell cul de sac. This leaves me no choice but to drive past. I park up at the next lay-by and walk back up the street. I enter the cul de sac and walk through looking for the car that I saw them in. I don't have to look to far as it's parked in the street in front of a driveway, where his taxi is parked. I walk back to Wully's taxi and looking around I realise that this is a five minute walk from the phone box where I was set up...coincidence?

I drive home feeling relieved, anxious, tired and shocked all at once. I curl up in bed with Kelly who is fast asleep with Biscuit lying like lord muck at the bottom of the bed. I lie for a long time waiting on everything going around in my head to settle down. I think back to when I smashed Macintosh, it was around the same time all this started. The run in I had with Mudro must have been a coincidence…ah fuck it, he had it coming.

Kelly lets me sleep late and when I eventually surface she has been busy all morning cleaning my flat and packing some of my things. We've decided to leave tomorrow morning and she's phoned up to put me on her insurance. The plan is to take turns and drive to Dover, catch the ferry to France and then drive onto Spain. I'm only taking my clothes and some personal things, I'll leave the keys with my mother who will pick up the TV and stereo and stuff. The rest has to stay as it will be rented out as a furnished flat. I want to tell Kelly about last night but I think it would be best if she didn't know as it would mean having to explain that I lied to her. It's at the back of my mind that I know I can't let him get away with it but I am leaving in less than twenty four hours which means something has to be done tonight.

After a cup of coffee handed to me with a large smile from Kelly I make a mental note of the things I have to do today. Kelly makes a comment that I appear a little anxious but this is explained away that I am excited about taking off with her. I don't like keeping this from her but the less people that know the better. As I leave the flat Kelly gives me a long kiss and a squeeze of the arse. I have Biscuit with me as Kate and Big Danny are going to take him. I struggle down the stairs with his food bowls and his basket, not that the wee bugger used it, as he was always curled up in my fucking bed. Kelly was quite sad to see him go and as much as I would love to take him with us it's just not possible. On the way I stop off at the stash to pick up Gaz's money. It's been moved around over the years to different places but it's been in here the longest. There are all different sizes of these storage containers and I drive into the yard where the smallest ones are. I park right outside leaving Biscuit sitting in the front seat. I unlock the door to the nine by five feet container to find the plastic bags still stashed in the same place as I left them. I pick them up without even looking inside. I lock the door and hand the keys back into the security office where I am given back the deposit. Before I go to Big Danny's I pull up into a quiet side street and start counting the money. They are wrapped in thousand pound rolls and I count one hundred and fifteen rolls. Fuck, I never knew there was that much. I put it all back into the one bag and hurry over to Big Danny's.

"Biscuit." Kate shouts as she opens the door.

"I've got his basket and stuff in the car, I'll go and get it."

I walk into the house and see that Biscuit has settled back into his own territory in no time, with his place on the sofa next to the window. He used to sit there all the time when Gaz wasn't in. For the first time in days I've felt the lump in my throat again thinking about Gaz as I know Biscuit must be missing him. He'll probably sit there every day now waiting on Gaz coming home. I remember Gaz used to jump the fence from around the side of the house and sneak up to the window so that Biscuit couldn't see him. When he stuck his head up to the window it was so funny watching Biscuit bolt to the door. I know he's more at home here and Big Danny will more than keep him occupied but it still makes me feel sad. I explain to them that I am leaving for a while and Big Danny takes the piss that I am running off with a burd.

"Yeah but she's loaded though."

"Ah well Eh guess that's ah that matters then."

I look at Big Danny and nod at the front door to signal that I need to see him on his own. He walks me out and I hand him the bags of money and tell him to put it in a safe place as this is to make sure Biscuit is taken care of. Big Danny looks in the bags.

"Eh telt ye we dinna want it. You'll make better use o it than we ever will."

"What if Biscuit ever gets sick, vets bills are not cheap. You know Gaz would want him to have the best of care."

I walk away before he has a chance to force it back on me.
I head straight across the road to my mothers, who, before I
even get a chance to sit down has the kettle on and is making
me a cup of tea. Jerry isn't in, thank fuck because I really
couldn't be doing with him just now

"Where's Jamie?"

"I don't know he said he had to nip out and that he would
be back later, you know what he's like, he's always up to
something."

"Eh, yeah."

"Eh saw ye ower the road, eh thought ye were keepin Biscuit?"

"I'm leaving mum."

"What do ye mean?" She says smiling unsure of what I am
on about.

"I'm leaving, I'm moving abroad."

"When?"

"Tomorrow."

"What? Why?"

"Quite a lot of reasons actually."

"It's no we that lassie fae the funeral is it?"

"Yeah."

"It's aboot time ye found a nice lassie."

"Mum." I say pausing as I think of how to tell her.

"What? What is it?

"Eh, You're eh, going to be a granny."

"She's pregnant."

"Yeah."

She doesn't say anything as she passes me the cup of tea
and sits down.

"So whare are ye goin?"

"I cant tell you mum, the less people that know the better."

"What aboot yer flat? Are ye sellin it?"

"I'll be renting it for a while, see how it goes."

"So this is ye here ti say cheerio."

"Sort of, I'll come past in the morning before I leave, I knew you would be on your own today so that's why I came. You know I can't talk to you when he's around."

She changes the subject quickly as usual, before I start ranting about how much of a wanker Jamie's dad is.

"Am eh ever gonna see this grandchild?"

"Of course, I'll be back to visit now and again."

I hear the front door open and Jamie comes in.

"Ahright, how's it goin?"

"No bad." I say gesturing him to head upstairs. I pick up the cup of tea and follow him upstairs to his room.

"I know who stabbed you."

"So do eh." Jamie says, smiling.

"How do you know?"

"Eh hae meh contacts." He says, quite smug like he's some sort of wide-o but I let it go.

"It wasn't Dek Murdo."

"Eh ken, bit that didna stop you thinkin that though did it?"

"How did you know I...Kyle told you."

"What? So you told Kyle before you told me." Jamie says angrily.

"What do you mean?...Kyle was with me."

"So you went eftir Dek an took a wimp like Kyle we ye an never thought aboot askin me."

"You were just out of hospital."

"So."

"Wait a minute. What are you getting worked up about?"

"Nothin." Jamie says like a spoiled child going in the huff.

"Look, it's a guy named Macintosh and I'm going to get him tonight. Do you want to help me?"

"Eh ken wah he is. He's the son o the guy you smashed a while back."

"How long have you known it was him?"

"Oh quite recent like." Jamie says with his smug look back on his face.

"I don't have my car anymore and I have to drop this taxi off on the way home. Macintosh finishes his shift about four and his old man picks him up. So if you be ready about half three I'll pick you up in Kelly's car."

Jamie laughs.

"You jist mak sure your ready." He says very smugly.

I head back downstairs to say cheerio to my mum. I fucking hate Jamie when he's being like that, all arrogant and thinking he's some sort of big man. He reminds me of his old man and if he ever tries to get wide with me like Jerry did, I wont be slow in putting him in his place. Actually that reminds me, I've still got to pull him up about what Gaz told me about the girl in the tent at T in the park. I promised Gaz I wouldn't say anything but if it needs to be said, it will. I use my mothers phone to call Kelly to meet me at Wully's when I drop off his Taxi. I say cheerio and tell her that I'll see her tomorrow. She has tears in her eyes, so here's to what she'll be like tomorrow.

29) Payback part 2

Shane didna ken what tae say when eh telt him eh kent wah stabbed is. He thinks eh found oot fae Kyle bit he's surely mistaken. Speakin aboot Kyle, eh need somebody we a half decent car. That heap o shite that Shane's burd has is nae good, there's a chance it could brak doon an that's the last thing eh need. Eh dinna ken what Shane's plans fir the night were bit he's gonna be well fuckin happy when eh phone him later on the night.

"Eh Kyle, is that you?"

"Yeah. Who's this?"

"It's Jamie. Eh need a favour the night."

"I'm listening."

Too fuckin right you're listening, you wee nonce. In a we while e'm gonna be the fuckin man an they'll ah be listenin ti me.

"Eh need somebody we a car."

"Sounds familiar. What time?"

"Late.Early oors mate."

"No problem. Just give me a phone and I'll pick you up."

"Cheers."

Too fuckin right you'll pick me up. Fae meh good sources, eh ken that Macintosh is feenishin an oor early on Sunday an he's no gittin picked up fae he's old man. He has the car cause his old man goes on the piss on a Sunday. Bit eh'm no interested in he's old man. Eh only want him.

"Ahright Kyle, bang on time eh."

He fuckin kens better.

"Right what's the plan?"

"Drev me up ti that taxi office but dinna go in. Jist sit aroond the corner fae it."

"And then what?"

"Jist fuckin wait an see."

We sit fir a wee while bit as soon as eh see that car comin roond the corner we the flet tyre eh ken it wis worth the wait.

"Right folly that car bit keep yer distance. Cause we'll hae ti pull in quick when it stops."

The car starts ti slow doon an then pulls ower ti the side o the road.

"Right pull in now an kill the lights."

The guy gets oot an goes aroond ti the passenger side. He opens the boot an taks oot the spare. He's bendin doon ti tak aff the punctured wheel. Eh ken this is meh chance ti get him, bit if eh dae it now it means eh'll hae ti cheenge the wheel...Fuck that, eh'll wait.

"Clever thinkin o is dein the passenger wheel eh Kyle."

The new wheel is on an he's tightenin up the bolts so eh git oot the car an run as fast as eh could we a steel bar in meh hand. Eh get close ti him an sweeng the bar oot ti the side. As eh run past him eh smack him in the haed as hard as eh could knockin him oot. Eh signal ti Kyle an he gets oot the car an comes ower.

"Come on you fuckin shift. Eh dinna want anybody ti see us."

We lift the cunt an put him in the boot. Eh tighten the rest o the bolts on the wheel an jump in ti he's car.

"Kyle folloy is."

"Where are you going?"

"JUST FUCKIN FOLLY IS, YOU'LL FIND OOT." Eh shout at the cunt.

Eh head for Shane's an phone him on the wey, the cunt better be fuckin ready.

"Yeah what is it?"

"We're on oor wey. Git yer arse doon the stairs an we'll pick ye up."

"Who's on the way?…"

Eh hang up on him before he starts ah he's questions. Eh drev up he's street we a the fancy expensive hooses. It'll no be lang afore eh hae ain o them. Eh thought he made he's money beyin an sellin hooses bit eftir a that time, him an Gaz were sellin gear an never even telt is. Eh always thought that Gaz was up ti no good bit eh never thought in a million years that Shane was at it. Eh guess Shane was the main man as he's the ain we the expensive flat an the fancy car. But Gaz, well Gaz was always pleadin poverty. Well eh'll show the cunt eh'm gonna be the man. That Glesgay cunt telt is how much money eh could be makin. If eh get mesel started up they'll see that eh'm no a cunt ti be fucked we. Shane is waitin at the corner o his block an eh drev up beside him.

"What's goin on?" He says.

Eh git oot the car an open the boot jist as Kyle pulls up behind is.

"Is that Macintosh?"

"Eh." Eh say we a big grin.

"How did you…"

"His old man wisnae pickin him up. He had the car at the office."

"I'll explain it ti ye on the wey. Come on."

"Where are we going?"

"You'll find oot."

Eh close the boot an drev aff headin fir Tempy woods we Kyle still follyin us. Eh onay need him so that eh could git a lift hame. Eh drev in as far as eh could so that naebody fae the main road could see us. As soon as Kyle parks an turns aff he's lights, eh open the boot. Bit ti meh surprise Macintosh launches oot an taks aff. Shane sprints eftir him an punches him ti the groond. Eh catch up we them an Shane is on top o him throwin punch eftir punch. He gits up an then eh start kickin him in the puss as he treys ti cover hesel. Eh look aroond ti see Kyle standin ower him we the steel bar that eh used earlier. Eh'm quite shocked as eh didna think Kyle had it in him. Macintosh is screamin an yelpin like a wounded animal until Kyle hits him in the haed we the bar.

"That's fir Gaz." He says as he turns an walks back towards the car. Eh gee him another kick in the puss bit he disna make a noise, no even a whimper.

"Is he daed?" Eh say.

"Don't think so."

Eh pull oot meh blade an walk towards him.

"What are you doing?"

"Awa ti feenish him aff."

"Oh no you're not."

"Well here ye go. You dae it."

"Nobody's fucking doing it."

"What? So you're gonna lit him aff we a hidin eftir stabbin me an killin Gaz…Yer best mate."

"We're not killin him an that's it Jamie."

"That fuckin burd o yours is makin ye saft."

What is we him. Eh canna believe what e'm hearin. For years when eh was growin up, ah eh ever heard wis 'You're brother is fuckin mental' 'Naebody messes we you're brother'. Eftir smashin Murdo eh thought he really is the fuckin man bit now he canna even feenish aff some piece o shit that killed he's best mate.

"Some fuckin mate your turnin oot ti be."

Shane takes a couple o steps towards is an smacks is in the mooth. Eh put the blade oot in front o is an he steps back.

"What are you going to do? Stab me now, are you? Well…What are you waiting on?"

Kyle walks ower fae the car we the bar still in he's hand, looking like he's ready ti use it. Well if he wants some he'll fuckin git it tae.

"Dae ye no realise that piece o shit lyin there tried ti kill you. It was you that he went ti stab, no Gaz...an you're jist gonna let him go."

"Jamie his time will come, believe me...But not like this."

Eh drap meh hand ti meh side we the blade in it an Shane walks towards the car. Fuck him. Eh dive forward an plunge Macintosh in the stomach. Eh pull oot the blade an plunge him again...An again...An again...An again, until eh feel masel bein thrown onto meh back we the knife still in meh hand.

"What's wrong with you." Shane says as he stands ower me.

"Gaz always warned me about you, for years he said there was something not right about you. I always thought he was taking the piss, I always took you're side and made excuses saying you were just young. We thought that letting you hang out with us that maybe you would change but after what he told me about you starting on that girl in the tent, I guess he was right all along."

"Fuck you. Ah they hidings you've gave people ower the years. You've got a fuckin hard neck."

"You just don't get it do you?"

"Git what?" Eh say but he doesna answer. He walks ower ti Macintosh an drags him towards he's car.

"Help is then." He shouts.

Kyle walks towards him.

"Not you Kyle. I don't want you to get any blood on you."

"What are ye dein?" Eh ask.

"Cleaning up you're fucking mess."

30) The cover up

I know I came out tonight to get Macintosh but I never intended on killing him. I know he killed Gaz and that he actually intended on killing me. Jamie is right about that but I just think this is all wrong. I would rather have gave him a hiding and set him up to suffer for the rest of his life. If we leave him here there will be a massive murder enquiry and no doubt they'll find some sort of evidence relating us to his murder so I'll have to make this look like an accident. I get Jamie to help me put Macintosh into the back seat and I open the boot, shit no petrol can.

"Kyle you wouldn't happen to have a petrol can in your car would you?"

"Yeah, why? What are you away to do Shane?"

"I told you, clean up his mess. Kyle i want you to drive to the petrol station just outside Dundee, the one at the start of Invergowrie."

"Yeah, I know where it is."

"Fill up your petrol can and meet me and psycho-boy here at Emmock road."

"Where is that?"

"Trottick, the hill as you head up to the old Bentleys farm."

"Eh'll go we Kyle."

"Will you fuck. This is your mess, you're fucking driving this car."

Kyle takes off sharpish and Jamie drives us to Trottick with Macintosh lying curled up in the back seat. I didn't even check to see if he was still alive, I wouldn't think so after Jamie's onslaught. Jamie tries to speak on the way but he is told to shut his fucking trap and drive. I had it all planned out. Wait until Macintosh gets home, kick his door in and set about him and his old man. No sneaking about and jumping him on his own when his back is turned. Just a toe to toe in his own house and break their legs to make sure they cant walk for a while. Just as they get their plaster off I would arrange to do it again and again. Now due to this nit wit of a half brother of mine I am now travelling in a car covered in blood with a suspected dead body in the back. Now I am on my way to try and make this all look like an accident. We arrive at Emmock road and Jamie pulls into the side with the lights off. We sit in silence but we don't have to wait long as Kyle's car pulls up behind us. I drive up the hill and Kyle follows behind me until I reach a place where there is a good stretch of straight road before it turns on a bend. We park up and I instruct Jamie to turn the car so that it faces back down the hill. Jamie helps me put Macintosh into the drivers seat while Kyle starts splashing the petrol all over the front and back seats. I strap Macintosh in with the seat belt and roll down the drivers window so that I can steer it from the outside. I turn the key to start the engine but leave it out of gear.

"Right start pushing." I say to them.

We slowly push the car until it is in the middle of the road and the wheels are straightened up. As I jog along the side of the car I pull out Kyle's lighter and ignite a piece of paper that was lying around in the car, I throw it onto the back seat and within seconds the inside of the car is ablaze. I let the car roll past and with the three of us pushing hard from the back we run as fast as we can until it takes off at speed down the hill. We watch the flames light up the inside of the car as it picks up more speed going down the hill towards the first bend. The car veers off the road and into a tree with a loud crashing sound. As we run back towards Kyle's car I think to myself that I am glad I strapped Macintosh in because if his body came out during that crash and police saw the stab wounds, then all this would be for nothing.

We get in Kyle's car and i look back before we take off up the hill to see Macintosh's car ablaze, lighting up the dark sky. We travel through several tight country roads that eventually lead us back into Dundee and to my mothers house. Kyle waits in the car as me and Jamie go into my mothers so that I could change clothes.

"Right Jamie, give me something to wear and put all your clothes into a plastic bag…Oh, and the blade."

As we are getting changed Jerry comes barging into the bedroom clocking the blood stained clothes.

"WHAT THE FUCK IS GOING ON? WHAT'S ALL THAT BLOOD FORM? WHAT THE FUCK HAVE YOU DONE NOW?" He shouts in his English accent while looking right at me with his menacing stare that I have encountered many times over the years.

"I've been sorting out your fucking sons mess. So if you don't want him ending up in jail I suggest you shut your puss and fuck off back to your bed."

And he does just that, he lowers his head and walks out without saying a word.

"Your boots too Jamie."

"What?"

"Put your boots in the bag as well."

"But eh've jist bought them."

"I don't give a shit, they've got blood on them."

"But they're meh brand new timberlands."

"Well you should have thought about that before you decided to turn into an evil bastard with that blade."

I put my trainers in the bag too and borrow a pair of Jamie's, which are two sizes too big, but they're only to get me home.

"I'll bring these back later" I say as I head out the door with the carrier bag over my shoulder and down to Kyle who is waiting impatiently in the car.

"Come on, what took you?"

"Settle down mate, I had to get everything we had on."

"What about mine?"

"You weren't near him or touched him so you should be alright, just give them a good wash anyway."

"Do you have any petrol left in that can?"

"A little bit."

"Good, go back to the woods."

Kyle drives us back into Templeton woods. I get out and take off Kyles car seat covers as they will also be covered in blood. I walk on my own, deep into the darkness to the same spot on the track that Jamie stabbed him. I dump the bag and the seat covers in the middle of the dirt track and pour what was left in the petrol can onto the clothes inside the bag. I light it up and watch it burst into flames. Walking back to the car I turn several times to see the flames settling down. All that will be left is the blade, but there will be no trace of anything on it. Kyle drops me off and I apologise for him being dragged into all this.

"It's not your fault, it's that fucking brother of yours."

"Hey, half brother, don't you forget…Half brother."

"It doesn't matter, he's still a fucking spacer and if it wasn't for you I would hate to see what he'd turn out like."

"I know. Kyle if he ever calls asking you to do anything for him again, do me a favour and tell him to fuck off. Even if it's only to give him a lift some place, just make your excuses."

"Don't worry."

"Listen Kyle you had better give the inside of this car a wipe down"

"I'll do it when I get home"

"Take care Kyle, I'll be in touch."

"Good luck mate."

I creep quietly back into the flat and have a quick shower before climbing into bed as I try hard not to wake up Kelly. I see the sun creeping through the curtains so I get my head down and try to get a few hours sleep as it's going to be a long day tomorrow.

Time to go

"Hey babe, time to get up." I hear Kelly say loudly and sounding quite excited.

"What time is it?"

"Nine o clock baby." She says as she climbs on top of me.

"I thought you were wanting to leave earlier."

"I was but after you disappearing during the night I thought you might need a few extra hours sleep."

I look at her and feel quite guilty as I didn't think she heard me leave.

"I don't know what you were up to and I don't want to know, but I do want you to move your arse as I need some breakfast."

"Yes sir." I shout.

"It's yes mam." She says smiling.

I pack my bags into Kelly's car and lock up the flat. We head into the town and I pick up a newspaper before going to a café for a large greasy breakfast and some strong coffee. I scan the paper thinking that I will see news about Macintosh but as it only happened several hours ago I know I am being stupid. I drive to my mothers but tell Kelly to wait in the car.

"I'll just be a minute." I say as I pick up a bag with Jamie's clothes and trainers.

Kelly blows me a kiss as I walk away.

"Mum." I say as I enter the kitchen.

"Shane, I thought you had left without saying cheerio."

"Don't be daft. Here, these are the keys to my flat. This is the list of things that has to stay, so you are welcome to the rest. This is the name of the solicitors to hand the keys into."

"So where's Kelly?"

"She's out in the car."

"Why didn't you bring her in?"

"Because we are not stopping. Is Jamie in? I have some of his things here."

"He has his new girlfriend in with him."

"What girlfriend?"

"I don't know, he's been seeing her for a few weeks now. She turned up about five this morning."

"Oh well, I won't bother him then."

What a relief I don't have to go and talk to him. If I see him it will just bring back all the bad feeling of last night. My mother walks back out with me to the car. Kate and Big Danny are out in their garden with Biscuit and they let him out the gate when they see me, he comes pounding over with his tail whizzing around ready to take off

"You'd better look after my boy." My mother says to Kelly.

"Oh I'm sure I'll manage."

I say my goodbyes and just as I am about to drive off Jamie comes out of the house in his boxer shorts.

"Shane." He says as he signals me to come over.

I get out the car and walk to the gate. He puts his hand out for me to shake it.

"Good luck."

"Cheers." I say as I shake his hand.

"Whare is it yer goin?"

"Just for a drive."

"Whare?"

"Nowhere." I say as I smile and walk back to the car.

You're the last fucking person I want to know.

As I go to drive off for the second time I look back to give them a wave and see that Jamie is now joined by his new girlfriend...Lisa.

"Shit...You stupid bastard."

"What?" Kelly says.

"Oh no sorry, I'm speaking to Jamie."

"Somehow I don't think he heard you."

"Fuck it, it's his problem now. Were out of here." I say as I smile at Kelly.

About a mile down the road Kelly pulls out a carrier bag from under the seat and opens it.

"Wow. What's all this?" She says as she pulls out some rolls of money.

"Where did you get that?"

"Big Danny gave it to me when you were in seeing your mum. He told me to hide it from you until we were on our way. He said it's your half and told me to buy the baby something nice."

"I can't believe him."

"Where is it from?"

"Gaz."

I smile and then laugh to myself as we hit the main road on our journey to a new life and leave behind all the drunks, minks, junkies, schemies, wide-o's, bullying bouncers, Tayside's finest and Dundee Council the most corrupted organisation in the world.